W9-BOF-597

Flowers in the Dust

A Novel

Myriam Alvarez

Para mi mamá,
Gracias por todo tu amor y tu apoyo.
And the loving memory of my grandmother,
Cholita, te extraño.

Chapter Index

6

Family Tree

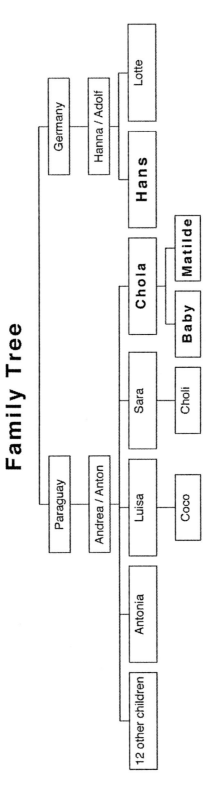

Prologue

I stopped the first taxi that drove by. It was dark and my heart was beating fast. I didn't know what I was doing or where I was going. My hands shook and beads of sweat covered my upper lip even though the night was unseasonably cold.

"Follow that car. Fast!" I ordered the driver. He must have thought I was a crazy woman. And he was right. I was desperate for answers I would probably never find. Everything I had built over the past twenty years could disintegrate in just a second. Everything—just gone. For the last two decades of my life, I tried so hard to keep it together and now I was so close to losing it all.

"Faster, faster," I kept screaming as if the stranger in the front seat could take me back in time. The taxi drove through the streets of Buenos Aires, and the city around me looked alive, vibrant, full of excitement. How ironic, I thought, I feel like dying inside—insignificant. All my life I felt as if my breathing could stop and no one would ever know.

I had no time to waste and the traffic was slowing us down. "Keep going! We can't lose them!" I insisted. My husband and his lover sat in the car in front of us, unaware we were following them. They were escaping from me, and I couldn't let that happen. I had invested my life in this marriage and I wasn't going to let him leave without looking me in the eyes one last time. He owed me that much. I had believed his promises. I had saved his family from the gas chambers. I had given him two daughters who loved him despite all his weaknesses. Our life was far from perfect, but it was the only life I knew, and I had to fight for it even if it meant driving like a lunatic through the streets of Buenos Aires.

The cold air came through the window and hit my face, swollen by the many tears I cried, and refreshed my memory. I remembered the day I met Hans in Asuncion, after his arrival from Germany. I remembered his first words in Spanish and how his thick German accent made me laugh. I remembered our wedding night—how nervous I was, his gentleness despite my inexperience, his soft touch. But the more I thought about our beginning, the more I hated our end. This couldn't be the ending of our story. We were supposed to grow old together, play with our grandchildren, be each other's pillars to the end of our lives.

Every traffic light that stopped us was like a death sentence. My heart threatened to explode inside my chest and there was nothing I could do about it. I tried to calm down, inhaling deeply and slowly, but with every breath I took, my fury worsened.

"Lady, please try to calm down or I will have to drive you to the nearest hospital," the driver pleaded with me. But I couldn't hear him. The voices inside my head screamed at me, blaming me for everything, calling me names.

"Stop talking and drive faster," I ordered the stranger, who by now was obviously losing his patience with me, regretting the moment he stopped his car in front of my old house to give me a ride. I was never like this. I never raised my voice to anyone, let alone a stranger who was trying to help me. I belonged to the generation of women who were taught to obey and be silent. But my silence all these years had brought me nothing but sadness and despair. The first years of my life I belonged to my father, and after that to my husband. I never had the chance to belong to myself.

I was the youngest of sixteen children. Growing up in Paraguay, under the tyrannical watch of my Eastern European father, wasn't easy. But being the youngest provided me with some invisibility and a bit of freedom. Compared to my oldest sisters, my life hadn't been that bad. Most of them remained single or heartbroken, waiting for a happiness that never arrived. They all faded away slowly like flowers without water or light until they all turned to dust.

Maybe that was my destiny at last, to be just one more flower in the dust.

The taxi stopped suddenly and I heard the driver asking me to get out of his car.

"The car we are following stopped a few meters ahead. I think they arrived. You need to get out now," he said, trying not to lose his temper with me. Probably the sight of my swollen face and the dried tears on my cheeks awakened some sympathy from the stranger behind the wheel. "I don't know what's going on, but don't do anything that you may regret later. If that man is your husband and he's leaving you for another woman, he may not be worthy of you. Let him go before he causes a tragedy," he said without looking at me.

"Thank you for your trouble," I replied and gave him double the amount on the meter. "You are a kind person," I said before exiting the car and closing its door behind me. I knew I might never see this man ever again in my life, but I should never forget his words.

Garbage and street vendors filled the sidewalks at the train station, and their loud voices confused me for a moment as they pushed their merchandise. It took me a minute to realize where I was standing and which direction I needed to go. Crowds of people walked by quickly. The Estación Constitución was the most important transit hub in the federal district of Buenos Aires. Most train lines from the interior of the country had their end stop here. It was the beginning or the end for thousands of people who arrived daily in the big city looking for a better life, just as we did a few years back. We arrived from the north, from neighboring Paraguay, with only a few boxes and suitcases to our name. The little money we had, we used to pay the expenses of our move. But I believed in him. I truly did.

A man wearing an expensive suit and a briefcase ran into me.

"Excuse me, *señora*," the stranger said, probably wondering if he was talking to a mental patient. I had a lost look on my face. "Can I help you find your way? Where are you heading? Do you need the ticket window?" he continued, trying to be helpful.

"Yes, the ticket window," I replied, still in a trance. From all the options I heard, that one made the most sense. It seemed like a good place to start looking. If Hans and Marta were leaving, they would need to buy a train ticket first.

The well-dressed man took my arm and gently walked me to the main hall. It was massive. The ceilings were high and vaulted, reminding me of an immense cathedral. There were signs everywhere pointing in different directions.

"Which city are you heading to?" he asked me. "Do you know where you are going?" he repeated, wondering if I could actually hear anything he was saying.

"Rosario," I said. It was the only place that came to my mind. Hans used to travel for business there regularly. It was only five hours away, in the Santa Fe province, which, after Buenos Aires, was one of the most prosperous places in the country.

We walked to the window and the stranger left me there without saying good-bye. I had no time to waste.

"When is your next train to Rosario?" I asked the attendant.

"There is a train leaving in fifteen minutes from platform five. But it's sold out. I just sold the last two tickets to a couple that came three minutes ago," he explained.

"Was the man tall and blonde, with a thick German accent?" I asked, my heart racing.

"Yes, *señora*, just like that," he replied.

My face turned white, and my hands started shaking. "I have to go," I said and started walking away.

"There is another train in an hour. Do you want to buy a ticket?" he asked, elevating the tone of his voice as he saw me walking away.

"Platform five, platform five," I kept repeating in my mind, afraid that I would forget where I was going. I ran into a conductor and asked for directions. He pointed at the platform right ahead of me. My legs shook but I started to jog slowly at first and then faster and faster. The clock was ticking against me. I was going to miss them. If they get on that train, my life will be over, I thought.

Big numbers hung over the platforms. I spotted the "5" quickly and ran as fast as I could.

And then, I heard them. The gun shots were loud and clear. One, two, three shots.

I fell on the floor, paralyzed with fear. Suddenly, I just knew. He's dead. Hans is dead.

Chapter One

I was just seventeen when I met Hans. My best—and only—friend Ana Maria had told me about a group of German visitors that had arrived in Asuncion a few days before. Her father, one of Paraguay's most successful businessmen, had organized a party in their honor and I was invited to attend. Ana Maria and I had been friends for as long as I could remember. Our fathers were both Eastern European and spoke the same language. The European community in Paraguay was relatively small in the 1920s and everyone knew each other. But there were two substantial differences between the two of us: she was an only child; I was the youngest of sixteen siblings. Her father was a loving and caring person; mine was a tyrant.

My father's rules were very strict. He didn't tolerate any disobedience from any of his children, especially from his daughters. By the time I was a teenager, I had already seen him destroy my sisters' chances for happiness. No one was good enough for his daughters. He considered himself superior to everyone, especially the locals, and wouldn't approve any marriage proposal from anyone of a lesser social condition. We were never wealthy—far from that. With sixteen mouths to feed, money was always tight. Yet that didn't stop him from feeling superior to everyone else.

I knew better than to provoke my father's rage. I grew up hiding behind my sisters' long and heavy skirts, afraid to look him in the eyes. For a very long time, I was scared of any adult man I came in contact with.

We never knew what would trigger his rage. We were not allowed to speak to him without his permission and could only address him as "Sir."

My father, Anton, a very gifted artist, had his studio at the back of our big house, where he worked on different restoration projects and portraits of rich Paraguayan families. The studio connected through a long corridor to the heart of our home, a roofless, red Spanish-tiled patio that provided a much-needed breeze in the summers and kept the rest of the rooms cool at night. The kitchen was relatively small but opened up to a large eating area. This was my favorite part of the house. It always smelled of fresh bread and spices. It was also the place where life unfolded every day. Our family was so large that when we finished with one meal, we had to immediately start preparing the next one.

There were eight bedrooms that we all shared. My parents had the smallest one. It was located next to the main entrance of the house and had a window that overlooked the cobblestone street we lived on. Situated this way, my father was able to hear if anyone tried to get in or out of the house, granting him further control over our moves.

Anton had a constant presence in our daily lives, though he would spend long hours locked up in his studio, working on his paintings and giving us an opportunity to breathe more freely.

My mother, Andrea, was his opposite. She always had a smile on her face and made sure that everyone had what they needed. At siesta time, she liked to rock with me on a hammock that used to hang between two old mango trees in our back yard and tell me stories about her childhood. We would spend the long, hot hours of the early afternoon rocking and holding each other tight. She even taught me secretly how to speak the indigenous language called *Guaraní,* making me promise that I would never speak it in front of my father or any other white person. Of course, I could make an exception every time my oldest sister Antonia took me to the market, where *Guaraní* women sold their goods while their children ran around half naked and covered in red dirt.

Those were the most wonderful moments I spent with my mother. We talked, laughed, and shared each other's company. But every time I asked her about her first baby, she would just keep silent.

"It's very painful to speak about the ones that are no longer with us," she would tell me.

I was a very curious child, though, and didn't give up so quickly. I knew I had other sources of information, like my aunts Paula and Nira, or my sisters Antonia and Luisa.

From an early age, it was very clear to me that my mother never healed. Losing her firstborn left a hole in her heart that never closed. I started to believe that the real cause behind my father's bitterness and rage was the early loss of his first son.

Every afternoon at siesta time, I would try to extract new bits of information from my mother.

"Why is father always mad?" I asked her one day.

"He had a very hard life. Sometimes you wear scars in your soul that never go away. No matter how much time goes by, you can't forget the past," my mother said.

"But I don't understand," I insisted.

"Your father was a refugee when he came to this country. He fell sick during the boat trip. He had to stay in quarantine for a long time until he was healthy again. That's when I met him at the hospital, where I worked as a nurse," she continued.

"What's a refugee, mother?" So many of the words she used were foreign to me.

"A refugee is a person who is forced to leave his own country because his life may be in danger. See, when your father was growing up, soldiers came to his house and took away his father and his two older brothers. They accused them of treason against the emperor and put them in jail. He never saw them again. The soldiers spared your father's life because he was too young and his own mother was very ill. He took care of her until she died, a few months after his father and brothers were taken away. Your father was all alone in the world and had to learn to survive by himself. He lived on the streets of Belgrade until a priest took pity on him and let him stay at the church. There, he worked for food, helping the priests clean the church, cooking for them, and doing anything that was needed. Some of the paintings and statues needed to be repaired and your father helped the artists responsible for the project. That's how he discovered how much he loved art," my mother told me.

"But why doesn't he love us?" I asked, still unable to understand the reason behind his rage. We didn't cause any of his sorrows or pains. Why was he punishing us for something that happened so long ago?

"Of course he loves you. You are his children, his own flesh and blood. But he doesn't know how to show love. He grew up alone, without the love of a family," my mother explained.

"But we are now his family and he's always mad at us."

"He's always worried about his work and how he is going to feed us all. Some of your brothers work too and that helps, but it's not enough. He's a very proud man, Chola, and he feels he needs to protect his children. He knows what it's like to go hungry, to end up living on the streets. He doesn't want that fate for any of you," she added. "Someday, you will have your own children, and you will understand. But now, close your eyes and try to take a nap. We need to get dinner started soon," she said.

It took a long time for me to understand.

So when Ana Maria invited me over to her house, my immediate reaction was one of fear.

"I don't think my father will allow that—you know how strict he is," I said to my friend.

"Don't worry, I already talked to my father and he will speak to yours. This way the invitation is coming directly from him. Relax, Chola, you will be fine. He has to let you come. He would never say no to my father," she insisted. Anton had needed his friend's help many times through the years and owed him many favors.

"You don't know him, Ana. He's very unpredictable. You know what he did to my sisters Luisa and Sara. He would never let that happen again. I think we should forget about the whole thing," I continued.

"Chola, you are beautiful and seventeen. If you don't start coming out of your shell, you will end up a sad, single old woman, just like Antonia," she said comparing me to my oldest sister, who was almost eighteen years older than me and still unmarried.

"Please don't speak that way about Antonia. You know how important she is to me. It's her choice not to marry. She had a few marriage proposals but always declined. I don't think she found the right man for her," I added, feeling sorry for my loving sister.

"And she never will. Your father will make sure of that. Chola, you need to think about yourself and your future. Come to the party, if anything just to be with me and save me from all that horrible socializing my mother forces me to do," she said with a big smile. She knew I could never say no to her.

Ana Maria was the only escape I had. When I wasn't doing chores at the house, cleaning or cooking with my mother in the kitchen or taking care of my niece and nephew, Choli and Coco, my friend's house was the only place I could find some peace.

My father decided after I turned fifteen that I had enough of an education for a woman and pulled me out of school. I needed to learn more about the responsibilities of a household and to prepare to be a decent and obedient wife. Of course, that was in the rare case of my finding a suitable husband who was up to my father's standards—a possibility that seemed remote to me.

My friend, on the other hand, knew all too well that she was approaching an age at which both her parents would start looking to arrange an acceptable marriage for her. She was a very beautiful woman with fair skin, blue eyes, and light brown hair. She was educated and kind. It wasn't going to take them long to find somebody right for the family.

To marry for love was out of the question. Rich people married for money, power, or social status. Love was a sign of weakness. Families formed alliances through marriages, solidified their fortunes, and moved up the social ladder. The sacred duty of procreation had nothing to do with love. Men knew their responsibility was to take care of their wives and children. If they wanted anything else, they found it in their mistresses. The rules were clear and everyone accepted them.

Chapter Two

The official invitation came to our door in a sealed envelope, with Ana Maria's father's initials. I received it nervously from the messenger and left it on Anton's dark oak desk, which sat next to the main door, like a guard dog. Anything of importance that arrived at the house was to be placed there until he took a break from his studio and came in for his afternoon tea.

I continued with my chores, ignoring the invitation and trying, unsuccessfully, to think about anything else. The idea of confronting him or asking him about it terrified me. I had to wait patiently until he decided to speak to me about it.

I saw firsthand how he ruined my older sisters' chances of happiness. I witnessed his fist in the air landing on my brothers' faces because they disrespected him. Being the youngest, I had the great advantage of learning from their mistakes.

But Anton was especially cruel when it came to his daughters. Nobody was good enough for them. Antonia, the oldest, decided never to marry, maybe to please him or maybe because she feared him too much. The rest of us tried to find happiness, but his shadow always came between us and the remote possibility to love and be loved.

Out of all of us, my sister Luisa was the one who suffered his injustice the most. She was two years younger than Antonia, and one of my favorite siblings.

When I was about six years old, something unexpected happened that changed the course of our lives.

My father's tyrannical rule over my sisters was very well known around Asuncion. Any man who showed interest in one of them had to be prepared to face the devil. I was still too young to understand what was going on, but I noticed a dramatic change in the atmosphere nevertheless.

The nuns of *El Sagrado Corazón*, who ran the small Catholic school that I attended, suddenly started treating me differently. They would stop and whisper in the hallways and give me long, hateful looks every time I walked by. I was afraid to ask what had changed, why they were so cold and distant. Physical punishment was a regular and normal way of discipline in those days, but the nuns at The Sacred Heart always treated me kindly. Yet I was scared to ask them any questions.

So I asked the only person I truly trusted: Antonia. She looked at me with compassion and said, "Chola, you have to learn from this. Something terrible happened, but you have to promise me you will never forget what I'm about to tell you."

I nodded silently, wondering what could be so bad, so terrible that my entire family was in a state of turmoil.

Luisa, who was one of Asuncion's most beautiful and sought-after bachelorettes, had fallen in love. But that wasn't the terrible thing that had everyone upset. She was pregnant out of wedlock, yet even that news wasn't so horrible. The reason that had everyone outraged was that the father of her child was half-*Guaraní*, half-white.

They met by chance at the *Deportivo Sajonia*, a local social and sports club. These clubs were very popular places and the only form of entertainment in Asuncion, before they opened the first cinema. Every neighborhood had a similar club. There were no memberships—people just showed up and paid a small admission fee to participate in their events. Older ladies met to play cards, older men preferred bocce, and children played soccer. Every Saturday night, a live outdoor band would play the typical Paraguayan polkas, a very fast dance that has couples turning around in circles on the dance floor. It was a popular style among the younger people. My older sisters had permission to go but were only allowed to dance with my brothers. Strange men were totally out of the question. Luisa didn't care; she was a free spirit. She loved to dance and was happy no matter who her partner was. Her blue eyes were so intense, men would turn around and stop everything to breathe her in. Her personality was sunny, affectionate, and caring. She never gave anybody the cold shoulder and that made her even more desirable. She kept her black hair long to her waist but always made sure it was properly tied high up in a bun when she went out.

One evening, the sight of a young army officer in a white summer uniform caught her eye. His eyes were black, as was his hair. You could see some Indian blood in his face, which made him even more interesting and exotic to her. He represented the forbidden fruit. If anything would make my father angry, it would be that one of his daughters had come in contact with an indigenous man. "*Guaranís* are dirty people and they don't belong in our society," Anton would say. But Luisa forgot those words the second Lauro Ross laid eyes on her. Her heart raced and her hands started to sweat.

He, too, was mesmerized by her beauty and didn't wait long before he approached her.

"You have the eyes of an angel," Lauro said shyly.

"Angels don't dance with strangers," she answered, giving him her most disarming smile.

"Maybe this angel would be willing to make an exception," he replied.

She knew this would mean trouble for her but he didn't let her think about it too long. He took her hand and walked her slowly to the dance floor, holding her tightly against his chest. She could smell his skin, as he could hers. That first embrace sealed their fates.

My two older brothers were too busy getting drunk and flirting with the other ladies to notice what had just happened. At the end of the night, Luisa and Lauro said goodbye from a distance.

Love grew fast between them. One morning, when we were finishing our breakfast, the doorbell rang. My father went to the door as usual and opened it only because he saw a man in uniform. He was very suspicious, but he let him in anyway. We all looked on in surprise from the kitchen. We didn't know who he was. Luisa wasn't home.

They walked into the main living room and my father asked him to sit down.

"My name is Lieutenant Lauro Ross. I'm with the second battalion of the army," he explained in a strong and determined voice.

"How can I help you?" said my father, looking him straight in the eyes, noticing his Indian features.

"I love your daughter Luisa, and I am here to ask for your permission to marry her," he said, not shying away from my father's burning gaze.

At that moment, we could see my father's fury burning in his face. We could imagine the questions racing through his mind: Who is this man? Who is he to ask for my daughter's hand in matrimony? Where is his family? Why does he look Indian? How dare he come to my house unannounced?

My mother knew he was about to explode and ran into the room to try to defuse the situation.

"Hello, I am Luisa's mother. I happened to hear your conversation. I think you should leave now. My husband and I will think about your request. Please, go now," she kindly pleaded.

Lauro couldn't say no to her and walked silently to the door. Before he stepped out, he added, "I will come back."

The door closed behind him and we were paralyzed. Nothing like this had happened before. None of my sisters had ever had a boyfriend before, let alone a marriage proposal. My father was not ready for this. He looked confused for the first time in his life. He turned around and walked toward his studio. My mother followed him and, even though we could hear their voices, we couldn't understand what they were saying. Their conversation didn't last long. My mother came out looking somber, but gave us no explanation of what had just happened.

The day went by quickly, with my father in his studio and my mother helping me fix an old dress. Luisa came home later than usual. She volunteered at the hospital a few times a week.

As she walked in, my father called her into his studio. We couldn't hear what they were saying—we could only imagine. She came out five minutes later, with a bruise on her cheek and tears in her eyes. My mother called us to dinner, but Luisa didn't join us at the table. In fact, she didn't come out of her bedroom that night or the day after. We all worried about her. My mother asked me to bring her some soup, hoping that she would eat something. But she refused to eat.

I couldn't understand so I decided to ask what was going on, to see if she was sick.

"She is sick from the heart," my mother said, "but she is young and will forget soon."

Luisa never forgot. She kept silent, but things were never the same. She wasn't allowed to work at the hospital anymore. She helped Antonia with her embroidery and did some cooking, but she never left the house.

The days went by slowly for her and her face began to pale. We noticed that she was losing weight and that her joyful demeanor had disappeared. None of that stopped my father from keeping her locked up inside the house.

Three months went by without word from Lauro. Then, one early morning, Luisa went to the door to pay the man who brought us fresh milk daily and she found a small piece of paper between the bottles.

"Meet me tonight, after midnight, at your neighbor's yard," it said.

There was no name on the note, but she knew who had written it.

She waited until it was dark. The lights were off at ten o'clock sharp. Nobody was allowed to come out of their bedrooms. Luisa waited until the house was in silence and everyone was asleep. With the light of the moon as her only guide, she found her way through the back yard. She knew her way well because one of her many chores was to take care of the garden. She knew there was a gap in the fence, and she went through it. Lauro was waiting on the other side for her. They kissed passionately, but he pulled her away softly.

"They are sending me away," Lauro said. "There is a military post at the border and they need me at the patrol. It will be for only one year. I will be back and we will get married, with or without your father's approval," he explained, trying to hide the pain and fear in his voice, and the fact that this might be their last time together.

Luisa was speechless, her heart breaking into pieces as she heard his words. All of a sudden her legs felt weak. She thought she would fall, but he held her tightly and pulled her against his chest. She kissed him between sobs. Their soft kisses turned into desperate ones. There was no turning back. Passion took over and he made love to her, while she was leaning against the neighbor's wall. Their bodies found each other in the dark and were perfectly united. Before she realized what had happened, she was back in her bed, her face wet with tears, and her legs sore and stained by the blood of her lost virginity. As she lay there, Luisa wondered if this would be the last time she would ever see him.

She kept her pregnancy a secret until it was obvious why she was gaining weight.

My father exploded with rage and this time locked her in a back room where we stored food. There, with no sunlight, Luisa spent the last two months of her pregnancy. She grew so weak, we thought she would die. My mother and Antonia tried in vain to convince him to let her come out of her cell. My father could not tolerate disobedience of any kind, especially from one of his daughters. But most of all, he couldn't forgive her for the shame he felt she had brought upon him and his name. He felt superior; his European blood made him different, better, more worthy. He would never let any of his children mix with the locals, who hardly spoke any Spanish, walked without shoes, and had dark skin. He was determined to control our lives and made sure we knew it.

One morning, mother heard the screaming and knew it was time. She sent me to call the midwife. I ran as fast as I could, as if my life depended on it, and brought the midwife back with me. I had never seen a woman in labor before and my heart broke for Luisa. The baby was born twelve hours later. It was a beautiful boy. My mother said it was a miracle of God that he survived inside the womb. Luisa was extremely weak and her condition got worse by the end of the day. We called the doctor and he said she had tuberculosis, which was as good as a death sentence.

My mother moved her back into the house despite my father's rage and took care of her, ignoring the warnings of the doctor that the disease could spread to the rest of the family. Luisa saw her baby only from a distance, while tears ran down her face. She wasn't allowed to nurse him, hold him, or be in the same room with him. For her this was a far worse punishment than being a captive in a small cell. Every day that passed in separation from her child was a new blow to her heart.

Four months later, she was able to hold him for the first time. Fortunately, her condition had improved dramatically. But this moment of happiness was bittersweet. We had news from the military that Lauro Ross had been killed in the line of duty. A few years went by before we found out that our father had orchestrated his transfer to a particularly dangerous border zone through his contacts with the local politicians. At that moment, despite the fact that they were never married, Luisa became a widow in her heart and mind. For the remainder of her life, Luisa never again looked at another man. Her heart closed up to any possibility of love. Her only love would always remain her son.

I was seven years old when Lauro Ross Filippi was born. Luisa decided to name him after his father, but we quickly realized that to hear his name was too painful for her. So we nicknamed him Coco.

Once Luisa got her health and strength back, she decided to move with her child to my aunts' farm. Anton wasn't speaking to her and she couldn't forgive him for ruining her life. Besides, rumors traveled fast in Asuncion and the stigma of being a single mother—of a half-indigenous child—was too much to bear. She found refuge in the only place where she knew nobody would judge her.

My mother's sisters, Nira and Paula, had moved out of Asuncion and worked a small farm not too far from the city. Every month, my siblings and I would travel for an hour along the riverbank of the Pilcomayo to visit them and pick up some fresh vegetables, fruits, or a chicken to eat.

Both my aunts welcomed Luisa and her baby with open arms. It brought them so much joy to have a child in their home. Tia Nira, my favorite aunt, never married nor had any children of her own. The farm and her sixteen nieces and nephews were enough to keep her busy. She had a soft spot for me though. She used to say that I was the only one who had inherited my mother's good looks. Until I was sixteen, you could only tell that I was a girl by my long dark hair and my dress. I was skinny, tall, and had no breasts. I didn't have the typical Latin body. I lacked a good pair of hips and my curves left a lot to be desired. But I didn't care much. Nira was exactly like that too, and she was a happy woman. I was the only one of us allowed to sleep over at her house, which was located on a little hill and had a wonderful view of the river. Tia Paula had her own small home on the same property. They were together, but apart. The sisters couldn't be more different. Paula loved to have fun and she rotated her affection among several different men, all of them married. She used to say that she preferred to be a happy lover than an unhappy wife. Of course, my mother and Nira disapproved of her lifestyle, but loved her nonetheless. No matter how each chose to live her life, they were tied as a knot. I never saw sisters more loving and supportive than those three. Their bond was hard to describe. The three of them were extremely different and yet they were the same. They were there for each other, and when times got hard, it was natural that they would help each other as much as they could.

Their farm was a haven to all of us. There were trees everywhere and the sweet smell of roses and lilies made their homes seem like paradise. They grew all kinds of vegetables and had fruit trees all over the property. They were famous at the farmer's market for the quality of their produce and they were proud of it. They kept only a few animals, mainly chickens and goats. Nira was obsessed with the smallest details, from the color of the flowers she picked every day to the way the table had to be set for breakfast.

She could work the farm as hard as any man and at the end of the day still look impeccable for afternoon tea. She kept a few parrots, which she treated as if they were the children she never had. She catered and looked after these birds as if they were her babies. She talked and sang to them—it was fascinating to watch. The birds responded to her as if they were children. Some of them learned fast and could speak some words very clearly. One of them especially would terrify us by mimicking one of the workers, a *Guaraní* Indian. He didn't speak any Spanish, only his native language. He was over six feet tall and had lost an eye in a fight. His voice was deep and his tone always sounded menacing to us.

Tia Nira insisted that he was a decent worker and a good man but Paula told us that he was cursed by bad spirits. That was enough to keep us up all night speculating about his life and telling scary stories. Paula was a master at this. She had an amazing imagination and always told the best stories. She could go on all night and never run out of new tales to tell. But, of course, we all preferred the scary ones.

Paula's premature death in her early forties shocked us and was devastating for her sisters. She lived an intense life and left this world the same way. The Spanish Influenza didn't give her a chance. It was quick and painful. And the farm was never the same without her.

Nira tried to move on and worked hard to avoid the sadness. She and I became even closer in the years after Paula's death. I spent long periods of time with her, trying to fill the void her

loving sister had left. I adored Nira. She was also a good seam-
stress, like my mother. Every time my sisters would stop wearing
a dress, she would fix it for me and make it look like new. I learned
watching her skilled fingers work on the fabric. Little did I know
that this skill would one day save my life.

Luisa spent three years in the country until my mother convinced her to come back to Asuncion. We all missed her and Coco
and couldn't wait for their return. After three long years, my father
finally agreed to let her move back but their relationship would be
forever damaged.

I was glad they were back, no matter what the conditions of their
return were.

It was very exciting not to be the youngest anymore. Coco and
I grew up together like siblings. I took him with me everywhere.
He followed me obediently and was happy to come along. Despite
the age difference, we shared games and friends. He always had
a smile on his face and was pretty content. It was impossible not
to like him. He looked a lot like his father, but he had his mother's
kindness and soft eyes.

When it was time to go to school, Coco grew insecure and shy.
He had a hard time reading and writing but he loved to paint. My
father tried to ignore Coco's talent for a long time, but slowly and
indirectly allowed him to come to his studio to watch him paint.
Despite Luisa's disapproval, Coco learned fast to use the brushes
that my father discarded. Sometimes, Anton would show Coco
how to master different techniques, but he remained cold and distant. Their relationship was strange and unique at the same time.
Unintentionally, Coco found a way to get to his grandfather's heart
and win his affection. On the other hand, Anton couldn't help but
see the irony in this situation, and how his own talent was passed
on to his illegitimate grandchild. None of his sixteen children had

shown any interest in his business. Eventually, Anton realized that Coco would continue his legacy as an artist, and that it was his responsibility to nurture his talent.

Soon, Coco became his disciple and companion. Both spent hours together, working on different pieces, restoring old church saints, painting portraits of rich people, or just talking about art. No one else was allowed in his studio.

The man my father hated so much had come back in the shape of his first grandson and was to become his closest friend.

The day my father died, Coco was the last person to leave his room and the one to inherit his paint and brushes. Maybe, Coco was the only one who truly loved him.

Chapter Three

The invitation requested the presence of Anton and Andrea Filippi, and their daughter Mariana de Jesus at a social gathering to honor the visit of a group of European comrades. I was very surprised to see my real name printed on paper. Nobody called me by that name except the nuns at the Sacred Heart. My Tia Nira gave me my nickname when I was just an infant, and it stayed with me for the rest of my life.

Right after breakfast, my father asked me to his studio.

"Ana Maria's father is having a party and he requested your presence," he said, his eyes focused on his work.

I remained silent, waiting for him to continue. He lifted his eyes from the painting he was working on and looked at me.

"You need to be ready by five on Saturday. Ask Antonia to help you find an appropriate dress. I don't tolerate tardiness, so make sure you are ready to go on time," he added and returned to his work.

"*Si, Señor,*" I replied quietly. I walked away with a smile on my face, trying hard not to jump for joy.

Once I reached the kitchen, I embraced my mother and told her the good news. I was finally going to attend my first social gathering! Antonia and Luisa were in the kitchen as well and celebrated with me. Immediately, they started looking for a dress that they could fix in time for the party. They may have needed to do a few alterations but both of them were quite skilled with scissors and needles.

I couldn't wait to tell Ana Maria that her plan had worked and my father had asked me to join them. It was nothing short of a miracle. She had been right all along. But that was the way she was—she wasn't paralyzed with fear, as I was. She was confident and knew how to get her way. I was the opposite. Ironically, we each envied the other for what she had. While she thought my home was a paradise of fun, filled with people of all ages, I thought her house was a wonderful, quiet place, where things were neat, clean, and organized. Our friendship became my favorite and only escape. She was my confidant, a person I could trust without fear of punishment or judgment. We spent the hot afternoons of summer dreaming of all the things we would do and places we would visit. We traveled in our minds to exotic locations where handsome men would cater to our every need. That thought made us break into laughter until our bellies ached.

"Aren't you afraid of it?" I asked her once.

"Afraid of what?" she replied with a certain confidence that I so lacked and envied.

"Afraid of getting married and hating your husband," I added, almost frozen with the idea.

"No, I'm not. My husband won't be my life. He will provide for me and make sure I have what I need, but he won't be everything to me," she replied coldly.

"How can you say that? Don't you want to marry someone you love?" I insisted.

"Oh, Chola, be realistic. That won't happen to us—" She stopped suddenly, noticing what she'd said and quickly corrected herself. "—at least to me. Love and marriage don't necessarily go together. I'll be glad to find someone who is kind and makes me happy. But love and passion are completely different things. I see my parents and I know they never loved each other that way. But they're good friends, and they understand each other well. I don't think they could ever live without one another now. They're so used to being together they couldn't have it any other way. But love wasn't the reason why they got married."

"That's exactly what scares me. How can you spend your life with a stranger?" I asked.

"Well, he's a stranger only for the first few years, I guess. After that you have children, you become more used to one another, and you feel more comfortable." She stopped, and I noticed that she was actually preoccupied with that thought. Maybe she was trying to believe her own words.

"So love is not important to you?" I wondered, surprised by her rational views of marriage.

"Of course it is, but look what love did to your sister! All I'm saying is that you need to be careful and choose your husband well. If you also love him, then you're one of the lucky ones. But love can sometimes blind you and make you see and believe things that are not true," she added as if she could see my future.

"Now you are talking like my mother," I said, and we both laughed and hugged.

"But I'm still scared," I added nervously between giggles.

I awakened early on Saturday. I was anxious and excited at the same time. I wished the clocks would run faster today and five o'clock would come sooner than normal. I had almost no sleep the night before, so I decided to make some fresh tea and wait until Antonia was up. She was always the first one in the family to get up and start the process of making breakfast for the younger siblings. She had stayed up last night to finish my dress and this morning she was catching up on her sleep.

I walked into the empty kitchen and looked around for some fresh tea leaves. I grabbed a few logs and started the fire in the stove. While I waited for the water to boil, anxiety started to build in my stomach. Maybe I wasn't ready for this, I thought. I was a shy girl who had never experienced anything remotely close to this. The only contact I had ever had with the opposite sex, besides growing up with my older brothers, had been a complete disaster. When I stopped attending the Sacred Heart, my mother insisted that at least I learn to play an instrument and because we had a piano in the house, the choice was an obvious one. She convinced my father to let me take a few lessons.

To all of our surprise, I turned out to be a decent player. Lessons were once a week a few blocks from the house. My teacher was a sweet old lady, with such bad arthritis in both hands that she couldn't pick up a cup of tea. But her soul was intact, and her passion for the instrument I loved so much was untouched by the crippling disease. One of my older brothers walked me to my lessons, just in case I decided to walk around on my own—something I was dying to do.

One afternoon, a few months after I started my lessons, I noticed an open window just in front of my teacher's house. I started fantasizing about who might be behind it. The following week, I decided to drop a little note in front of the window, asking to meet whoever was on the other side. I didn't hear anything for a while, but one day my teacher handed me an envelope. I opened it quickly, almost ripping the whole thing apart.

"My name is Manuel. I am fifteen. I like you."

That was all it said. I was very excited to have a new mystery friend. The next few months we kept communicating through my teacher. She thought it was an innocent child's game and became my secret's keeper. Every week I would write Manuel a little note, just a line or two, and he would send one back to me. I would tell him about a new piece of music I was learning to play and he would tell me about his hobbies or his day. After a while we decided to meet in person, but I didn't know how to get rid of my brother's supervision and asked again for my teacher's help. She kindly agreed to let him meet me at the back of her house for five minutes before I was supposed to be picked up.

The adventure fascinated me. The night before, I couldn't sleep, thinking about what he might look like, what he would say to me, how we would keep seeing each other. That day I arrived early and told my brother to pick me up ten minutes later than usual. But, of course, he showed up early and demanded to see me. My teacher tried to find an excuse while he forced his way in and found me and my new friend sitting next to each other, holding hands shyly. He took me by the hair and pulled me all the way home. Once we reached the house, I was in tears, begging him to keep my secret. He called me a little whore and went straight to my father, who demanded to know who the boy was. After locking me up in my bedroom, he went to my teacher's house, screamed insults at her, and told her that was the end of my career as a pianist. As for the boy, Anton went to his house and demanded that his father punish him for such unacceptable and indecent behavior.

I wasn't allowed to leave the house for more than a month. My mother kept me busy in the kitchen, helping her with the cooking and drying my tears.

I never took another piano lesson, but its music stayed deep within me.

The day of the party went by smoothly, but slowly. Once we cleaned the kitchen after lunch, Antonia called me to her bedroom to help me get ready. She wanted to flat iron my wavy black hair and make sure my dress didn't need any last-minute touch-ups. She had taken one of Luisa's favorite dresses and adapted it to my figure. I was smaller than Luisa, and Antonia had to work diligently to make the adjustments. It was a long, white summer dress, with lace appliqués at the collar and a beautiful lace back that accentuated my pale skin. My sister Asuncion made me a hat especially for the occasion, and my mother let me wear her pearl earrings. It looked as if I was getting ready to walk down the aisle.

It was a glorious day. The tables at Ana Maria's house were set outside under a canopy of vines. There were flowers everywhere. Everything looked perfect. The smell of roses was intoxicating. We were the first ones to arrive and the last to leave. I couldn't have enough of this ideal picture. I didn't want to go back to my own life. I just wished it could always be like this day. Most of the guests were people from the Eastern European community of Asuncion whom my father knew well. The group of foreigners, in whose honor the party had been organized, looked completely out of place. They seemed overwhelmed by the local hospitality and yet they were enjoying themselves. They had arrived a few days earlier, hoping to start an exporting business with Ana Maria's father. Rumors of a possible war in Europe were strengthening, and they were looking to take advantage of the situation by exporting iron from South America to fuel the factories back home.

The foreigners didn't speak a word of Spanish but were busy trying to communicate with the locals, especially the girls. I made sure I stayed away from them, because my father's possessive gaze was burning on my skin. The party was almost over when Ana Maria asked me to play something on the piano. I played Beethoven's "Fuer Elise." Everyone was impressed and gave me a standing ovation. I was proud of myself but felt shy under the scrutiny of the guests, especially the Germans. My father looked pleased and happy to hear everyone's compliments. He was busy talking to a group of friends when one of the foreigners approached me. After a few minutes trying to communicate without any success, he left and asked Ana Maria to translate for him.

"His name is Hans. He wants to know if you have someone special in your life," she told me.

I couldn't help but laugh out loud—just the thought of it seemed ridiculous to me.

"Of course not," I replied after I stopped laughing.

"He says he wants to ask your father permission to see you," Ana Maria continued.

Suddenly, the smile disappeared from my face and the color from my cheeks. I was completely petrified. I didn't know what to say.

"I don't think it's a good idea," I answered.

"But, Chola, why don't you try? The worst thing that can happen is that your father says no and locks you up in the attic for the rest of your days," said Ana Maria, trying to hold back the laughter.

"Very funny," I replied. "But no, thank you. I don't want to date a stranger who needs a translator to tell me he had fun and in a few days will return to his country and will never see me again. Besides, my father will never allow it. Tell him not to waste his time on me and to find himself another candidate," I insisted.

"That is a mean thing to say. I think his intentions are noble," my friend said, this time speaking for herself.

As we spoke, he kept watching us, trying to guess our words but probably knowing what we were saying just by the look on our faces.

Just in time, Ana Maria's father interrupted our conversation and took her away, saying he had a big announcement to make and her presence was needed immediately. A shiver ran down my spine as Hans and I were left alone in the music room. I smiled at him and excused myself, leaving the room as fast as I could without running and praying that my father didn't notice our conversation. I stayed away from him for the rest of the evening and blushed every time I met his penetrating gaze.

What does he see in me? I wondered. I was nothing to look at. Too skinny. Too plain. Too simple. The room was full of Asuncion's most desired bachelorettes, all of them from wealthy, influential families, and he had eyes only for me. It was ridiculous, I thought. He'll forget about me the minute the party is over and will move on to someone else. But why did I worry? Why did this stranger make me so uncomfortably nervous? Why were my hands moist with perspiration? Why did his intense stare make me feel naked, exposed? I had never experienced anything like it before. It was a strange but intoxicating feeling. I was terrified and intrigued at the same time. How could such contradicting feelings overwhelm me? It was all too new, too different. But I liked it. I liked feeling wanted. I enjoyed the sweet taste of attraction.

We all gathered in the main room under a heavy crystal chandelier to listen to Ana Maria's father. He asked everyone to raise their glasses for a toast.

"We are honored with the presence of these distinguished gentlemen, and we welcome them to our country and to our humble home. We look forward to a very long and fruitful relationship. We wish them the best in their future enterprises and a safe journey back to their homeland," he said with pride.

"There is something else I would like to add if you'd allow me a few more minutes. My wife and I are very proud to announce the marriage engagement of our daughter Ana Maria to Carlos Lopez Martinez, a dear friend of our family and proud descendant of our beloved hero, the Mariscal Lopez," he added. The crowd broke out in a loud applause as the sound of clinking glasses overwhelmed the room.

As he finished his speech, my stomach sank and I almost dropped my champagne glass filled with lemonade. I looked around the room for my friend, but all I could see was a group of people surrounding her and her parents, waiting for their turn to congratulate the happy couple.

I couldn't see her face, but I could imagine the overwhelming flood of emotions she must have been feeling inside. Ana Maria getting married? It was finally happening. All these years just talking about it and now it would become a reality. Our friendship would forever be changed. Our paths would turn in different directions. I panicked with the thought that this could mean I would lose my best friend forever.

I pushed my way through the crowd until I reached Ana Maria. I stood speechless in front of her, incapable of moving. She came closer and gave me a big hug.

"I'm sorry I didn't warn you earlier," she whispered. "Don't worry about me. I'm happy. It's what's best for my family," she added as she kissed both my cheeks and moved on to the next guest.

I stood there as if waiting for someone to wake me up from a bad dream. That person turned out to be my father. He called my name and told me it was time to go home.

As strange as it seemed, I was glad to leave and be back in the bedroom I shared with my nephew and niece, Coco and Choli. Staring up at the ceiling, I went through every detail in my mind.

I couldn't help feeling betrayed by my dearest friend. All these years, I had kept no secrets from her, and she had kept the biggest one from me. On the other hand, my head was spinning with thoughts of the stranger I had met that night.

I remembered his blue eyes, his intense gaze, his pale skin, his blonde and curly hair. When did I have a chance to take in all these details about him? How could he have an impact on me in such a brief moment? I was so tired, but I couldn't let my mind go and give in to sleep.

That evening seemed like a dream, and I was afraid it would all disappear the minute I woke up.

Chapter Four

Life went back to normal in the following weeks. Ana Maria was busy with preparations for her wedding, and we hardly had any time to see each other. My mother sent me away to my aunt Nira's place to pick up some things for her, and I decided to stay with her for a few extra days. She was getting older, and she missed the time when we all went to fish and play at the river and pick apples from her trees. Now most of my brothers worked, and my sisters were busy around the house. Besides, there were two more mouths to feed, and father's business wasn't doing very well. So everybody was expected to help out.

I enjoyed the days with my aunt and our walks in her garden. Time seemed to have a different pace at her farm, giving me an opportunity to put my thoughts in order, to think about my feelings and what had happened a few weeks ago.

I wanted so badly to tell her about my brief encounter with the German, but I didn't trust myself. Maybe by now he had forgotten all about me, just as I thought he would.

When I returned home a few days later, I went straight into the kitchen looking for my mother to tell her about my days in the country. I brought a lot of things back from the farm. Coco and Choli were already waiting to see if I had some homemade sweets for them. Everything seemed normal, but I saw worry on my mother's face. Before I could ask, my father walked in the room and looked at me intently with his deep brown eyes.

"A young German man came asking for you," he said drily.

My heart dropped to the floor, my body paralyzed.

"He wanted my permission to come and visit you on Sunday. I believe he was at Ana Maria's engagement party. I told him that Europeans are always welcome in our home. So you better look nice and be very polite when he arrives," he added as he sat down at the kitchen table to read the newspaper.

I couldn't understand what he was talking about. My mind raced, and my heart beat so fast, I thought my chest would explode.

"*Si, Señor*," I said, looking down, avoiding eye contact.

"He is a German businessman who's staying with Ana Maria's father. Your relationship with him may improve our financial situation. I want you to be nice to him. His name is Hans Silbermann," he added, with his eyes focused on the paper.

"But he doesn't speak any Spanish," I said carefully.

"You don't need to talk, just smile and look pretty," he replied, looking irritated. The conversation was over, so I just nodded my head. I was too afraid to say anything. This was the first time Anton had let any of us meet a man at his house. I didn't know what to think or what to expect. He was breaking his own rules and I didn't know why.

Mother looked even more confused than I. She stayed in the kitchen after he left and tried to change the subject. She asked me about my aunt, the farm, and the food. Finally she said, "Don't upset your father. Be very polite to this man." She gave me no chance to answer and quickly left the room.

On Sunday, I decided to wear the same dress I had worn for Ana Maria's engagement party. It was the only one I had that looked special. Of course, I was very nervous. Antonia came to tell me that Hans had arrived and was sitting in the living room, waiting for me.

To my surprise, he looked very relaxed, as if he had done this many times before. He wore a custom-made, white summer suit with a white straw hat, which he probably bought at a local store. He was very tall, but that didn't bother me. I was a tall girl, compared with the other girls in school, and his size didn't intimidate me. What scared me the most was his way of showing me how sure he was of himself.

We were two complete strangers, yet he looked at me as if he already knew me. I couldn't do the same. I was very shy and didn't look him in the eyes. Suddenly he held my face between his hands and forced me to look up. When I did, I saw his face up close, and he was smiling at me. I saw once again his intense blue eyes and noticed that his hair looked messy. I felt like laughing but swallowed instead. I kept wondering if he could actually read my mind and what he would be thinking.

My thoughts raced and I could not make much sense of them. I had so many questions. I wanted to know every detail of his life, but I didn't know how to communicate with him. Words between us were not yet possible, and I didn't know if he would stay long enough in Asuncion to learn some Spanish. I wondered if people were capable of communicating in other ways, like animals do. But I didn't know, so I limited myself to what I did know. I offered him some iced tea, and he nodded. Not bad, I thought. This could be the start. I walked away and came back with the glass and gave him a big smile, feeling suddenly very proud. I asked him if he liked Paraguay and all I got was a puzzled look. So I stopped talking. What was the point?

Our meeting lasted less than one hour. We didn't speak; we just looked into each other's eyes. After he finished his iced tea, he stood up, thanked me with a strongly accented "*gracias*" and left the house.

At that moment, not knowing how or why, I felt a connection. And I immediately knew—we were no longer strangers.

Two weeks went by until we heard from him again. Anton was in a good mood because he had had a productive week. He had finished a few portraits and had cashed his commissions. He came to tell me that I was going to be picked up next weekend to go to a picnic, organized by Ana Maria's family at their country estate. My sister Antonia would be my chaperone, he said. As was his way, he never asked me—he simply informed me.

I was glad about the news, but kept my emotions to myself. That night I brought Antonia's dinner into her bedroom, and she offered to read the Tarot cards for me. The cards had become her favorite hobby, and she was very good at it—so good it was a little scary! I accepted willingly because the curiosity was killing me.

She handed me the cards and asked me to choose five. She took the cards and put them on the table. Then she asked for another five. She looked serious, focused. After a few minutes of silence, she said slowly, measuring her words, "This new man in your life is here to stay," she announced.

"But he doesn't live here. He will soon go back to his country," I explained, as if it was obvious that what she was saying was impossible.

"No, he will stay with you and make you his wife," she replied.

"Are you sure? How can that be possible? I don't speak his language and he doesn't understand mine," I insisted.

"Love doesn't need words. You will find a way to communicate," she said.

"But we are not in love. I only saw him twice," I said, and for the first time I wondered if my strange feelings meant I was falling for him.

"That is how it starts. Love finds a way into your heart, even when it seems impossible," she answered. "You just have to let it in," she added.

It all seemed too wild for my imagination. How could I love a man who didn't understand me or know my culture; who would probably leave soon and never return?

I left her room more confused than before and decided never to let her read the cards for me again. The future was already scary enough. I didn't need added stress from an amateur Tarot reader.

The day of the picnic we left early before it got too hot to walk on the streets. We took the trolley to Ana Maria's house, where we met with her family and other guests. Her father had arranged for a few cars to pick us up, and we drove for an hour before arriving at their estate, north of Asuncion. Their property was a few hundred acres surrounding a crystal clear lake. The main house had the style of an old Spanish hacienda, its walls a bright orange terracotta with blue and white ceramic details on the windows and door frames. A small group of servants awaited our arrival and had set up long picnic tables on the shady side of the lawn with an idyllic view of the lake. It was spring and the weather was sunny and breezy.

The Germans were very friendly and did their best to speak a little Spanish with us. Hans had his eyes on me and spoke softly into my ear, like he didn't want anyone to hear him. I couldn't understand a word he said but I didn't care. His soft voice, his warm breath, his lips so close to my face—it was more than enough for me. I didn't care about his words. I remembered what Antonia had said about finding a way to communicate and it was true: we surely did find one.

He kept repeating one phrase in my ear: "*Du bist mein Schatz.*"

I made an effort to remember it so that I could ask Ana Maria later what it meant.

Antonia was very happy drinking wine and eating all the sweets that she could, so she didn't notice when he kissed my cheek and I blushed. All the excitement I was holding back went straight up to my face and gave me away. I was aware of my blushing and didn't know how to hide it. So I hid my face against his shoulder hoping that the red on my cheeks would soon disappear. That was when I smelled him for the first time. I had never been so close to a man before, except for my own brothers and Coco, but they all smelled like the outdoors. And in Paraguay's high temperatures, nobody ever smelled pleasant to me, especially the men. But this was different.

I inhaled the sweet, soft, comforting smell of cologne. It reminded me of the way a baby smells just after a bath or when fresh-baked bread comes out of the oven. I wanted to keep my face buried in his shoulder. I wanted to breathe it all in and let myself get lost in his shirt. He noticed I wasn't pulling away from him and he stroked my cheek softly. I closed my eyes and we stayed like that for a few minutes. Everything else suddenly disappeared. There was nobody else but us, sitting on the grass, breathing and feeling each other.

When it was time to go, Hans told Ana Maria he wanted to take me home. We sat next to each other in the car ride home, and he held my hand all the way. When we arrived, he asked if he could talk to my father. Antonia went to get him while I waited anxiously with him in the living room.

When Anton came, Antonia and I immediately left the room. We sat patiently in the kitchen for half an hour until we heard the front door closing.

We looked at each other, trying to guess what had just happened. Anton walked in a minute later and said that Hans would be gone for a while.

My heart stopped. I didn't understand. I had so many questions. Why was he leaving? Where was he going? When would he be back? What was he going to do?

Antonia held my hand and squeezed my fingers, reminding me to keep quiet. But I couldn't.

"Is Hans coming back?" I finally asked shyly.

"Yes, but not for a while," said my father, and he walked away without explanation.

For a few days, I tried hard to forget everything about Hans and move on with my life. My father never explained the content of their conversation and I didn't dare ask. Not even my mother could help me get information out of him. My only hope was to speak to my friend and try to find out something through her.

One afternoon, the doorbell rang and Ana Maria came looking for me. I let her in and without saying a word I took her hand and walked her to my bedroom. Once the door closed behind us, I made sure it was locked and gave my friend an anxious look.

"I'm so sorry it took me this long to come to see you. You know how crazy things are around the house these days," she spoke quickly as if she was in a rush to get back to her chores and didn't have much time for me.

"I know," I said, trying to hide my resentment and disappointment.

"Hans gave me a note for you before he left, but I couldn't find time to sit down and translate it until now. Here it is. Don't let anyone read it. I promised him you would be the only one to see it," she said.

I took the letter, but my hands shook so badly Ana Maria had to open the envelope for me.

Dear Chola,

I didn't want to leave without giving you an explanation. I told your father I would come back for you after I made enough money to give you a decent life. I loved you since the first time I saw you and nothing would make me happier than to marry you. Please find in your heart the patience to wait for me. The thought of you will keep me strong and bring me back to you as soon as possible.

With love and respect, I remain sincerely yours,

Hans

I looked silently at his words. After a few minutes, I asked my friend if she knew when he was coming back, but she said no. How long could I wait? I remembered the words he said in my ear the day of the picnic, and I asked Ana Maria what they meant. *"You are my treasure,"* she translated. These were his words to me.

His letter had confirmed what I already suspected: he was in love with me. But how could he have fallen in love in only a few short weeks? I never expected it to happen this way. He was a foreigner; he belonged to a world very different from mine. What could I offer him? He was European. He was an educated, worldly man. I was nothing. My world was small, my life insignificant.

Ana Maria saw the confusion in my eyes.

"What is it?" she asked.

"He's in love with me," I replied slowly, barely able to hear my own words.

"Aren't you happy?"

"Yes, but I don't know if I love him back."

"What do you mean?" she replied, taking my hands in hers.

"I don't know what love feels like. I've never been in love before," I tried to explain.

"Why? You've never felt butterflies in your stomach before?" she asked, almost laughing.

"Yes I have, but those were childish feelings. This is real. It's different from anything I've experienced before. He is not like anyone I've ever met. But how can I be sure?" I insisted.

"That's the beauty of love, Chola—you don't have to be sure. It almost happens without trying. It should feel very natural, almost effortless, but exciting at the same time. It's as if you don't know yourself anymore. Everything old looks new. Your fears go away. Your life seems incomplete without him. That's what love feels like," she said.

"How do you know so much, Ana Maria? I thought you didn't believe in love."

"I do. I've been in love before, but I never told anyone. It was an impossible situation and we both knew it. It didn't last long, and now I'm engaged. So I have to move on—I can't think of him anymore," she replied as she looked down, trying to hide her pain.

"Why didn't you tell me? You know you can trust me," I said, wondering how many secrets my friend was keeping to herself.

"We both knew the consequences of our relationship. I promised him I wouldn't tell anyone. But I will never forget him. No matter how long my marriage lasts or how long I live, I will always love him," she said and her voice broke down.

"Would you tell me who he is?" I wondered if I really knew my friend.

"Maybe one day I will. Now it doesn't matter. I'm getting married. It's over," she said, looking down and accepting a fate that was not fair. "So," she continued, "are you in love with Hans?"

"I think I am," I said as I folded his letter and hid it inside my blouse.

"There is something else you should know about him," she said, and I expected to hear the worst. In a few seconds I thought of a thousand possible answers: that he had an incurable disease or that he was a murderer. Anything but what came next. "He's a Jew," she continued and waited to see my reaction.

I stood there, a little disappointed with the simplicity of her answer, and wondered what this meant. "I never met a Jew before. Should I be worried?" I finally asked Ana Maria, more curious than concerned.

"No, my dear friend. It doesn't change the fact that he loves you. You should not worry about it at all," she replied with a smile that gave me back my confidence. She hugged me and rushed out of the house to finish her chores, leaving me with a smile on my face and Hans' words in my hands.

Because I wasn't sure when he would be back, the only way not to go crazy while I waited was to do as much work as possible around the house: helping my older sisters with their jobs, cleaning my father's studio, helping my friend with her wedding, or taking care of the younger ones, especially Choli.

She had always been a fragile child who needed extra care and attention. She was my sister Sara's daughter. She was a twin, born prematurely. Her brother had been adopted by her father's family after Sara died in childbirth. They had refused to take Choli because she was a very sick little girl and only agreed to take her twin.

Of all my other fifteen siblings, Sara was the smartest. She was the best and brightest of her class, and her teachers recognized her talents early on. It took them a long time and a lot of effort, but they finally convinced my father to let her continue her education. She knew from the start she wanted to be a women's doctor. Anton agreed to let her attend medical school, despite his strong opposition. "That's no place for a girl from a decent family," he used to say. But Sara didn't listen. She was the first one of us to leave the household, even before my older brothers did. Her school was far from home, but she was able to room with a distant relative of my mother, an old lady who was blind and needed the company and the help.

Sara wasn't as beautiful as Luisa but her heart was made of gold. Once a week, after school and before she went back home, she made a stop at a local reservation to help the Indian families with their health issues. At the beginning, they trusted only the medicine man who promised to cure everything with his witchcraft. But after seeing Sara in action, taking care of sick children, women and old people, they made a special place for her in their community. She became well known throughout the whole region. By the time she finished medical school and had to decide where to practice, she didn't think twice and returned to the reservation.

Despite the fact that the *Guaranís* had no money to pay her, she stayed with them and after a few years became a part of their community, feeling almost like one of their own.

Sara was beloved, and her reputation as a young doctor working with the indigenous community attracted the attention of another talented physician, Pablo Fernandez Lozano. He came from a rich family and couldn't be more different from Sara, but their mutual attraction was immediate. He started visiting the reservation to observe her work and ended up staying with her permanently. Their romance grew fast and they married a year later. Their passion for medicine was the main reason they were together. But, of course, his family never quite accepted a woman who preferred to work with *Guaranís* than sip tea at charitable events.

Sara didn't care. She became pregnant shortly after their wedding, but her long hours at the reservation didn't make it easy on her. She never stopped, not even when the early signs of labor started. Her husband found her lying on the floor, sweating and aching with every contraction. He rushed her to the nearest hospital, a few miles away. By the time they got there, she was ready to give birth. The labor went well and she gave birth to twins, a boy and a girl. But she started losing too much blood and died a few hours later, holding her husband's hand and looking at her babies.

Pablo was devastated. Her death made him a hollowed man. He found relief only in his work and could not take care of the twins. The babies were born prematurely and needed special care, but their father refused to give up his responsibilities at the reservation. His family agreed to raise only the boy, who would carry on the family name, but they didn't want the baby girl. She was too little and fragile and looked just like Sara. My mother was outraged when she found out and welcomed the new baby with open arms.

Sara wanted to name her Andrea, after our mother. Soon after her arrival, we realized that I was the only one with whom she didn't cry, so my siblings started calling her Choli—a diminutive of my own nickname.

Choli and Coco were both conceived in love but started their lives under tragic circumstances. They reminded me of what my sisters went through to have them. I loved them dearly, and I knew my life would always be connected to theirs.

Almost a year went by without a word from Hans. Through Ana Maria I found out that he was trying to get a business started and that he was working hard to make some money. His friends had left a long time ago and were back in Germany. He stayed behind with the conviction that his destiny was in South America with me. The first few months I waited anxiously for the postman to arrive with news, but after a while I gave up. I kept thinking of all the reasons why he would never want to be with me—I was worthless and insignificant compared with him and knew a man with his class would never look twice at a girl like me. Deep inside, I wished my life could be more like my friend's.

Unexpectedly, his second letter came just before Ana Maria's wedding. I was at her house helping prepare dinner for two hundred guests. My friend came looking for me in the kitchen with such excitement in her face that I had to stop everything I was doing. She pushed me to a corner, away from the others.

"Hans wrote you," she said, showing me his letter and looking at me with complicity. "I didn't have a chance to translate it, so I will try to do it while I read," she continued, unable to hide her joy.

I still couldn't say a word. My hands were dirty with the flour and eggs I was using to cook, and I didn't dare touch his letter.

Dear Chola,

My days without you have been lonely but things are going well. We started a business taking apart old ships and selling the iron to factories in Europe. We work very hard and I'm trying to save as much money as possible. If things keep this way, we could get married in less than a year. Please forgive me for not writing more, but it is hard to find a moment alone to sit and do it.

Your face is the first thing I think of every morning and the last I see in my mind every night. Send me a few words through Ana Maria when you have a chance. To read about you will help me through my days until we meet again.

With love and respect, I remain sincerely yours,

Hans

I realized that his letters were giving me slowly a picture of who he was. Until that moment, we had never said so much in words to each other. I was happy but remained cautious. I was falling in love with a man I barely knew. Ana Maria noticed my preoccupation.

"Don't worry so much!" she said. "He wants to marry you. Aren't you happy?"

"I don't know him, Ana Maria," I repeated. "He's far away. I don't know when he'll come back. So much can happen until then. Besides, I'm no good for him. I don't speak his language and don't even know what it means to be Jewish."

"I'm marrying a man I hardly know, so don't worry about it. Hans loves you and I think you love him too. You are already doing so much better than I," Ana Maria said, giving me a big hug and ignoring the fact that I was covered in flour dust.

"Now, I have to go get ready or my mother will kill me. I'll see you tonight. I'm so happy for you, Chola," she exclaimed and ran upstairs. I sat for a moment, wondering what unexpected turn my life would take. My friend was getting married to a man she didn't love, and I was falling in love with a man I hardly knew.

Ana Maria's wedding was one of the biggest social events that year in Asuncion. But my mind was somewhere else, far away with Hans. Waiting to hear from him proved harder than I thought. My patience was tested daily.

That night I was allowed to sleep over at Ana Maria's house because the party was going to last until the early hours of the morning, and I wanted to enjoy it as much as possible. After all, it was the first time in my life I was going to witness such an exquisite event. Ana Maria's parents insisted I stay over, and my father couldn't refuse.

The religious ceremony took place at Asuncion's cathedral. Located in the middle of the colonial town, the magnificent church represented the heart of the city. Everything was built around it. A Spanish-style square, shaded by hundred-year-old trees, was directly across from its marble steps. Before I entered the church, I could smell the sweet scent of the hundreds of white roses that decorated the main altar.

The guests started to arrive early to make sure they could find a good seat and not miss a thing. Before long, even a needle wouldn't have fit in the room. All of Asuncion's high society was there, and everyone who wanted to be was there as well. Ana Maria arrived at the church with her father. I was waiting for her at the main entrance to help her with her train, which was several feet long and looked like a beautiful, crystal-clear cascade of water. The bride looked radiant and for a brief moment I saw myself in her, walking down the aisle followed by a path of rose petals. I walked quickly to the spot my parents saved for me, anxious to see my friend getting married and wishing I could read her mind. As she walked slowly past me, I tried to look into her deep blue eyes. They were empty. I couldn't help but feel sorry for her and blew her a kiss as I whispered silently, "I love you." She nodded her head and kept walking solemnly.

The wedding reception was at her family's house. They lived in an old colonial home in the more affluent part of town. The party was held outside and the festivities didn't start until ten o'clock that night, when the heat of the day finally gave in to a cooler breeze. Every detail was carefully planned, leaving nothing out. There were color-coordinated flowers, white cotton tablecloths, and shiny silverware. Giant bowls filled with wild orchids and white candles decorated the tables. A fifteen-piece band played music all night long.

It was like a dream that shouldn't end. My friend looked content and her family was enjoying every minute of it. I wondered if her mind was somewhere else, somewhere far away with the man who truly loved her.

Because my father hated these types of social events, my parents decided to leave right after the dinner was over. While everyone danced and laughed, I kept to myself. My emotions seemed like a rollercoaster, feeling happy one moment and miserable the next. Ana Maria took a moment to sit with me, and she noticed that I wasn't enjoying myself. She hugged me gently.

"Don't worry—he'll come back soon," she whispered in my ear.

I made an effort to be more sociable and look happy for my friend's sake, but she knew me better than that. I was surprised to realize that she was actually thinking of my feelings during the biggest, most important night of her life. She was supposed to be the center of attention and yet she was worried about me.

This wonderful evening seemed to last forever. I observed the couples dancing and laughing together and wondered if that would ever be me.

I was finally ready to call it a night when one of the waiters came looking for me. "Señorita Chola, there is someone asking for you at the door," he told me.

Puzzled, I walked to the door, my heart beating fast and my breath accelerating. Impossible! But there he was, tired and dirty after a ten-hour trip. Despite his condition, Hans looked as handsome as the last time I saw him.

We kissed and hugged each other, not noticing that it was the first time we were doing it. I wanted to tell him so many things, but I didn't know where to begin. He just looked me in the eyes and pressed me against his chest. We stayed like that for a few minutes and then he kissed me goodbye. Right there I knew we belonged together, and without saying a word, we agreed to never separate again.

The day after the wedding, I returned home, feeling complete again. I couldn't wait to tell Antonia that Hans was back. Some of my brothers had gone to the country to help Tia Nira, and the house seemed suddenly empty. I found my mother in the kitchen preparing breakfast, and I tried to control my excitement before walking into the room.

"He is back," I finally said, unable to hide the joy in my voice.

"I know," replied my mother. "He was here last night looking for you and wanted to talk to your father. He asked for your hand in matrimony," she added. As I heard the news, my legs became soft and I looked for a chair to sit down. "I was waiting for you to come back from Ana Maria's to tell you that your father said yes and that they will meet again to set up a date for the wedding." She spoke slowly and carefully, waiting to see my reaction, not sure what to expect.

I was listening carefully as if she was talking about somebody else. The whole scene seemed unreal.

The sound of the boiling water steaming through the kettle brought me back to the kitchen, returning my thoughts to the matter at hand. I never thought I would marry so soon, if ever. I never thought my father would agree to give my hand in matrimony to a foreigner. I never thought this day would come.

"Your father wants to wait until fall," said my mother, breaking the silence. "The weather will be nicer and the house won't be so hot for the ceremony," she continued, as if we were talking about some insignificant thing.

Still shocked with the news of my sudden engagement and not sure I could speak at all, I asked: "Does Father know he's Jewish?"

"He knows. They had a long conversation about it. Your father agreed to the marriage under one condition—that you will raise your children Catholic," she explained.

"And what did Hans say?" I wondered.

"He told us that the children are Jewish only if their mother is Jewish and since you are not going to convert, that makes them Catholic anyway. He said that he loved you and that was the only thing that mattered to him. He just asked your father to let a rabbi be present at the ceremony. He's a man of few words," she said.

"And what do you think, Mother?" I asked, looking into her eyes, searching for an honest answer.

"I don't want to force you into marrying someone you don't love. I don't care to which religion he belongs. Marriage can be difficult with a man you love. I can't imagine how hard it would be if you are with somebody you don't want. I will talk to your father if you don't want to marry. I will not let him ruin your life like he did your sisters'," she protested, letting me see for the first time that she was willing and capable of confronting my father when needed.

I got up and walked to her. I stroked her face gently and smiled. She looked at me with concern in her eyes and finally asked, "Chola, *mi hija,* are you sure you want to do this? Do you really love him?"

"*Sí, madre,* I do."

Chapter Five

Our wedding was small and simple. We married in my parent's living room, as was usual in those days. My sisters decorated the house with wildflowers they brought from Tia Nira's garden, and we dined under the shade of the mango and orange trees on our patio. Hans agreed to have a Catholic ceremony but requested the presence of a rabbi. I was only nineteen.

My sister Josefina made my dress and Antonia embroidered it. They agreed to my request of no train, but they insisted on the veil, despite my strong objection. I didn't want an elaborate wedding; it was simply not me. My mother gave me her only piece of jewelry, a pearl necklace she received from her absent father on her fifteenth birthday, and Luisa let me borrow her pearl earrings. Hans had given me an engagement ring with a white pearl on it, as was customary. Maybe I wasn't the most beautiful bride, but I surely felt like the luckiest one.

The weather was pleasant but the heat of the summer wasn't completely gone. Everyone I loved was there, including my dear friend Ana Maria. It had been a few months since her wedding, but already it felt like an eternity. Married life had changed her and her many duties took her away from spending time with me as we used to. Our friendship was no longer the same.

When it was time to start the ceremony, my father held my arm and walked slowly next to me. We reached our homemade altar, and he put my hand in Hans'. For the first time in my life, he gave me a brief hug and let me go quickly, almost embarrassed by the physical contact with his youngest daughter.

It was hard to believe that the words I heard in so many other weddings were finally read to me. But this time I was the one promising to spend the rest of my life with the man standing at my side. Hans remained still, trying to follow the words in Spanish and waiting until I gave him the signal to say "*I do.*" Despite the fact that he was six years older, I felt like I was in charge, speaking for the two of us.

It had been more than a year since his arrival in this remote part of the world, where he decided to finally settle down. He could make himself understood, though he still had a hard time keeping up with a conversation. But language didn't matter anymore. He knew what he wanted and he made sure he would have it. I always admired his focus and ambition and the way he achieved his goals. He looked strong, sure of himself, and was devastatingly handsome. As we heard our wedding vows, his eyes locked with mine in an intense gaze. He held my hand throughout the ceremony as if he was making sure I wasn't going to run away. Or maybe it was his way of claiming his new possession. She is mine, now and forever. He kissed me gently after the priest pronounced us "*marido y mujer*", husband and wife.

The wedding reception started immediately after the ceremony. The dinner menu included a few of my favorite Paraguayan dishes, all deliciously prepared by my mother and sisters. Josefina baked a wedding cake and decorated it with a cascade of small pink roses. My father was proud and kept telling all his friends how wonderful it was that one of his daughters finally married a *true* European. He congratulated Hans several times, but didn't speak much to me. At the end of the evening, he came to me and said coldly, "Take good care of your husband. Now you belong to him."

The sun came down that day, like any other day, and yet my life would never be the same. I was a married woman. My new marital status put me in a different social category, but with it, new responsibilities came attached. Especially in the bedroom.

My oldest sisters had talked briefly to me about my obligations as a wife and my duty to obey and please my husband. But they explained very little about what happens after the wedding festivities come to an end. I knew from Ana Maria that the groom takes the bride to his room, but that was it. What happened next, behind closed doors in the bedroom, was every married woman's secret. Nobody talked about it, nobody asked. Despite my curiosity and fear of the unknown, I knew I wasn't going to be the first one to ask these questions.

My mother gave us a room in the back of the house because we had no place of our own yet. It was small and had only one piece of furniture, but Luisa made sure it felt welcoming. She made the bed with fresh, white cotton sheets, and spread some red rose petals on it. The smell of roses lingered sweetly in the air when I arrived to change into my pink silk nightgown, embroidered by Antonia, and wait for my new husband. The anxiety I had been able to keep under control all day came back with a rush. My heart beat fast, and I thought I was about to die. Maybe this is what sex feels like, I thought, like death.

As I was trying to calm down, Hans walked in the room and smiled at me. He moved slowly toward me, as if to show me that he was not going to hurt me. We sat in silence and after a few minutes, he started to take his clothes off. I closed my eyes. I was afraid to look. I was afraid of feeling him; I was afraid of him. Completely naked, he extended his hand and invited me to join him under the sheets. Without the need for words, I followed him obediently. He lay next to me in silence and kissed my forehead. He took my hand and put it on his chest. He moved my hand slowly, letting me explore his body, speaking softly in his language. It didn't take too long for his hands to explore me in the same way. He undressed me without a hurry, savoring every step of the way. He kissed me gently as he took off each layer. The room was warm and a mild breeze caressed my skin, reminding me of my nakedness. I could feel my tense muscles begin to relax and my warm body wanting more.

It was a strange new feeling to want someone that way. I thought it was sinful to feel like this. I had been raised to think that sex was a sin, so why was I feeling so wonderful? Why was touching a man's body so electrifying? There were too many questions I couldn't answer myself, so I let my mind go. I simply let go of every thought and gave myself to him for the first time, as I would do for the rest of my life, without limits.

Shortly after our wedding, Hans was able to rent a modest home, not far from my parents' house. Built at the turn of the century and framed by a thick, black iron fence, it had a brick façade and two large windows. My greatest joy was the small backyard where I could grow my favorite flowers and some vegetables. The only shade we had was provided by an old orange tree that was too tired and frail to give us any fruit, but it filled the entire house with a fresh, citrusy scent.

We didn't have enough money to buy furniture, so the house stayed almost empty for a long time. Between a few wedding gifts and my mother's generosity, we were able to get a mattress, a table, and two chairs. Our official honeymoon lasted only a weekend, but I felt like a honeymooner throughout our first year together.

Hans kept traveling to keep his business afloat and each homecoming was a reason for celebration. The intensity of our passion grew with every absence. It was during that first year that I truly fell in love with him. We made love every chance we had, and we were never in a hurry to leave our bed. I tried to keep occupied while he was away, but it was useless. I missed him terribly and I couldn't wait for his return. My anxiety grew stronger with every trip and it made me feel very possessive of him. I didn't care; I never envisioned married life would be this way. I did not expect to be so crazy for my husband. He made me discover a physical and emotional need I never thought I possessed. I felt strong when I was with him, yet extremely weak when he was not around. I felt vulnerable and helpless without him. On the other hand, he made me feel loved and wanted, something I had not experienced before. When I agreed to marry him, I knew I was doing it in part to please my father, but I hoped that maybe one day I would learn to love him. That day arrived sooner than I imagined.

Before we could celebrate our first anniversary, war broke out in Europe. The news shocked and devastated us at the same time. Hans had left his country thinking that the political situation would improve eventually, and like many others he was outraged after Hitler's invasion of Poland. Not long after that, we received a telegram from his father in Germany explaining that his family was in danger and that they would try to seek asylum in South America.

Terrified about what could happen to his loved ones, Hans went to my father and asked him for help to bring his family into the country through his connections with the local authorities. For weeks, Hans would spend entire days waiting at the Ministry of Foreign Affairs for a confirmation or a sign of hope. When permission for their arrival was finally granted, we noticed it was only for his immediate family: his parents and his only sister and her husband. The rest of his family would have to find other ways out of Nazi Germany, we were told.

At the ministry, they explained that the quotas for Jews had been filled and that there was no possible way to let more people come into the country. There were long waiting lists and very little hope. Countries in South America opened their doors to desperate Jews from all over Europe, but the need was greater than anticipated. Thousands were able to emigrate, while millions perished in Hitler's gas chambers. Our efforts to save Hans' aunts and uncles, or maybe some of his younger cousins, were lost in a sea of burocracy. Not even my father's connections helped much. Most of them died.

Hans arranged for his immediate family to come on a cargo ship. It was in very poor condition, but it was safe. He had dealt with this shipping company through his iron business, and he knew he could trust them. Still we were not sure if his parents and sister could make the trip from Berlin to Amsterdam in time to board the ship. We didn't have a way to keep in touch with them. We would know only after they arrived in Amsterdam and contacted the shipping company.

I tried to prepare the house and asked my mother for extra beds. I didn't know much about my in-laws, just the few things Hans told me in his broken Spanish.

His father, Adolf Silbermann, belonged to a family of tailors in Berlin that had amassed a small fortune through the years, thanks to their family-run factory that produced men's suits and hats. They enjoyed an agreeable life, lived in a comfortable apartment in Charlotteburg—one of the city's nicest neighborhoods—and had a country home near a lake, where they would go ice skating in the winters and sailing in the summers. His father was Jewish but his mother, Hanna, was Protestant, and even though she converted and kept the Jewish traditions at home, Hans was educated at a private Protestant school.

Maybe that was the reason my husband remained neutral to any religion throughout his life, even after we had children of our own.

His only sister, Lotte, who was older than he, was married to a very wealthy and influential German banker and was used to a very extravagant lifestyle. She was the one I was most nervous to meet.

For reasons I never knew, Hans didn't like to talk about his childhood. He rarely mentioned his family and did it only when it was absolutely necessary. Sometimes I could see the sorrow and desperation in his eyes, but he never admitted it. It didn't matter how many times I asked him the same questions, he always avoided having a conversation about his past.

Once we received confirmation of their departure from Amsterdam, it was a month before the ship finally arrived in Uruguay. From there, Hans' family took a bus to Asuncion, surviving the many hours on dirt roads in the heat. They had seen only a picture of me, taken on my wedding day. I had lost some weight since then and wasn't feeling my best. A week before their arrival I found out I was pregnant. I had been feeling different for a while but thought it was just my anxiety playing tricks on me. Receiving and hosting my husband's family had not been in my plans. But now it was a fact that I needed to accept, and I didn't know what to expect. Worried about my health, I described my symptoms to my mother, and after seventeen pregnancies, she was quick to tell me that my morning sickness was not due to indigestion or gas.

Hans was happy and excited when he found out, but the good news was eclipsed by more urgent events. The fighting in Europe and Hitler's latest conquests constantly preoccupied my husband's mind. Once again, my mother filled the void and celebrated with me as if she herself was pregnant. I went to her house to share the news with the rest of the family. My father smiled at me and said, "*I hope it's a boy.*" Overwhelmed with joy, my sisters hugged me as if they were welcoming me as a new member of their club. Luisa was especially moved by my new state. She didn't have fond memories of her own pregnancy, but I could see her happiness when she found out that I was expecting my first child. And despite the fact that she had never been pregnant in her life and was probably still a virgin, Antonia wrapped her arms around me and touched my still-flat belly, trying to read any future omen. "*She will be a girl. Another flower in the family,*" she exclaimed with excitement and kissed me on both cheeks.

I spent the rest of the day with the most important women in my life, sharing stories of morning sickness, swollen feet, and sore breasts.

The night before Hans' family arrived, I went through the house, cleaning and making sure that I had everything ready for them. I moved fast between the few pieces of furniture we owned, dusting and shifting them around until I was completely satisfied with their arrangement. But even that wouldn't calm my nerves. I cooked extra food, made sure linens and towels were washed and pressed. I checked every corner of the house, washed every dish, and swept the floors twice. My anxiety was obvious to Hans and he tried to calm me down, unsuccessfully.

"Everything looks great. You've done a good job with the house," he told me.

"I hope they feel welcome," I replied, looking for any specks of dust I might have missed.

"I'm sure they will. They've been homeless for too long now, trying to escape this nightmare. Our home will be their safe haven," he replied, taking my broom out of my hands and forcing me to look at him.

"What if they don't like it here? What if they hate our home? What if they hate me?" I finally asked, admitting my biggest fear out loud.

"Chola, you are my wife, you are my life now and you are expecting my child, their first grandchild. How could they ever hate you? Thanks to you, they will have a place they can now call home."

"But I'm not Jewish. Your mother will be very disappointed," I cried.

"Your heart is what matters," he replied. "Look at what is happening in Europe because of hate. If I hadn't married you, they would have never been able to escape the concentration camps. You represent life, a future. That is the only thing that matters."

He spoke softly, with a kindness and love that were strange to me. His voice was soothing and his eyes gentle. I had never seen so much compassion in his face before.

"Now, I want you to rest and forget about tomorrow. They will be forever grateful to you, Chola, for opening the doors of your home and giving them a second chance at a peaceful life."

And then he came closer, wrapping me in his arms and speaking in my ear.

"I will be forever grateful to you, my love. *Te amo.*"

The day of my in-laws' arrival, I put on my best dress and went with Hans to wait for them at the bus terminal. It was unbearably hot and some of the ripe mangos lying on the dirt roads were starting to smell. I could feel the sweat dripping down my spine, but it wasn't because of the heat. My heart started to race as I saw the bus approaching. I could feel Hans' excitement to finally see his family after worrying for so long.

We had been waiting anxiously for this moment, but I was still terrified to meet them. What if they didn't like me? Maybe I wasn't good enough for them. I didn't come from a wealthy family, nor did I have any Jewish heritage. It could all go wrong so quickly, and there would be nothing I could do about it. I took a deep breath. It was too late for regrets, too late for fears. I stood tall and lifted my head up, so they could see me better.

Hanna, Hans' mother, was the first one to come off the bus. She was a very small lady. She looked tired but relieved, and her face lit up when she saw her son. They embraced each other, my six-foot husband holding his tiny mother, standing on the bus platform as if they were trying to turn back time. With tears in her eyes, she turned to me and gave me a warm smile. She kissed me and spoke in German, while tears ran down her cheeks. Her expression of gratitude was more powerful than a thousand words. Suddenly, all my fears went away.

My father-in-law, Adolf, came to greet me as well, followed by Lotte's husband, Heinrich. Lotte came out last, looking very irritated and upset. She gave me one quick look of disgust and moved on to hug her brother. That moment defined the kind of relationship we would have until the day we found out she had taken her own life.

The first few weeks together were strange and uncomfortable. With almost no privacy at all, I felt my own house had been invaded. My mother-in-law always had a very positive attitude and tried to communicate somehow with me. My father-in-law kept to himself most of the time, absorbed in his own thoughts. Every evening, after dinner, he and Hans would have long and heated conversations that would go late into the night. I couldn't understand what they were saying, but I imagined their discussions were about the war in Europe.

Lotte didn't even know I existed. To her, I was a maid whose only job was to clean and cook. She never made eye contact. She would ask her brother to tell me what she wanted and spent most of her time sleeping or reading in bed the few German books she was able to bring along. Her husband, Heinrich, on the other hand, was kind and tried to always be helpful, despite the obvious limitations.

Gambling was the family tradition. They played a game of cards every night after dinner, and because I didn't understand the game or the language, I felt completely excluded.

There were no casinos in Asuncion, but they liked to talk about and remember the days when the family would go once a year to the city of Baden, in the south of Germany, to relax at the natural springs during the day and gamble at some of Europe's most distinguished establishments during the night.

Hans and Lotte seemed possessed every time they sat down for a game of poker. They would bet fictitious money and write down in a little book how much they owed each other to make sure they could pay it in the future, when they got their fortune back.

My mother-in-law, Hanna, was the kind of woman who was always a step ahead of everybody else. She didn't bring much from her home, just a few clothes and her jewelry, which helped pay for the trip. But she managed to bring the deeds to their homes and factories and all kinds of documents that described their assets in Berlin. She told me that one day, they would return to Germany and reclaim their right to their properties. She was convinced that they would find a way back. She missed her home and even though she didn't say it out loud, I could sense that longing in her eyes.

It made me sad to think of all the things she left behind or lost on the way, and I couldn't even imagine the pain she felt when she saw her loved ones shipped away to concentration camps, never to return. Nobody survived; all she had left was her immediate family. I tried to picture in my head my own family: my siblings, my parents, my aunts, all of them here today and gone tomorrow. I realized that the price that Hans' family had to pay was far greater than anything I could ever imagine. My heart sunk in my chest. I had so much respect for Hanna and her husband.

Shortly after my in-laws' arrival, we moved out of our rental and into our first home. Hans was able to get a loan, thanks to Ana Maria's father, and we bought a small, three-bedroom house in a new, up-and-coming neighborhood called *Sajonia*, a few minutes' distance from the Pilcomayo River. In the beginning we were uncomfortable in such a small place, but we all grew accustomed to the situation and learned to live with it.

Every time Hans was away on business, I would go crazy trying to communicate with my hands and feet. Heinrich was funny and had a great sense of humor, and when we had a language problem, he would find a way to make us laugh about it. Hans' family wasn't used to the extreme temperatures of a Paraguayan summer, and I tried to teach them the few tricks we had that helped us survive the heat. First, I explained that we usually took a nap during the hot hours of the afternoon after eating a light lunch, but they preferred heavy lunches and lighter dinners, which made them very uncomfortable during the rest of the day. Another recipe to combat the heat was to keep hydrated. In order to do that, Paraguayans drink a special ice tea called *Tereré*, made with yerba mate, herbs, and lemon. The first time I made it for them, Lotte almost threw up on me, while Hanna and Adolf's faces turned green with disgust. The only one who happily gulped a few glasses was Heinrich.

"*Mucho bueno!*" he kept yelling and laughing, while his wife puked her guts out.

Lotte was my biggest problem. She expected clean sheets every day and the finest china I had—a wedding gift—on the table every night. Her clothes had to be washed and pressed in a certain, specific way. She never said thank you and she always looked down on me. During my pregnancy, especially when I became very heavy with the baby, she would make no efforts to make my job easier. She would throw her clothes on the floor knowing that I could hardly bend, she would make me clean the bathtub on my knees, and she expected breakfast in bed every morning. I knew it was my fault; I knew I should have said no to her demands, but I couldn't. I was afraid of her, intimidated by her aristocratic manner. In contrast, I was ashamed of my humble origins. I wished I would have been braver or stronger, but I wasn't. All I had were my own hands and I worked them to the bone to make my husband's family feel welcome.

Between my non-existent German and their broken Spanish, I was able to find out a few details about my husband's childhood and previous life. His mother called him a spoiled but loveable child. Pictures showed he was good-looking from a young age, always with a big smile on his face. They paid for the best education money could buy in Berlin, but he never showed any interest in books. Women were another story. In that subject he excelled. He was breaking hearts before he wore long pants. In fact, love was the reason he had left Germany in 1935, after Hitler took power. Until that moment he had lived the carefree lifestyle of a playboy, frequenting Berlin's famous cabarets and enjoying its nightlife to the fullest. He was Marlene Dietrich's biggest fan and would never miss her performances. His life was so extremely different from mine that I couldn't possibly imagine why he fell in love with me. While I was being educated to serve and respect my future husband

and going to Church every Sunday, he was enjoying Berlin's sexual freedom and a lifestyle of excess. While I was attending Catholic school, he was frequenting transvestite cabarets and whorehouses.

It made sense when he decided to leave his beloved city in pursuit of a woman. He was in love with the youngest daughter of the president of the German Communist Party. They were among the first ones to escape to Austria once it was clear that Hitler was becoming a powerful man and started to persecute and jail his opposition. The political mood in Berlin changed dramatically during those years, forcing people to take sides, to leave or face the consequences. Hans followed the girl's family to Austria and stayed with them for a while until the patriarch found out he was sleeping with his daughter. That was the end of the affair, and Hans decided Vienna was too boring for his wanderlust and left for Paris.

In the City of Lights he met a group of old friends and partied carelessly until they all ran out of money. By then, they knew that going back to Berlin wasn't an option. With whatever money they had left, they decided to board a ship and go on an adventure until things calmed down in Europe. They had heard that there was good money to be made in South America, exporting iron and other goods. Nobody ever imagined that a devastating war would break out and kill most of their loved ones. At that moment, they just wanted to get as far away as possible, to the most remote place on Earth. That was how they arrived in Paraguay.

Chapter Six

Our first daughter was born in June 1940. The labor pains started in the middle of the night. I didn't know exactly what to expect, but after a while the signs were clear. I woke Hans up and he rushed out of the house to get the midwife, who lived just a few blocks away. In my entire life, I had never experienced pain like this. My mother-in-law, Hanna, kept me company, holding my hand until the midwife arrived. I had asked Hans to send word to my mother and sisters, hoping that they could get to me in time to help with the birth. When they finally arrived, I was ready to start pushing. The baby was ready to come into this world and saw the light for the first time after the third push. She was small and looked so fragile we were afraid to hold her. My mother wrapped her in a white cotton blanket and handed her to me. I was mesmerized! She had Hans' deep blue eyes and my pale white skin.

We named her Anita Juana, in honor of the saint's day of her birth. Hans simply called her "*Baby*."

The birth of Anita brought so much joy to the house, especially in light of the devastating news coming from Europe. Bombs were falling all over the Old Continent, as Hitler's army left a trail of death and destruction behind. Around that time, we stopped receiving missives from Hans' relatives and we began to expect the worst.

But all of that was a world away from me. With the baby and Hans' family in the house, my life was as busy as could be. There was no time for me to rest. In addition, Hans' business picked up and he began to spend most of his time away from us, working at the docks, and leaving me alone for long periods of time.

Motherhood became my new challenge. Nothing I had done before could have prepared me for it. I saw my sisters taking care of their own children, and I helped raise Coco and Choli, but at that time, I was a child myself. I now realized that being a mother was the most difficult job I would ever have. Though Baby was a good child, when you are as naïve as I was, things can get a little complicated. Hanna tried to help me, but she probably had had her own babysitters and baby nurses because she seemed to know less than I did. Lotte was completely out of sight. My mother visited us regularly, and Antonia tried to give me a hand whenever she could. But they had their own busy lives, and I knew I was responsible for mine. I prayed that mothering would come naturally; after all, every woman should know how to take care of her own child.

The eve after I gave birth, I woke up in the middle of the night thinking that Baby was actually part of a dream and that my reality was back to our normal life, just Hans and I. It took me a few minutes and a loud cry from her for food to realize that I was sleeping next to my child and that she was here to stay. But my love for her grew stronger every day—to the point that it became unthinkable to love another human being so much. She gave a purpose to my life, a meaning that I didn't know existed. She made me proud.

If I was able to create something so beautiful, so perfect, then maybe, just maybe, I was special, too.

About that time, we received a letter from the German Consulate in Asuncion informing us that all German Jewish citizens were expected to turn in their passports and other documents because the Third Reich no longer recognized them as nationals of that country.

They had thirty days to comply or face legal consequences. Hans and his family were outraged. Their first reaction was to reject and destroy the letter. Hans was furious. He was one hundred per cent German. How could they take away his citizenship? That was his birth right! His family had lived on German soil for generations.

He felt humiliated, his pride violated. It was Adolf who calmed him down and reminded him that he had a daughter to think of. After long discussions, they all decided to turn their documents in and apply for Paraguayan citizenship. This process could take a long time and we needed to be patient. But the tension in the house grew more intolerable by the day.

Hans found refuge in his work and traveled regularly, which was very hard on me. The only advantage was that his business picked up—especially with Europe's immense appetite for iron—and the money slowly started coming in.

For the first time in my life, I had money to buy a crib and some extra furniture for the house. I still remember the first dress Hans brought me from one of his trips. It was off-white, with small pink flowers. He told me there was a parade in town, and he was looking forward to taking me. He picked me up in a convertible filled with fresh roses. There were so many roses, I was afraid I was going to have to sit on them. I thought it was all a big joke made at my expense, but as we drove slowly into town, I started to see more and more vehicles with beautiful women inside who would throw flowers and candy to the crowd. Every car had a number and was lined up on the main road. We went down this long avenue, greeting everyone. I was a little shy at the beginning, but soon I was waving my arms in the air and throwing roses left and right. I had never had so much fun in my life. At the end of the event, they announced my name as the queen of the parade and put a small toy crown on my head. I was embarrassed by the whole situation and gave Hans a furious look. He knew how shy I was and how much I hated the extra attention—though I had to admit, I had fun. When I came back from the podium, I walked right by him with my head up high, as if I was looking down at one of my royal subjects. I stopped next to him and said:

"Will you swear loyalty to your Queen?"

"Of course, my love, you will always be my Queen," he replied before we both broke down laughing.

Unfortunately, my royal dream didn't last long.

Hans kept making good money. But with the money came a side of him I had not seen before. He didn't trust the local banks run by corrupt managers, he said, so most of our savings were in a shoe box on the top shelf of my closet. It didn't take long until he started playing cards, with friends first, and with professional gamblers soon after. He would go away after dinner and come back a few times during the night, depending on his luck. If the night was good, he would return and put the money he won in the box. If luck wasn't on his side, he would come a few times to get more money until it would either run out or he won his bet back.

These nights were very long and lonely. I would wait up for him and beg him to return to his senses. I would implore him to stay home with me and the baby, to think of our family, of our future. I would cry and yell. But nothing worked. "You don't understand," he would tell me without making eye contact. I kept telling myself that things would change. It was very hard for me to understand why he was doing this. His behavior seemed to go against everything I believed in—our marriage, our lives. Every time he gambled, he was a different man, as if he was in a trance. He would enter a different world, where nobody mattered, not even his own family.

I finally realized that he would probably never change. I could see very clearly that he could not control the urge to gamble and that this weakness ran in his family. I began to take small amounts of money out of the box and hid it, ensuring that we had enough money to last through each month.

Whatever money my in-laws were able to bring with them when they escaped from Berlin ran out quickly, and they depended on us financially for a long time. Heinrich tried to get a job at a local bank with the help of my father, but the language barrier was almost impossible to overcome. He ended up helping Hans with his business at the docks, despite Lotte's refusal and fury that her husband was getting his hands dirty doing a lower-class job.

All I could do was try to raise my young child, keep our family together, and take care of our finances.

Every day became a guessing game with Hans. I never knew what to expect. Most of the time he was a loving husband, but I began to notice that we were not his priority. Money burned in his pocket. He had this urge to buy unnecessary things and take superfluous risks. I was the opposite. I was always worried that we were not going to have enough money to feed my now seven-member family. We went from two to seven in the blink of an eye, and I had no idea how we were going to provide for everyone. Since Baby was born, my outlook on life had taken a dramatic turn, and I was more stressed than ever about our future. War times were always difficult, I told myself, trying to find some consolation. The war may have been taking place on the other side of the world, but I felt its impact directly under my feet.

My mother-in-law saw the tension building in me and always tried to show me some affection.

"You wonderful wife, Hans very lucky man," she used to say in her broken Spanish.

I believed she knew something I didn't; she seemed to understand Hans' nature better than I and showed me a lot of compassion. I kept wondering how she was able to sit and watch from a distance and not tell me how to change him. I never had the courage to ask her directly. She belonged to my mother's generation, I thought, when women just accepted their fate and didn't do anything about it. Sadly, I wasn't any better.

I was raised to believe that men knew best and that they would always provide for their families, but the more I saw, the better I understood how things really worked in a marriage. I chose not to confront Hans, but rather I kept hiding money, taking care of the house, and watching silently as his true personality unveiled itself before my eyes. In time, I realized that I was doing the same thing my own mother did to survive her own marriage: she just endured.

Hans never drank. Alcohol wasn't his drug of preference. He loved gambling and women—all kinds of women. Sex was his second-favorite drug. I didn't know details, but I could tell when he had just spent a few hours with a woman. I could smell it. I could taste it. I didn't have the courage to ask him about it though. I was aware that married men were not always faithful to their wives. In Paraguay's society, it was almost an accepted fact of life. Every man had the right to his sexual freedom. It didn't matter the emotional cost of their adventures or if they left bastard children around the world. That they were committing adultery never even crossed their minds. I knew a few cases in which the wife was forced to take her husband's offspring and adopt them as her own without asking any questions. It never happened with my father, or maybe my mother was never honest enough to admit it. But that thought haunted me. It was always in the back of my mind.

I tried very hard to satisfy my husband sexually, but with me he was different. There was a big difference between his wife and the rest of them: sex with me became a duty, with the others it was fun. With them he used a condom, with me he didn't.

"Condoms are for whores," he used to say. So I kept praying that I wouldn't get pregnant and it didn't happen for four years.

Our second daughter was born in March of 1944. We called her Matilde. She didn't look anything like Baby. She had a head full of black hair, small brown eyes, and was skinny. But there was no doubt she was his daughter. There was an expression in her face, a look in her eyes, the way she stared at me that was exactly like Hans. After more than four years of being an only child, Baby didn't welcome her sister with open arms. Sometimes her jealousy would get out of control and I would fear for Matilde's life. So she went everywhere I went. She was always strapped to me and became an extra limb. I managed to do all my chores with her hanging from my waist. I loved having her so close to me all the time. We were one, moving together, eating together, and sleeping together. I nursed her well beyond her first year and the day she finally stopped it broke my heart. The bond between us was very hard to describe. It amazed me that she became such an independent woman later on in life, having depended on me every minute of her first years.

It became obvious to me that Hans and his family had a soft spot for Baby and would almost ignore Matilde. It pained me to see the way they acted toward our younger daughter, but she didn't seem to care. She was just a happy child. Of course, I showered her with love and affection, and she became my own mother's favorite grandchild. My children were complete opposites: Baby was beautiful, Matilde was plain; Baby was sensitive, Matilde was tough; Baby was insecure, Matilde was independent. It was very hard for me to understand how two sisters could be such extreme opposites. With my own sisters, I felt we were all diverse but we shared a common factor. I didn't see it with my daughters. They lived in different worlds. But I knew how important the bond between sisters could be. In my case, they were like mothers to me. They helped raise me, they taught me everything I knew, they were my confidantes—my best friends. I wished my own children would one day discover the power of the sisters' bond and how it can shape your life in ways that nothing else can.

When Matilde was still an infant, my brother Juan made Hans a business proposal and convinced him to invest all of our savings to buy a few trucks that he and a few drivers would drive through the border to Argentina, transporting goods between the two countries. Hans was tired of all the traveling and the hard work at the docks and seemed interested in a new venture. My brother Juan had been in the trucking business for a few years and told us there was a lot of money to be made. He was one of the younger ones in the family, and I knew him well. His work ethic had never been the best, but he had a charming personality. He was funny and good looking, a free spirit. I couldn't picture him as a manager running his own company or being the boss of anybody. He could be a good drinking buddy, yes, but not a good business partner. He had never married and was happy as a bachelor. For him, life had too much to offer to spend it in one place, with just one woman. Maybe this aspect of his personality was what most attracted Hans. I was afraid that Hans identified himself with Juan's way of life and even envied his freedom.

Juan's proposal sounded interesting at the beginning until Hans told me that we had to move to the Argentinean side of the border, a few hours away from Asuncion. How could I leave my family? There was no way in the world I would leave my mother, my sisters, my house, my life. I was going to lose too much, but then I realized that maybe a new place would cure Hans' weaknesses. Besides, he'd be so occupied with his new business venture that he wouldn't have time to gamble or sleep around. Asuncion was a small city and word had started to spread. Hans' reputation grew quickly. Gossip about his infidelities started to take on a life of their own, and the more I found out, the more I wanted to escape the shame. Even my friend Ana Maria visited less and less, and I knew she was avoiding me. My back was against the wall. I had no choice; I had to do something drastic to change our situation.

By then the war was over and my in-laws were in the process of reclaiming part of their fortune. They were able to get some money back, but with Europe in ruins they figured it was madness to try to return to Berlin. They decided instead to move to Argentina's capital city, Buenos Aires, which they found to be more European and civilized than Asuncion. Lotte and her husband moved with them initially but returned to Germany as soon as they could. With the Marshall Plan in effect, Heinrich was able to be a part of the reconstruction efforts and would become a very successful banker.

Sadly, he passed away from heart failure only a few years after returning. Lotte didn't waste any time and remarried almost immediately to another wealthy business man who kept financing her gambling habits, fur coats, and expensive taste.

After five long years, it was back to me, Hans, and the girls. My house felt empty and I especially missed my mother-in-law. In all these years her Spanish hadn't improved very much, but I still loved having her with me. She was very close to our children and gave them a lot of love and affection, as had my father-in-law. She even tried to teach them to say some words in German, but that didn't go well. Hans' family arrived suddenly in my life and left the same way, leaving an empty feeling in my heart. All of a sudden the idea of moving away didn't seem so crazy. I told myself I wasn't going to be that far away and could visit any time that I wanted or needed to. On the other hand, Hans was very excited about his new venture and kept talking about the money he would make and the palace he would buy me. He would always dream big, and I would always keep him grounded.

Chapter Seven

The floor of my new palace was made of mud. In fact, there was no floor. All I could see was dirt. There was no point in cleaning as the wind blew dust around constantly and I became obsessed with the broom. The more I swept, the more dirt I found. It was useless but I was determined to tame the beast. Our house sat on a dirt road, off the main road, which was also dirt.

The town of Clorinda was more than 600 miles northeast from Buenos Aires and completely disconnected from the Argentinian capital. It had just a handful of streets and was populated by a few hundred people, most of them employed in some border-trade related activity. Because there was some illegal trafficking taking place, the border police were a constant presence in the town. Of course, they were the first ones involved in any illegal activity and looked the other way if there was money in it for them. It was important to be friends with the right people if you wanted your business to be successful. I found this interaction—between the good guys and bad guys—fascinating. In no time, Hans charmed them all with his accent, his sense of humor, and his street smarts.

He was busy with his new enterprise and spent most of his time building it. He had a few extra drivers besides my brother and himself. They all came to my house to eat and I discovered a new passion: cooking.

I loved spending my days in the kitchen and realized that if I kept myself busy I wouldn't miss Asuncion and my sisters so much.

With little to no success, I tried to grow my flower garden in the back of our new home. No matter how much I tried, I couldn't get anything to grow. How can you grow flowers in the dust? How can you survive without the proper soil? I felt like one of my flowers, fighting every day to survive in a place that was nothing but dust.

The girls, however, adapted much faster than I. Baby went to a little Catholic school every day for a few hours and Matilde kept me company. I was settling, despite the facts that we had no money, we lived in a hut, and I missed my family back in Paraguay terribly.

Away from everything that had been familiar to him till that moment, away from the temptation of the women he had met and his infidelities, Hans started to pay more attention to me. He began to make love to me with an unusual tenderness, as if he needed to recapture our long-lost intimacy. It had been years since I felt close to him. The passion we once felt for one another had been slowly disappearing, as parenthood, obligations and resentments took over our daily lives. We shared a bed every night, but he felt like a stranger to me. Many times I wondered if I was the right woman for him, if he fell in love with me out of necessity or loneliness. All these years together and I still didn't know why he chose me. I liked to think that deep down in his heart and soul, he longed for a family, for a normal life next to a woman he could love unconditionally. But there were two sides to Hans. One was the man from Berlin who missed a lifestyle that was now gone; the other was a man who struggled to be happy in a world that wasn't his own.

My life was very different from his, but I did love him and I wanted to be loved in return. So I forgave him, just to feel a brief moment of happiness when he gave himself to me.

I was still physically attracted to him, even when I knew he wasn't faithful to me. He fed me the crumbs, and I was satisfied. In my heart I wished that I was all he wanted, all that he needed. I tried to convince myself that we had a chance, that our marriage could be again what it used to be.

Between his trips we spent very little time together. He brought money home regularly, and I went back to my old habit of hiding some of it in a box under our bed. I made sure that we had enough for our daily expenses and whatever I had left, I saved for building a real floor. I could feel his trips pulling us apart, and it hurt to remember the days when we couldn't wait to be together again.

Every so often, I would get a ride with the girls in one of the trucks and go visit my mother and sisters. Most of them were still in the house, keeping each other company with no hope of finding a husband. My father had died the past year at the age of 81 and they were still in mourning. He had been sick for a while and his condition had deteriorated quickly even though the doctors couldn't tell us exactly what was wrong with him.

"All those years of bitterness and anger. He poisoned his own blood," was Luisa's conclusion.

My mother took care of him until his final breath, and he died peacefully in her arms. She and Coco were the only people allowed in his room. I found it very ironic that he left this world so peacefully after a life of tormenting everyone around him.

The mood of the house had changed dramatically after his death. My brothers left to start their own families, but my sisters remained in a strange state of paralysis. My father's ghost still lingered inside those walls. They were numb after all the misery he had caused them, as if they had no sense of self. I was probably the only one whose marriage was blessed by him and left the house on good terms. No other female member of my family had the same luck. Antonia and Luisa remained single. My other sisters, Josefina and Asuncion, didn't have much luck either. Josefina married a low-ranking military officer who turned out to be a wife beater. They had four children, three girls and a boy, and many years later we found out he had another family. Of course Josefina never left him and he died by her side. On the other hand, my sister Asuncion was left standing at the altar on the day of her wedding. Her fiancé ran away to Brazil. She never married and ended up adopting and rais-ing the baby of one of our maids who had died at childbirth. When her adoptive daughter got married, Asuncion moved in with her and her husband and stayed with them until the end of her days.

After Anton's death, my mother's health started to deteriorate fast. A lifetime of heartache was finally taking its toll on her. With-out a man to look after and children to protect, she found herself lost in this world. She missed a sense of purpose. But our visits became a reason for joy, and she looked forward to having the girls around her. She would take care of them as if they were her own children. The older she got, the more she wanted to live in the past. She could remember everything that happened twenty or thirty years ago, but she had a hard time remembering yesterday.

I never understood how she survived all those years with my father. "Life has many mysteries," she used to tell me, "and a woman's heart is full of secrets."

Tia Nira, my mother's sister, had passed away a few years ear-lier. She left her farm to my mother, but one of my older brothers was working it. His wife had just one condition before moving to the country: get rid of the parrots. So my mother adopted them and had them in her patio, right outside her kitchen. She talked to them, sang to them, fed them, and looked after them, just as Tia Nira had. They were her best friends; they listened and didn't ask questions. They kept her company during the long summer after-noons, when the pain caused by her arthritis didn't let her sleep her siesta anymore.

Despite her age, Andrea was still a beautiful woman. Her hair had turned grey a long time ago, but her skin refused to show the passage of time. As a wife and a mother, I could see myself in her more and more. But when it came to forgiving my father, I could not do it. The news of his death brought me relief instead of grief. After we came back from his funeral mass, I felt like the rope we had around our necks during our childhood was gone once and for all. Not even when I got married and moved out of the house did I feel this liberated. Yet even after his death, I couldn't forgive him for all the damage he had caused, how he had ruined my sisters' chances of happiness, how he had tortured us on a daily basis to feel superior.

"Your father has a tormented soul," my mother used to say. But why would he go against us? Why were we the victims of his fury? No one knew what drove him to such madness. Maybe he felt we were his punishment for not having the courage to stay behind in his country to fight for his ideals, maybe he was just a miserable man who probably hated himself more than anybody else. The pride he felt inside, his unwillingness to forgive, and his incapacity to love made him a sad and lonely old man. None of his children felt close to him. He was never a real father to us, just a tyrant that imposed his ways no matter the consequences. He built a family on bricks of hate and pride.

Luisa's son, who almost died in his mother's womb because of our father's fury, was the only one who seemed to miss him. After my father's death, Coco took over his studio and finished the few pieces he had been working on. Coco did such an amazing job that my father's clients kept coming back for more and his reputation started to grow as Paraguay's most talented artist and restoration specialist. He also enjoyed decorating people's homes and soon the rich were calling him to work in their mansions. His specialties were laminating furniture and picture frames with gold, and restoring statues of saints and altars.

In those days, people had their own altars at home and for Christmas they would compete with one another for who had the most beautiful Nativity scene. Usually, people would open the doors and windows of their magnificent homes and show off their figures of the three holy Kings, Jesus, Joseph, and Mary. But Coco decided to take it to the next level. He created almost life-size statues for his Nativity scene, including animals and dunes. His became the most famous one in Asuncion, and people from all over the country came just to see it. My mother's house had to be open almost all day and night to let visitors admire Coco's work. He changed it from year to year so that everyone had an excuse to return. Not even the heat of summer stopped people from coming to our house. Soon after, his clients started demanding the same type of work for their own Nativities; that way neighbors could spend the entire Christmas season visiting each other's homes, drinking iced tea, and tasting some traditional holiday dishes.

But Coco's life was lonely. He spent most of his time working and never showed any interest in women. We all had very high hopes for him because his work was making him a wealthy man. But the stigma of growing up without a father was still strong among the upper-class families, and we knew it was always going to follow him if he ever decided to get married. His mother, Luisa, didn't think anything of her son being single. In fact, she preferred it that way. She overprotected him throughout his life and she was not ready to let go. She would constantly check on him, asking him where he was going, which clients he was visiting, what projects to take. She had started to run his business as well as his private life.

I always felt a special connection with Coco, and it made me sad to see him surrounded by older women who were counting on him to take care of them until they died. So I decided to ask Luisa to come spend some time with me and the girls, as a way to liberate him from her asphyxiating control.

"How can I leave Coco? He needs me here," she replied to my invitation.

"Listen, Luisa, come for a few weeks. I need you too. I need help with the girls, and they never spend time with the family anymore. You will like it too. It's a chance for you to take a little break," I insisted, knowing that she probably couldn't resist the temptation of making us the subject of her obsession.

"Fine, but only a few weeks. I don't know what Coco will do without me," she said reluctantly.

"He'll survive. He's a grown man now, and you need to let him have a life," I replied, stepping into dangerous territory.

"He has a life with me. He is happy like this. Not everyone is destined for marriage. Look at me—I don't miss being with a man," she said.

"It's not fair to compare yourself with him. He's your son and you are his mother, not his wife. Sooner or later you will have to realize that you can't take that place in his life. You don't want him to end up alone," I pressed.

"He will never be alone. As long as I live, he will have me," she concluded, and I could tell that she was getting upset. There was no point in continuing the discussion. It was only a matter of time until Coco found the right woman and Luisa would have to accept it.

"You are right," I said. "He has you and he's very lucky to have such a caring and loving mother. You did an amazing job raising him. I'm sure he's very grateful," I added, trying to calm her. I realized that neither of us was going to give in today so I decided to leave the discussion for another day.

My visit to Asuncion was brief but invigorating. My mother was sad to see us go—especially Matilde, whom she nicknamed "*Palolo*". She adored her. It was a beautiful thing to see how well they connected and how symbiotic their connection was. I always wondered how such a bond could happen between a child and an older person. Somehow they were in a similar place, even though they were on opposite ends of the life cycle.

I was deeply moved every time I saw them playing together. Matilde didn't speak yet, but words weren't necessary. They had only to look at each other to know exactly what the other wanted. My mother would make the parrots talk and sing just to watch Matilde giggle. They would spend hours outside in the garden playing with dirt, singing old songs, or just watching clouds go by. Baby was older and preferred to play with the other kids in the neighborhood, so Matilde had her grandma all to herself. I wished my mother could come with us, but her health wasn't good. It worried me to be away from her. What if something happened and I was not with her? I couldn't even imagine my life without her, so I pushed that thought out of my mind and told myself to focus on the time I still had with her.

We drove back in one of Hans' trucks with Luisa and the kids. The dirt roads had potholes everywhere. It was a long and tiresome trip. We had to make several stops along the way because Baby got sick to her stomach and had to throw up. But even with all the motion sickness, the trip was an escape for me. I loved driving through different towns and watching farmers work the land. The geography of northeastern Argentina can be breathtaking. The furious green of the tropical forest mixes itself with the red dirt of the plains while rivers and streams bring life to the most remote corners of the region. The humidity made the air dense and filled it with the strange smells of nature. But the most powerful thing for me was the immensity of the sky. Nowhere else had I seen a sky so blue and infinite, with no beginning and no end. It reminded me of all the things we have absolutely no control over.

We passed a few indigenous communities along the way, with their colorful mud houses and children playing beside the road. The fiery red dust stuck everywhere: in our clothes, on cars, in the children's hands and feet, even on their faces. Nothing could take the red out of clothes. I tried several secret recipes my mother gave me, but nothing worked. It ended up not bothering me at all. I accepted life in red. Everything becomes so much easier when you learn to accept it.

I guess that was what happened with me and Hans. He was a good man but a bad husband, and I had to accept it. I just didn't realize how much I was going to have to suffer before I finally did.

Having Luisa around was a blessing. She helped me with the girls and in the kitchen, when it was time to cook for the drivers. One of them especially had his eye on her. He would come every morning to drink his coffee and stared at Luisa while we got ready for lunch. His name was Emanuel. He was tall and good looking, but very shy. He would never say a word. He just sat there until his cup was empty. Then he would get up, wish us a good day, and leave. Every morning the ritual was the same, until one day Luisa lost her patience and faced him.

"I don't know what you are after, but let me tell you, you are not going to get it," she said.

He didn't say a word. He just got up and left. I was shocked to see such a reaction from my beloved sister. It left me speechless.

"How can you be so cruel?" I asked her finally. "He didn't do anything wrong," I said.

"I could see it in his eyes. He wanted something from me that I no longer possess."

"And what is that?"

"My womanhood," she replied simply.

I walked away from the kitchen not to let her see the tears in my eyes. Luisa was in her late forties, but more beautiful than ever. She always walked tall, with her head up and her shoulders straight. I admired her and loved her deeply, and it just broke my heart to see that she had closed the door to her heart. Happiness was just not a possibility for her. At least not with a man. She came looking for me and hugged me.

"Chola, why are you crying? You're not feeling sorry for me, are you?" she asked, giving me a big smile.

I couldn't talk. My throat was knotted up with tears that I tried unsuccessfully to hide from her.

"Don't worry for me. I have loved and I was loved. And Coco reminds me every day of that love. I'm a very lucky woman and I have found my peace. I don't need a man to feel complete. I lost my man too soon, but he didn't lose me," she explained softly as if she was consoling a little girl.

The days turned into weeks, and the weeks into months. Luisa's presence became a part of our daily lives. She became my pillar, my confidant, my best friend. There was a big age difference between us, but it didn't matter. Hans also got along well with her. I think he admired her sense of independence and her strong personality. He treated her as an equal, which was a rare thing between a man and a woman at the time. This made me a little jealous; I was, after all, his wife and the woman of the house. But Luisa made us feel loved and we needed it. She taught me her favorite recipes. She even taught me how to dance. In return, I tried to teach her how to play the piano and make clothes, neither with success. She showed no interest in learning anything new; she was content with herself just as she was.

"I'm too old for this," she would say. "But look at you—you can do anything!"

I smiled and wished in silence that her words were true. I felt there was nothing I could do right and I found pleasure in very little. What was wrong with me? Why couldn't I just accept my life and be happy? Why did I always want more? Why couldn't I just be content?

Many answers popped into my head but the most important was Hans' late nights. As much as I ignored it, it killed me inside to think that he preferred to be away from me rather than spend time together. His trips didn't help either. The business was going well, and his route often took him to Buenos Aires where his parents had finally settled in an elderly home run by the local Jewish community. They were both getting older and his father's health hadn't been good the past few years. His mother was still strong and always kept her darling personality. I missed her. Hans brought us letters from her in German, which he would translate for me and the girls.

After the war ended, the German government paid them enough money to have a comfortable life and she always sent some cash for her grandchildren. She never forgot all the years that we provided for her and her family and let me know in small ways her constant gratitude.

Hans missed them too but didn't like to talk about his family with me. The Germany where he grew up no longer existed, and he vowed never to go back until Berlin was united again. He broke his promise only once, many years later, when he was forced to return to read his sister's will.

For now, everything German was bad. I begged him to teach his language to our daughters, but he replied the same way every time: "What for? We'll never go there anyway."

He buried his culture in a deep, dark place of his soul, like it never existed. Yet his accent was so strong, everyone called him "*el alemán*", the German. He kept a few European friends whom he met regularly to play cards and drink "*schnapps.*" One tradition he kept until the day he died: he always had iced coffee in the evening with a scoop of vanilla ice cream. On this side of the world, coffee was always hot, so his eccentricity never went unnoticed.

So many times I tried to help him open his heart, wishing that he could find some closure. So many wounds were still open and I knew that they were killing him.

"There is nothing to talk about," he would reply, avoiding the conversation.

"You can't deny who you are or where you came from," I insisted, trying to help ease his pain and confront his fears and frustrations.

"I know who I am. My past doesn't exist anymore. Most of the people I cared about, besides my parents and my sister, are gone. So what's the point of talking about them?"

"You would feel better if you just tried. Maybe remembering them is a way to honor their lives," I insisted.

"Chola, they were all murdered; they were killed like animals. I will only be happy the day those Nazis are dead. Every single one of them. And to make things worse, they are hiding in South America, living a perfectly normal life, when they should be brought to justice and sentenced to death for genocide. They should pay with their own lives for what they've done. I was proud to be a German. Now it's humiliating to even say where I come from," he replied, his eyes filled with hatred.

"You were the one who told me hate gets you nowhere, remember? How can you be so hateful? Don't you see that the only one who really suffers is you? What they did is out of your control. You need to let it go," I insisted, knowing that the conversation was going nowhere but still feeling it was necessary.

Talking about the war and the horrors of the concentration camps was extremely difficult for Hans. The devastation and death left behind was inconceivable. His cousins, his aunts and uncles—no one made it. I knew the guilt was making him crazy. He hadn't stayed behind to fight or protect any of his family members, and that probably made him feel like a coward. But on the other hand, if he hadn't married me and stayed in Paraguay, he and his parents and sister would all have died like the rest of them. I didn't know how to help him. He was a mystery to me. This was going to be a very slow process that he would have to go through. I promised him that I would stand by his side, but he had to find the courage to forgive himself first.

The country he grew up loving, feeling proud of, didn't exist anymore. His citizenship was taken away from him, along with his pride and his history. He belonged nowhere. Rejected and expelled by his own country, he was forced to create a new identity, a new life. With a broken heart and soul, he embraced his new home and swore never to go back.

Chapter Eight

After her second month with us, Luisa's visit came to an abrupt end when we had word from Asuncion that Coco was very ill. He was admitted to a local hospital, and no one seemed to know what was wrong with him. When we first heard the news, they told us that he probably had polio. My heart sank and I cried inconsolably. But Luisa picked me up and said, "Enough! He needs us to be strong. I'll leave tomorrow and once I'm there, I will let you know what you can do. I don't want your tears. Go make us some tea and after that we'll go to church to say a prayer," she ordered, looking into my eyes with a burning intensity.

I did as she told me. I got the girls dressed and we all went to church, where we lit a candle and prayed throughout the evening. Hans never went to church with me; he hated the religious rituals, especially the priests. He could not understand how God expected a man to go through life without a woman. Celibacy was a big joke to him, and he kept assuring me that priests and nuns were probably having a big orgy every night. Of course, I couldn't bear to hear him talk so disrespectfully about my faith. But when Coco got sick, he asked me to light a candle in his name. We all needed God sometimes.

Luisa left the next morning, and it took a few days until her telegram reached us. Coco was in stable condition but critically ill. Polio was now ruled out, but he was fighting a severe infection in his lungs. The doctors thought that it had something to do with all the oils and acids he used in his paintings and restoration projects and that it might take a few weeks until he was out of danger. For now, there was not much we could do but pray for him. So that was what I did. Every day. Coco was more than a nephew to me. I had helped raise him. Everything I learned in school I passed on to him and Choli. The three of us were inseparable; we played together and grew up together. The thought of him dying was killing me inside, and I wished I could be there with him to ease his pain.

But I couldn't leave. Hans' trips were long and the girls had finally settled in at our local Catholic school. Baby was a very good student and the teacher's favorite. Matilde, on the other hand, was too much of a free spirit. She loved to listen to my old classical music records and she loved the sound of the piano. Baby was interested in music as well, but not like Matilde, who was obsessed with it. She liked playing on my old piano, the one my parents gave me when I was a child. It was old, but it played nicely and in tune. It was my only distraction. We both sat together and played on the keys, finding new melodies and creating new sounds. Music was our common language; everything else about Matilde seemed a mystery to me.

Matilde and Baby didn't get along well, but I attributed it to simple sibling rivalry. I had been focused on my own sorrows until I found Matilde crying and hiding inside my closet one morning. She refused to tell me what was going on at first, but slowly she started to let it all out.

"Baby says I am not your daughter," she cried.

"That is not true," I said as I was trying to dry the tears on her face.

"She said you found me inside a garbage can and took me home with you," she explained between inconsolable sobs.

"That is nonsense. How could you believe such a lie? Look at us, we look so alike, you and I," I insisted, but I could tell she was not satisfied with my explanation.

"But I'm not like Baby. She's blonde and her eyes are blue. She says I look like a native girl. My hair is dark and so are my eyes," she replied.

"Matilde, I want you to listen to me carefully," I said, feeling angrier by the minute. "It doesn't matter what you look like—you are my daughter; you are a part of me. I will always love you, even if your hair were pink. I don't want you to listen to what your sister tells you anymore. Just listen to your heart, and you will know what is true."

She gave me a brief smile and cuddled in my arms for a while. I always knew that Baby was a jealous child, but never to this extreme. To do this to her own sister was cruel and I wasn't going to allow it. But I knew she couldn't control those emotions; after all, she had had everybody's attention for four years before her sister was born. I felt responsible for not having seen this before, for not protecting Matilde better, for not demanding that both girls be treated the same way. But this could not go unpunished. So I grounded Baby for a month: no friends, no games, no candy. She didn't cry when she heard the sentence; she just stared at me with her cold blue eyes. She knew what she had done was wrong, but in her head it was justified. So I told her from now on, Matilde would be included in everything she did. She was going to have to take her little sister along when she played with her friends. Their relationship didn't improve for a long time. In fact, they didn't become true friends until after they were both married.

It seemed like an eternity until I finally received a telegram from Luisa. It was a brief message, but to the point: Coco was out of the hospital and in good health, but weak. He would have to be taken care of by a nurse at home.

Of course I was overjoyed to know that he was out of danger but could hardly imagine that Luisa was going to let another woman—even a professional nurse—take care of her beloved son. I'm sure she couldn't say no to the doctor's orders, or maybe she was softened by the whole ordeal, or maybe she was finally coming to her senses, which I truly doubted.

The news of Coco's health arrived with another surprising one: Choli was engaged. I was very surprised because I didn't know she had met a man. But I was happy for her. It was time for her to move on with her life. The years had flown by fast and by now most of us were out of the house, with our own lives and our own destinies. Still, I missed the days when we were all under one roof.

Choli never seemed interested in studying or working out of the house. She wasn't lazy; she just preferred to stay where she felt safe. She didn't enjoy doing anything that made her leave the safety of our home. We all teased her and told her that she would never meet a man if she insisted on staying behind closed doors. So a man finally came to her. His name was Mateo. His family was Swiss, but he was born in Asuncion. They had commissioned Coco to make a family portrait and came a few times to his studio to pose. Sometimes Choli would help Coco get his materials ready. And that was how they met. Mateo saw her briefly in Coco's studio and immediately wanted to know about her. He convinced Coco to help him get to know her better and begged him to arrange their first date. Coco even agreed to chaperone. They all went to see a movie at the local theater, but Choli didn't say a word all night.

Coco thought that was the end of the affair and didn't try to get them together again, but Mateo kept coming back to visit him at his studio. So it was inside the walls she knew and trusted that she and Mateo started to get to know each other. She would wait for him with iced tea ready, and they would sit at the kitchen table for hours, talking about their lives and their dreams. Antonia was the first one who realized what was going on; the rest of the household didn't care much. Choli was the youngest in the family and no one paid attention to her. Since she was an infant, I was the one person responsible for her, and after I got married and left Asuncion, no one took my place. She grew quietly, to the point of almost becoming invisible. For that reason, her engagement came as a big surprise not only to me but to the entire family.

Mateo was a lot like her, shy but likeable. His family came from a small town in the Alps and they preferred to keep to themselves. They made a small fortune running their own chain of convenience stores, where you could buy almost anything you needed, from buttons to powdered milk. Mateo worked with his father at the stores and because he was the oldest son, his father expected him to take over the family business one day. But he was a dreamer. He wanted much more than that from life. He wanted to travel the world. He wanted to escape with Choli. He dreamed of taking her away and starting somewhere new. But he never would because Choli could never leave.

The wedding was planned rather quickly—nothing lavish, just a plain church ceremony and a small reception at Mateo's family home. Coco was supposed to decorate the place and design the catering menu—food was his second passion after art.

I was excited to have an excuse to go back to Asuncion and escape my routine, even for a few days. I missed my mother and my sisters terribly and couldn't wait to catch up with them. Our only communication was through letters that took several weeks to reach each other. By the time I found out how things were going, it was already old news. I was also anxious to see how Coco's health was coming along and if he was truly getting better. I always feared that my sisters kept things from me to spare me the pain and sorrow of worrying too much. I needed to see for myself. The girls were happy to attend their first wedding, and we all started preparing for our trip and planning which dresses we should make.

Time flew by and before we knew it, we were climbing in one of Hans' trucks. The trip took longer than usual because the driver had a few scheduled stops along the way. But the girls and I didn't mind; we were excited about the upcoming events.

We arrived in the middle of a rain storm. Because the truck got stuck in the mud a few meters away from my mother's house, I decided to walk the rest of the way. I took one girl at a time and protected her under the umbrella as well as I could. As we were approaching the house, I noticed that all the windows were closed, but with such furious rain that didn't seem strange. I opened the door and yelled my mother's name. Nobody was home. The house was dark and smelled funny. I told Baby and Matilde to wait for me at the front door because the driver was holding our luggage and was waiting to get back on the road. As I walked to the truck, protecting my face with the umbrella, a stranger stopped me.

"I am so sorry for your loss. You probably don't remember me because I moved next door after you married. Your mother was a wonderful woman. We will miss her very much," he said.

The umbrella fell from my hands as I stood under the rain. I couldn't move. My feet were sinking in the mud. I was paralyzed.

The driver ran to me with panic in his eyes and I heard the girls screaming my name.

All I could feel was the water hitting my face. He picked me up in his arms and brought me inside the house. I left a trail of water coming in. Matilde jumped at me and held on to my neck. She knew something was wrong. My daughters had never seen me in such a state. I held them both as the tears came. My face was still soaked from the rain and my tears mingled with it on my skin, dripping down my cheeks.

My mother had died the day before our arrival. The telegram crossed paths with us on our way to the wedding. The smell of death was still lingering inside the walls and was mixing with the flowers that inundated the living room. That was the strange smell I noticed when I first walked into the house.

The neighbor offered to take us to the funeral home, where my mother's body had been lying since the night before. I tried to get on my feet again and noticed my children's faces for the first time since our arrival. They were looking at me with compassion and anxiety at the same time. I felt weak, fragile, and vulnerable. At that moment, I realized I wasn't their mother—I was my mother's daughter.

The funeral home was only a few blocks from the house, but the roads were so muddy that the only way to get there was to walk. Both men walked beside me, each one holding one of my arms so I would not fall. The girls followed silently. I had a hard time picking up my feet; it was as if the weight of the world was pushing me down. It took us a long time to get there, but we made it under the torrential rain.

My siblings were gathered inside a large, windowless hall that looked more like a hospital waiting room than a funeral home. The walls were covered in white tiles as were the floors. It was cold, and when I saw her coffin in the middle of the room, a chill went down my spine. It was closed and I couldn't see her. I walked slowly, ignoring everyone in the room, and just went to her. I tried to pull open the lid but my brother Andres stopped me.

"You don't want to see her. She doesn't look like the person we knew," he said.

"But I need to see her face. I want to remember her," I said and stopped before I could finish my sentence.

"Chola, she's gone. This is not her anymore. She left her body and what you will see is not going to be what you expect. Please, let me help you find a seat and you can think about it," he insisted.

"I was supposed to see her one more time, just one more time. I have so much to tell her," I cried.

"I know you do, but all you can do now is pray and talk to her from your heart. She will always be there for you," Andres replied.

My hands were shaking and I was shivering from the cold of my wet clothes. The girls were looking at me puzzled, and I realized I had to go to them and explain what was happening. I wiped my face with my hands and sat down next to them.

"Grandma is in heaven now," I said.

Matilde hugged me and replied, "We know. She's an angel now, and she is with Jesus."

Her words brought some peace to my heart, and I stayed in my child's arms for a few minutes, wishing this was a bad dream. But the sounds of my sisters' cries were too strong. Everyone was wearing black, except for me and the girls. We had our traveling clothes on, dirty with red dust from the road and sweaty from the long hours inside cabin of the hot truck.

We sat in silence for a while, holding hands and praying. But I couldn't stop shaking, so I decided to take the girls back to the house to change out of our wet clothes.

By then, the rain had stopped. We walked slowly, trying to avoid the big puddles of water.

The house was open, so we went to the kitchen to make some tea. Hans was sitting at the table, waiting for me. The girls ran to him.

"I received the telegram only a few hours after you left. *Lo lamento mucho*, I'm so sorry, Chola," he said and came closer to hold me.

"If I had left a few days before, I would have seen her alive," I sobbed.

"How could you know something like this would happen? She was fine the last time you saw her. No one expected this," he replied.

"I should have been here," I repeated. "We should have never moved away. Why did you take me away from my family? Why did you take me away from my mother?" I said, not realizing that I was shouting at him.

"Chola, there is nothing you can do now. You can blame me if it makes you feel better, but death is a part of life and you know it. I'm not a religious man, but I believe that our loved ones continue to live through us as long as we feel their presence."

He held me and I broke down in his arms. My legs gave in and my entire weight fell onto his body.

The four of us sat on the kitchen floor for a very long time. We were never more united than on that day. Grief made us whole, it made us a family.

The morning after, we walked slowly to the cemetery, my brothers in front of us carrying the coffin. It was a slow procession, but it gave me a chance to think about my life, my hopes for my children and for myself, and the dreams I used to have and couldn't remember anymore. My life so far seemed full of surprises, and

I was the first one to admit that I had never imagined this ending. But then I realized it wasn't an ending, only the beginning. Hans was walking by my side for the first time. He had always walked in front of me, never beside me. My mother's death awakened me to my own misery; it gave me my life back, my sense of self, my need for belonging. Walking behind her body, I decided I needed to find my way back.

Hans had to leave directly after the funeral to get back to his routes, and I chose to return with him. The wedding was postponed for a year, and I had nothing else to do in Asuncion. I knew if I went back to my life, I would find what I was searching for, or so I thought.

The trip back was slow because the rain had made all the dirt roads difficult to travel. But I viewed it as family time. We had never spent so much time together, ever. The girls and I were one part of the family, and Hans was a member who came in and out of our inner circle. It shocked me to think that his drivers were closer to our children than he was. He was never a family man—not because he didn't love our daughters but because his head was always somewhere else: in cards, in business, in other adventures. I still wondered why he decided to marry me and have a family. He was a nomad who never meant to stay in one place. Maybe I was just an illusion that he had for a brief moment, an illusion that he thought he could love and hold on to. But illusions have a short life span. They usually die quickly, especially when reality hits you in the face. And my life was hitting me hard.

Chapter Nine

After my mother's death, time seemed to go by slower than usual. Hans went back to his work and I went back to my routine. The most important event was that we were able to make our first friends. We met Felipe and his wife Leonora because of a fight. One of Hans' drivers got drunk one night and decided to pick a fight at a bar. It got ugly very quickly and both drunk men ended up fighting in the street. One of them threw a rock at the other, which missed his head but landed against a neighbor's window, breaking it in the middle of the night. The police showed up at the scene and took both guys away. They later called Hans to pick up his employee from jail and repay the damage. Hans paid part of the damage and agreed to give a formal apology to the owner of the broken window, Felipe.

It turned out that Felipe's family was German as well and both men ended up having too many things in common, mainly their passion for women. Their friendship was immediate. They were so similar, it was scary.

Felipe's wife, Leonora, was a tall blonde woman, very elegant and European-looking, which was rare in Clorinda. Most women were dark and short, or very plain. Both of their families had settled in this border town at the turn of the century and they seemed to like it here. I couldn't understand why, but I respected it. We started meeting regularly for dinner or drinks. Of course, I felt like the ugly duckling next to Leonora, but I didn't care that much anymore. It was nice to have friends for the first time.

I found myself looking forward to our gatherings. Most of the time, we went to visit them because our home was not worth showing off. Often I found myself thinking of ways to make it look better, but the truth was brutal: we lived in a pathetic hut.

Hans didn't seem to care much. He was gone most of the time, and as long as he had a clean bed, everything else was unnecessary. For me, my home was a part of who I was, and that house was definitely not me. I was able to put new floors down, but the walls were still unfinished and our doors didn't match. I put my heart and soul in that house, but no matter how hard I tried, it always looked shabby and shameful to me.

So we visited our friends more than usual and they didn't mind. Their house was on a busy street, with a beautiful garden full of colorful flowers. You could smell the roses and jasmine a few blocks away. The front was white with a tint of red from the dust that gave it a sweet look of pink. The galleries were wide and open to help cool down the house in the summers. The columns that framed the main entrance were covered with ivy and lilies. Every time I walked through the entrance, I transported myself into another time and space where worries didn't exist. Felipe's wife always gave me a small bouquet of fresh flowers to take home.

Although Leonora and I appreciated each other's company, we never became close friends. Our worlds were simply too different, and we were opposites in many ways. The only thing we had in common was our husbands. Hans and Felipe understood each other without even speaking. They finished each other's sentences and laughed at the same jokes. If they had been brothers, they would probably not have been so similar. I used to envy their strong connection, for the last time I had something like that was with Ana Maria, and that was now gone. She belonged to Asuncion's high society, and I lived in a mud hut.

As I couldn't get another life, I decided to make this one work, at least for me and the girls.

Leonora was always kind to invite us when Hans was on the road. Because they never had children of their own, our visits were always celebrated. We spent many Sundays on her patio, sitting under the shade, drinking iced tea, and watching the girls have fun with their two dogs. Felipe always had a soft spot for me. He looked at me in ways that were completely new to me. His eyes were so intense and his grip strong. Every time we met, he would kiss me on both cheeks and squeeze both my arms with his hands, sending an electrifying sensation down my spine. I could feel his eyes going under my skin, discovering every one of my secrets and taking them away. At the beginning I didn't know how to act around him, but it all soon became a flirting game between the two of us. And I liked it. I liked being noticed. I liked that a man would find me attractive. I liked that his eyes would explore every inch of my body. It made me feel a better woman somehow. I started dressing up more every time we went to see them, and I was more careful with my makeup and my hair.

"I don't understand why you get all dressed up to go down the road to see friends," Hans would say.

"It's because I'm bored wearing the same old rags all day," I would simply reply, knowing what my true intentions were.

Our game went unnoticed for a very long time, and I loved every minute of it. I found myself wondering about things that had never crossed my mind. What would it feel like to be alone with another man?

"I don't like the way you act around Felipe," said Hans one afternoon before we were supposed to meet them for dinner.

"What do you mean? I act like I do every day," I replied.

"You are different around him. You smile too much. Since when do you smile so much?" he asked.

"Since we have friends. I don't know why my smiling bothers you so much. You should be happy that I'm finally having a good time outside this horrible house you put me in," I said, venting some of my frustration after years of silence.

"Happy is fine, but what you are doing is not acceptable. You are a married woman, and you are behaving like a whore."

"Well, I'm starting to realize why whores have more fun than I do. Maybe if you cared to spend more time with me than with them, or if you were more interested in our life together, I wouldn't be so happy when somebody else pays attention to me." I knew my words were hurting him.

He became very silent and walked out of the room. I started blaming myself for everything, for liking Felipe's attention, for dreaming of a life that wasn't possible, for thinking that one man could make me happy for the rest of my life. I kept wondering what my mother would have thought of me at that moment, disrespecting my husband, thinking about another man. But I couldn't hold back any longer. Hans had to hear loud and clear what I thought, what I needed. But I knew well enough that men only hear what they want to hear.

We canceled our visit that night. Hans told them I wasn't feeling well and needed to rest.

The morning after, he left on a long trip that included a visit to Buenos Aires where his parents lived. So I was alone again with my guilt. I kept making up excuses not to go to Felipe's house. One morning, he came to me.

"Chola, I know what's going on," he said, after kissing me on both cheeks. "We offended you somehow."

"No, you didn't," I explained surprised.

"Leonora and I are very fond of you and the girls. We don't want to lose your friendship, so tell us what we did wrong," he pleaded.

"There is nothing wrong with you or Leonora. This is between Hans and me."

"Are you two having problems?" he asked.

"It's just life. We spend too much time apart and it's very hard for both of us to pick up where we left. I don't think he sees me the way you do."

"Chola, he does see you, he just doesn't know how to put it in words. He loves you more than you can imagine. He just doesn't know how to say it," he explained, talking as if he had known Hans all his life.

"I don't know why he can't talk to me, but if he doesn't start trying, I will have to leave him. I feel empty and lonely inside. Felipe, I want to have a life with him, but I know I can also have a life without him."

"Do you want me to speak to him when he comes back?" he asked.

"No, this is something between us both. I appreciate your offer, but you need to stay out of it or it will be worse," I said.

He kissed me goodbye and left without saying another word. I knew he would respect my request, but I wasn't sure about what I was going to do next.

Heavy rains delayed my husband's return by a few weeks. The roads were almost flooded, and the heavy vehicles had to wait on the side until the mud was dry enough to continue. These few weeks alone gave me a chance to think long and hard about the next step. I was confused, but I knew I could no longer live like this, so I decided to wait for his first move.

He managed to come home in the middle of summer rain storms and bad weather. What I saw shocked me. He had lost a lot of weight, and his bones were showing everywhere. He wasn't the same man who left. Something deep had transformed him into this dilapidated human being. Something had sucked the life out of him, leaving him in an infinite vacuum.

At that moment, he looked like a stranger to me. I greeted him and asked him to sit down. I went to get his favorite iced coffee with vanilla ice cream, praying in my head that his favorite food would bring him back.

"Chola, my father died," he finally said.

I left the kitchen and ran to him. This big man melted in my arms, sobbing tears as I was holding him.

"You are the best thing in my life. I don't deserve you," he said, wiping his face as he looked at me as if he were doing it for the first time in his life.

I still could not find the right words to comfort him. He put his head on my lap.

"Chola, I promise you I will be the husband you deserve. I've been selfish all these years not knowing that I was hurting the person I love the most. Please forgive me," he sobbed.

It broke my heart to see a grown man cry like a baby. He looked helpless and vulnerable. But he wasn't crying only for his father, he was crying for everything that went wrong in his life. And he asked for my forgiveness. How could I not forgive him? I did, once more, as I would keep doing until the day he died.

The next few weeks, I worked hard, cooking for him, trying to fill in his big empty frame. He started to look healthier, but his face had changed forever. I thought this was what sorrow did to us: it slowly steals our soul, penetrates our body, and refuses to leave, sucking up our youth and turning us into an old person. I wondered what it was doing to me and the woman I was turning into. But he was more important right now. I felt a deep necessity to have my old lover back, the man who promised me the moon and filled my life with roses. That wish never left my heart, even when I knew what we had was never coming back.

My father-in-law had died shortly after Hans' arrival. He had been sick the past few years, deteriorating slowly of a cancer that was eating him inside. Hanna and he had moved to an elderly home outside of the city, where a few old Jewish Germans had settled. The last few years of his life were happy, except for the fact that his old Berlin had been cut in two. He refused to go back as long as the city wasn't unified. My husband always felt strongly about the same issue, explaining to me over and over again what a unique and vibrant place Berlin had been before the war.

My mother-in-law was very content in her new home and never talked about going back, or anything related to her old life in Europe. She pretended that that part of her existence had never happened. She erased every trace of her past, except for the fact that she never learned to speak Spanish. She managed to make a few good German friends. They met regularly and satisfied her necessity to speak her own language. With me she tried hard to say a few words in Spanish but always gave up, using Hans as her personal translator.

After her husband's death, Hans insisted that she move in with us, but she refused. She lived many more years by herself, in peace with her life. That was what I admired the most in her: her peace. It was like a contagious state. After every visit, I felt it coming along with me and staying for a while, reminding me of her struggle for survival and her amazing resilience. None of her relatives were able to survive the camps. Her sisters and their husbands, nieces and nephews, all of them found a tragic end in the gas chambers. She knew through her daughter, Lotte, that a cousin had escaped, and after many years in the United States, had decided to move back to Germany, where he married and had children.

But she never understood the reason to go back. She kept telling me a new life needs a new place to flourish. We all need fresh soil under our feet, she would say. I knew going back was just too painful for her. She would constantly be reminded of her loss and her despair. Here, at least she had a son and a daughter-in-law who adored her and grandchildren to love.

Lotte wasn't an affectionate daughter and never had any children. After her return to Germany, she never looked back. She came to visit us a handful of times, and every time she did, she had a new, richer husband. She married a total of five men, but she never seemed happy or satisfied. When Lotte asked Matilde a few weeks before her wedding what she would like as a gift, Matilde asked for a silk nightgown to wear on her wedding night. Lotte told her it was a very expensive request and instead gave her an old cotton sleeping dress.

Every time I thought of her, I felt nothing but sadness. I saw her unhappiness, her emptiness, her selfishness. In my heart, I knew she would die alone and sad. That's maybe why the news of her suicide many years later didn't surprise me. Her lifeless body was found in the bathtub, blue after days of lying there with no one interested in her well-being. Her cleaning lady found her and alerted the authorities. Thank God, my mother-in-law was no longer in this world when her daughter took her own life. After surviving the most violent war, it would have broken her heart in a million pieces.

But the fact that she never was a big part of our lives was always a blessing. Sadly, she was never going to be missed.

The death of his father was a big shock for Hans. They were never really close, but that was the norm in those days. He admired his father deeply, but knew he could never be like him. Hans grew up in a wealthy and affluent world, where the sky was the limit. But after the war, everything disappeared: the money, the power, the parties, the travels, the excitement. Hans felt cheated by fate. First it gave him everything, and later it took it all away. Seeing his father become a fragile old man, happy but without any possessions, made him realize his own humanity and vulnerability. Hans knew he had his own ambition and drive, but lacked his father's personality. He knew his limitations were many and his weaknesses crippled him. His father never approved of his lifestyle, though their relationship improved after our marriage.

Adolf came from a family of tailors. He was the oldest of seven brothers and had only one sister. As the head of the brood, he took over the family business early on in his life after completing his high school studies. His dream had always been to dedicate his life to science and travel to exotic places in the world to find cures for obscure diseases. But his fate was already decided. He would become the businessman his father expected of him and make sure the family trade would survive through the next generations. So he set out to do the best job possible and turned the little tailor shop into an efficient and exclusive men's suit factory. There was a waiting list that included the names of Berlin's most powerful citizens to have their suits made to order. Adolf trained his employees and was very fair to them, getting back in return a strong loyalty from all his workers.

His business thrived until the Gestapo asked him to make its top officials' uniforms. It was 1933 and Hitler was just revealing himself to the world. Adolf knew this would be the perfect relationship he needed to ensure the survival of his factory, but he couldn't bring himself to do business with the Fuehrer's secret police and, knowing that he was risking his entire family's safety, he declined.

The following years were very scary. Hans had already left for South America as the persecution of Jews increased. Their shops were closed. They were stripped of their titles, jobs, and positions of influence. Adolf decided to move his immediate family away from Nazi Germany. All his brothers had already left Berlin, and he was the only one holding on to whatever was left of his business. But there was no point. No one knew how long the nightmare would last. Adolf, Hanna, and Lotte, who was already married to Heinrich, decided it was time to leave and contacted Hans for help, fearing it was already too late. They packed a few belongings and managed to get a ride hiding in the back of one of Adolf's employee's trucks. They made it to Amsterdam, where they stayed, waiting to hear from Hans. After a few weeks, they received word that the government of Paraguay had granted them asylum and gave them visas. The next morning, they boarded a cargo ship whose captain had helped transport some of the iron for Hans' business. Their journey was long, painful, and dirty. All they could do was hope that they would be able to see their son again and meet his new wife.

On the other end, for Hans, fear and guilt made his heart heavy, and although he knew it was thanks to him that his family was able to find peace in a new land, he felt a deep sense of failure. His careless lifestyle was not the reason for his parents' misfortunes, but he knew he had enjoyed it without regrets while it lasted, never worrying if his parents disapproved. But life far away from Berlin gave him a clean slate. He could start from scratch and prove himself worthy of his father's name. Though his weaknesses were many, he was trying to make this new life work.

He never asked me about Felipe again or commented on my clothes or my smile. I tried a few times to have a conversation about it, but he changed the subject every time. When our friends invited us over for the first time since his return, I was extremely nervous. I asked my neighbor to watch the girls for us that evening, not sure of what his reaction would be once he met his friend again.

But I was determined to continue life as usual, convinced that I did nothing wrong and that his friend's attention was as harmless as could be. So I chose a new dress I had just finished sewing the previous week while he was away, and made sure my hair was not overdone and my makeup not too obvious.

When I was ready to go, I looked for him in the living room and found him wearing his white summer suit, which reminded me of the times when we were dating.

"I haven't seen you in that suit since we got married," I said, trying hard not to show him how much I wanted him at that moment.

"I know. It's been sitting in the closet for years so I thought it was about time to wear it again. You look very nice too," he replied, looking too uncomfortable to pay me a compliment.

"Well, I'm ready if you are," I said.

"I'm ready. Let's go."

We walked the few blocks between our houses without saying a word, but half way there he took my hand.

Our friends greeted us with affection, as they had not seen us in a very long time.

"So sorry for your loss, Hans," they both said while we all hugged and kissed each other.

Hans thanked them and I could see his eyes filling with tears; he pushed them back almost immediately. It was a relief to see that he was actually touched and moved by our friend's sincere condolences. It was not very often that I saw his softer side. Most of the time, he tried not to show any emotions that would make him look weak, and with the years, I started to believe that he had lost almost all sensitivity.

The evening went better than expected. I noticed that Hans was more interested in me than usual and that he kept a close eye on me, especially when Felipe would get closer or would start a conversation. I liked his newfound jealousy, but most of all I loved the power that came with it. For the first time, I realized that he had felt threatened by his friend and the possibility of losing me scared him. For that reason, I decided to keep playing the game. The more I played hard to get, the more he would want me back.

For the next few weeks, Hans decided to cancel his trips and spend more time with us. It was good to have him around, but it took some time for us to get used to the new routine. At the beginning he tried to be helpful, but I didn't know what to do with him. He was in my way all the time, and soon I started to feel frustrated. The girls, on the other hand, thought it was wonderful to have their father around. They shared a lot of time together, and for a brief moment, we all had the feeling that this fantasy would last.

But soon enough Hans started to go out more, especially in the evenings, and my worst fears came back. His true nature never left him. All the guilt he felt after his father's death had disappeared. All the empty promises were forgotten. How could this be possible? Why was he promising me one thing and soon after that turning on his own word? It was as if two different persons lived in the same body. One wanted badly to have a life with me—the other one wanted to escape.

One evening, I couldn't take it anymore and confronted him.

"I notice you are going out a lot," I said, obviously upset.

"Well, you know I like to do that," he answered, avoiding eye contact.

"Maybe I can come with you."

"Respectable women don't go out at night," he added, making no effort to hide his annoyance.

"If you went to a respectable place, maybe I could join you," I insisted.

"There are no women where we go. It's a men's club. They will not let you in. Besides, it's better this way. You need to stay home with the children."

"Hans, are you gambling again?" I finally asked, fearing his answer.

"Just for fun, nothing to worry about. Now I'm late," he said and started toward the door.

"You have to stop. We can't afford it, please," I pleaded in a broken voice.

"I have to go," he repeated firmly.

"Hans, I'm pregnant," I said as he walked to the door.

He stopped suddenly, turned around, and faced me. After a long silence he spoke softly but firmly.

"We can't have another child—it's out of the question," he said, without a hint of remorse in his eyes.

"What are you talking about? Don't you want to have a son?" I got dizzy with confusion.

"We can hardly feed the two children we have and you want to have more. Are you crazy? How are we supposed to do it? I don't want to discuss this any further. I'm your husband, and you do as I say."

"I can't kill an innocent life," I managed to say between sobs.

"You don't have an option. Can't you understand I don't want another child?" he repeated, again without a hint of remorse. His words cut through my soul.

He didn't give me a chance to reply and walked away. I felt my world falling apart in front of me. My legs shook and my stomach rolled. I ran to the kitchen and threw up.

I knew I had to pull myself together. The girls were sleeping in the room next door, and I didn't want them to hear me cry.

With a broken heart, I cried myself to sleep. If it wasn't for my two daughters, I would have left him that night, never to return. But I wasn't alone anymore. My children depended on me. I felt helpless and betrayed. Hans was their father and they loved him. I couldn't take that away from them, and besides, how was I going to be able to feed them by myself? I was his wife. I had to accept his decision and move forward. I had no choice.

The morning after, I took the girls to school and walked to the midwife's house with the little money I was able to save selling the eggs from my chicken. She invited me in and offered me some iced tea. She was an older woman but I couldn't guess her age. She seemed very soft and gentle.

It took me a long time to explain why I was there, but she listened patiently, holding my hands and letting me cry without interrupting me.

When I was done, she gave me a few minutes to catch my breath.

"You are a young, healthy woman. You will be able to get over this. You shouldn't let this dictate your future. You are not the only one. Many women come to me with the same problem. You are doing what's best for your family. There is nothing more selfless than that," she explained.

Listening to her speak gave me some peace of mind, as if I was listening to my own mother giving me advice. We talked for hours about my hopes and dreams and the life I wanted to have. She lifted the weight that had pressed on my chest for years, eating up my life.

After our long conversation, she explained to me what I had to do to stop my pregnancy and invited me to come back to talk again.

I walked home with a heavy heart, feeling guilty for what I was about to do to an innocent life. As a Catholic, I knew it was wrong and it went against all my beliefs. But I couldn't bring a child into this world like this, with a father who hated him and a future with so much uncertainty.

I tried unsuccessfully to convince myself that I was obeying my husband , that one day I would forget about it, that one day I would forgive myself. But how could I?

After completing all my chores, I waited to be alone in the house and did what the midwife told me. Immediately, I started to bleed and my heart raced. What had I done! The pain in my abdomen reminded me of the terrible sin I just committed and how I would pay for it for the rest of my life. I spent the day in bed, trying to rest before the girls and Hans came home, but the pain was too intense. I got up just in time to cook some dinner and held the tears back when the rest of the family was home.

Hans greeted me like always, not knowing how much I hated him that day. The girls did their homework and ate supper as usual, before going to bed.

Finally, I had the courage to speak.

"It's done."

"I'm glad. You did the right thing, Chola. You are a good wife," he said without meeting my eyes.

"No, I'm not." I walked away from him.

Hans went back to his truck the morning after, and we didn't see or speak to each other for three weeks.

Chapter Ten

The first anniversary of my mother's death was approaching and with it came back the plans for a new wedding. Choli was supposed to announce her wedding date sometime soon and that gave me something to look forward to. But it also reminded me of my loss and the pain I could still feel in my heart. The memories of my mother were still fresh in my mind, and it was painful to remember that I hadn't been there with her during her last days.

I often wondered what she would think about me and my life now and what words of advice she would have. She was a strong woman—she would probably give me hope and courage. It hurt to think that I didn't have her anymore. I started to remember her more vividly around that first anniversary and often found myself speaking to her out loud, hoping and praying that she could hear me. But the sound of my own voice always made me sad, amplifying my own loneliness and desperation.

What would she say to me? What would she think? Would she judge me for being so weak? Would she disapprove? Too many questions floated around in my head, not letting me sleep, taking me to the darkest places of my soul, making me face things I couldn't deal with at the moment.

The midwife had given me a calming tea to drink at night before bedtime, and that usually helped me sleep a few hours every night. But I still could not escape my reality every morning when I woke up. I started going to church every day, asking for forgiveness. I felt responsible for the life I chose to live and the way I was living it. That still didn't change anything. Hans and I grew more distant and his trips grew longer. I knew about the cards and the other women, but it was all out of my control. So I decided instead to focus on the girls.

They were growing up beautifully and they both helped me hold onto my sanity. Baby still adored her father over everything. She idealized him in a way that only a child can do and I let her do it. Matilde was more sensitive and her intuition told her that something wasn't right. She kept asking me questions. She could read my face like a book. She could tell my state of mind, even when I worked so hard to hide my feelings from her.

Baby was very focused on her studies, always trying to prove that she was better than the rest of the girls in her class. Matilde, on the other hand, seemed happy with herself and was more free-spirited.

I noticed Matilde's love for music early on, and I decided it was about time that she learned to play the piano, as I once did many years ago.

So, in our forsaken border town, I found a lady who played the organ at church who was willing to give her a few lessons. It didn't take long before Matilde could play better than her teacher, but there was nowhere to go to continue with her music studies, so we kept on going to her.

It was amazing to see my own child enjoy the keyboard as much as I did. It filled my heart with joy every time I heard her practice. Every penny invested in her passion was a pleasure to me. The eggs I collected from my chickens were paying off, and I was extremely happy to be able to do this for my own daughter.

To see myself in her was bittersweet because I didn't wish her my destiny. But she seemed strong and tenacious, and my heart was sure that she would have a much better life than mine. My child was destined for a bigger world and that was reason enough for me to be excited.

While Baby was intellectually gifted, Matilde was blessed with street smarts. She knew everyone on our little street. She could go to the store by herself and run errands for me. On the other hand, Baby was more insecure. She knew her good looks got people's attention, especially the men's, and that made her very uncomfortable. She preferred to stay home and help me around the house. For me, it was the perfect combination. Both my children were there for me and we supported each other. They knew I longed to go back to Asuncion to see my sisters, and they felt the same way.

So when the telegram finally arrived with some fresh news from Paraguay, we couldn't wait to open it. Luisa sent me news regularly, but this time it took her longer than usual. Her telegram was brief:

"Choli got married last week. They wanted a small wedding. Will tell you more when I see you. Coco decided to get married next spring. Hope you and the girls can come."

I had to read her message three times to believe my eyes. I was in shock! My disappointment in missing Choli's wedding lasted only a few seconds before I started to jump for joy for Coco's engagement. Unbelievable! Coco finally found someone to share his life with that Luisa approved of. I couldn't wait to hear every detail and started planning a trip to Asuncion right away.

A lot had happened in Asuncion since my last visit. My mother's death was a terrible blow to all my siblings, but especially to Luisa, and it took her a long time to move on. It made her rethink her role as a mother and the importance of seeing her only child happy as long as she was around. After Coco's long and dangerous illness, the doctor ordered, against Luisa's wishes, that Coco be taken care of by a professional nurse at home, at least as long as he was in a fragile condition. It took him a few months to start feeling better and for that long he had a nurse at his side. Her name was Elsa and she was a few years older than he was. She was smart and had a very strong personality, which caused a lot of friction between her and Luisa. She spent many hours caring for Coco, and they started to feel affection for each other. Coco saw her more as a mother than a nurse, which made Luisa even more upset. But on the other hand, she was very professional and made sure that Coco's health was a priority in the house. That was the only reason why Luisa kept her mouth shut every time she wanted to send her away. Another one was simply the truth: she couldn't have taken care of him so well. The idea of losing him to another woman was extremely painful, but the idea of him dying was inconceivable.

Coco kept seeing Elsa after he no longer needed her services. First he did it behind Luisa's back, afraid of her reaction. But my mother's death brought up her sensible self. For the first time, Coco saw a softer side to his own mother. The mourning period was long and Coco knew he couldn't make any announcements until it was over. But he decided to propose to Elsa in secret and wait for his mother's blessing. Soon enough, she would have to accept their engagement. He was an adult and was entitled to a life of happiness, and he was determined to make this relationship work.

All his previous girlfriends—and there weren't many—were never good enough for Luisa. Most of them never really became anything to begin with, and he was never very interested in dating. Elsa was the first woman who made him feel comfortable. All those months of vulnerability had opened him to a new world of possibilities. He was for the first time excited to be able to share time with someone other than his own mother or aunts. His career had made him a very respectable man, and he had a lot of friends in powerful places. But still he couldn't find his place. The stigma of being a bastard never really left him, despite all of Luisa's efforts to make his life as normal as possible. For as long as he could remember, he always lived in the family house, with his grandmother, mother, and oldest aunt. His only father figure had been his grandfather, a tyrant who ruined his mother's only chance for happiness, and yet he was also the man who had given him his greatest gift: his art.

Coco lived for many years with these conflicting feelings. He knew he owed his life to an uncontrollable passion, a love so strong that his mother closed the door of her heart just to keep it alive inside of her. But he felt guilty at the same time, thinking that maybe he was the real reason why his mother could never move on with her life after his father's tragic death. Elsa was his ticket out. She represented his only chance for a different life, a life he desperately needed.

Choli also suffered terribly after my mother's death. They had become very close, especially after I moved out of house. When she finally was able to set a date again for her wedding, she decided, out of respect for my mother's memory, to have a small event. Choli and her fiancé got married on a Sunday morning during a regular mass, and after that they celebrated with close relatives and a handful of friends.

Coco's dream to help Choli organize a big social event was shattered, but this ignited the desire in him to plan his own wedding. He talked about it with Choli, whom he considered a sister, and they both agreed that Coco needed the social status more than she did. He kept his engagement secret—even from me—for as long as Luisa was in mourning.

Months later, I learned from Choli the details of the day in which Coco announced his decision to marry. Hoping not to cause unnecessary anxiety in his mother, Coco decided to keep the evening casual and invite a few family members for an informal dinner. Antonia and Luisa prepared the house, which had been closed to the public for twelve long months. They uncovered the mirrors, wiped the furniture, brought fresh flowers from the garden, and put away all the black curtains that covered the windows from top to bottom. With the mourning period officially over, they felt ready for a new start in their lives. Of course, they would have never imagined what was in store for them.

They had raised Coco together and seeing him depart was simply unthinkable.

As always, Coco treated everyone like royalty, taking out his best dinnerware and silver. His cooking was superb. He focused on every detail, as if his wedding was taking place that same evening.

After a few glasses of wine and a delicious meal, he stood up in front of the family and said, "You all know that my mother has been the most important woman in my life. And that will never change. But it is time for me to start a new phase, and I found the right partner to do just that."

Luisa was looking at him first with pride but then, slowly, with suspicion. She kept smiling, but her facial expression was frozen.

"Elsa brought me back to health, and she will help me walk through this next stage of my life. She agreed to marry me and be my wife," he concluded.

The whole room went silent, as if what had just happened was an illusion. Choli was the first one to get up and congratulate the couple. Soon everyone followed, some with tears in their eyes, and others with cheers of happiness. Luisa remained very quiet in a corner of the room until the family turned to her to congratulate her on the good news.

She didn't show much emotion, simply standing there receiving hugs and kisses from everyone present. She nodded, forcing herself to smile, her gaze never leaving Coco's sight. She went to Elsa and gave her a hug in front of the family, just as a formality and to make sure that no one talked badly about her that night. But in her heart she had only resentment for her.

Soon the evening was over, and Coco was left alone in the house with his mother.

"I guess I never said congratulations," she said, almost emotionless.

"Mom, I know this is a shock to you, but it was going to happen eventually," he replied, trying to explain himself.

"I know," she said, not changing the expression on her face. "I wish you and Elsa the best of happiness, but you could have warned me before you embarrassed me in front of all our guests," she added. "I guess, I will be dying alone after all," she continued, stabbing her son right in the heart.

"You will never be alone. You and Antonia can live with us. I'm making enough money to buy a bigger house where you will have your independence and we'll have our privacy. Besides, my studio is growing, and I need more space for work. You'll see—it'll all work out fine," he insisted.

For the first time since the announcement, Luisa's face relaxed. As long as she had him close by her side, she would be able to survive and control him. She knew sharing him wouldn't be easy, but this gave her a chance to keep a close eye on her future daughter-in-law and make sure she didn't displace her from her son's life.

Coco started working on the wedding plans right away, paying attention to every detail. He wanted to make this an occasion that people in Asuncion would talk about for years to come, and hopefully never forget.

He chose everything with exquisite taste, from the wine, to the food, the flowers and the invitations.

His was going to be the wedding of the year, if not the decade. The only other event that dared compete with his was the wedding of the daughter of Paraguay's dictator, President Alfredo Stroessner, but it happened years later.

His list of guests included Asuncion's most influential politicians, military officers, and wealthy families. Once the word was out, no one wanted to be excluded.

I started to plan our trip to Asuncion immediately, excited to see my older siblings. The girls helped me make new dresses for all of us. We were able to find some beautiful remnants of fabric that I turned into very glamorous pieces. A few times a year, I would buy a monthly magazine that came from Spain with the latest looks from Paris and Madrid. I couldn't afford it on a regular basis, so I bought it only when I needed to come up with a fresh idea for a new dress. It was my connection to the world. I loved reading about the lives of all the royal families of Europe and the Hollywood movie stars. My personal favorite was Princess Grace, a former actress who fell in love with Prince Rainier of Monaco and now lived in a beautiful castle on the French Riviera. Her beauty and sense of style fascinated me. She had the perfect life, with the perfect husband, and three perfect little children. Even her tragic death in a car accident, a few decades later, seemed fit for a celebrity.

For myself, I chose light blue and for the girls I chose pale yellow and pink. The dresses were nice and tied in the waist, with big fluffy skirts. We all looked very sophisticated. It fascinated me how a simple dress could transport me to another dimension, how it could make me feel like someone completely different. I could be anything and anyone I wanted to be, even if it was just for a brief moment. All thanks to a dress.

I had a lot of work to do until Coco's wedding. I had to get my life organized and take care of my garden, my chickens, and the house. Because we were going to be away for over a week, I made an arrangement with a local restaurant, where Hans' drivers could stop by and eat while I was away. In return, I was going to bring them fresh eggs every day for a month. They accepted my offer immediately because my chickens were famous for laying the biggest eggs in town. I guess chickens show their happiness through their eggs. Hans wasn't happy though. He kept asking me why was I leaving for so long, telling me there was too much work to be done and accusing me of not caring enough about the well-being of our business. I simply replied that my family came first to me and Coco was one of the closest persons to my heart.

I knew he hated that. He hated to be number two. But there was nothing he could do. I had made up my mind and prepared everything so that he wouldn't notice my absence.

I asked him many times to come with me and the girls, but he just refused and made always with the same excuses. This time I didn't care. I wasn't going to let him spoil this important moment in our family's life.

I kept busy until the last minute. When the moment to pack our things came, I was already tired. Our new dresses took up so much space that we couldn't bring much else. The girls picked a toy each to keep entertained on the long drive, and I just managed to take my magazines. It was hard to read inside the loud cabin of the truck, but I embraced that time as an opportunity to spend it with the girls and catch up on some of my reading. I never finished school, so my reading skills were not the best. It was my deep sense of curiosity that made me want to have a book in my hands. Baby had a brilliant mind, but Matilde had my natural curiosity. Baby devoured textbooks, while Matilde loved comic books, children's magazines, and even some of her father's newspapers.

We all loved to listen to the radio. Music was virtually everywhere in my house. The radio was on all day long, and when it was off, either Matilde or I would sit at the piano and try to play some of the most popular songs we heard on the radio that day.

The girls loved the radio novellas, and I preferred to listen to the tangos. I knew them all by heart. I would sing them in my head when I was cooking in the kitchen. Their stories about fatal love affairs, lost love, and endless heartache seemed very familiar to me and helped me believe that I wasn't alone after all.

The long drive to Asuncion wasn't so bad. We arrived five days before the big event, with plenty of time to get ready and help out. The entire house was upside down. Rooms had been rearranged, new furniture was brought in, carpets were being cleaned, and walls were freshened up. An entire army of workers moved around the house like ants in an ant hole, and their sole mission was to make everything look beautiful. By the time we got there, there wasn't much else to be done, so I decided to park myself in the kitchen with Luisa, Antonia, and Josefina and help them cook for the more than two hundred guests. Of course, that number wasn't even close to the four hundred people that were usually invited to big weddings, but Coco's house couldn't accommodate more than that, and he was determined to host the event there. It was so much fun to be with my sisters again, hands covered with flour and eggs, talking and laughing like old times. We knew Luisa had preferred to keep Coco for herself, but she was so busy with the wedding preparations she forgot for a few days that she was going to be somebody's mother-in-law. I pitied the poor woman because Luisa was going to make her life a living hell; though for a second I hoped and prayed it wouldn't be that way after all.

The bride, Elsa, was smart to stay away from the kitchen while we worked. She only went to Coco when she had questions about the wedding details. Her family was scheduled to arrive from the country the day before the ceremony, and they all planned to stay at the house. I kept wondering where all of her relatives were going to sleep, so I offered my bed and asked Josefina if we could stay at her place instead.

The bride's immediate family wasn't big. She had only one older brother, who married late in life and never had any children. Her father had passed away after a long and debilitating illness and her mother was in a wheelchair. Elsa had stayed with them until her father's death, when she decided to become a nurse. She looked after her mother for many years and visited her at her brother's house regularly. She had a few aunts and uncles, all of them farmers from the interior of the country. You could tell immediately that they had indigenous blood in their veins and spoke Spanish with an accent. But we welcomed everyone as if they already belonged to the family.

Coco's father was half *Guaraní* himself, and Luisa thought it was a good sign that her son fell in love with a woman who had similar roots.

I was so excited and busy with the wedding I suddenly realized I hadn't had the chance to get to know Elsa better. We had talked a couple of times but always about some formality or family business—never woman to woman. It was important to me that I look into her heart before the wedding. I needed to confirm that she was the right woman for Coco.

I waited for the right occasion, when everyone would be busy with something else and wouldn't notice my absence. The morning before the wedding, I invited her to sit with me outside and help me with some flower arrangements.

She seemed grateful to have something to keep her mind occupied and sat next to me under the shade of the eucalyptus trees.

"Are you nervous?" I finally asked after we had sorted the flowers by colors and sizes.

"Not really. I never thought I would get married, so the fact that it's actually happening is very exciting. I'm actually more nervous to live in this house with Luisa and Antonia. I know both of them are very possessive women," she said without taking her eyes away from our task.

"I agree. My sisters can be a little overwhelming. But it all comes from a place of love. We have all adored Coco since the day he was born. That's why his happiness means so much to us," I replied, trying to explain to her what this event meant for all of us but making her feel welcome at the same time.

"Believe me—his happiness is also very important to me. He's a wonderful and generous man. He has the most precious heart I've ever seen. I never thought a man like him, so successful and creative, would fall for a woman like me."

"Well, love doesn't make distinctions. You took care of him when he needed you most and you won a place in his heart," I said, trying to be cheerful.

"But I don't know if I will be able to fit in his circle of clients and friends. I'm a simple woman, Chola. All I want is to be happy with him. I don't belong with the high society. And Coco's livelihood depends on it." She seemed worried.

"I guess they will have to adapt to you then. Don't let them intimidate you. You have a strong will. Just follow your instincts and all will fall in place," I insisted.

"Chola, thank you for your kind words. They mean a lot to me. I wish you lived closer to us. I don't have anyone to talk to around here."

"You are more than welcome to come to visit me and the girls. When you feel you need someone to talk to, write to me. I love getting letters," I said.

I gave her a hug and she got up quickly, saying she had to start getting ready for the wedding. I think she was a little overwhelmed. Maybe I opened a box that should have stayed closed. But I felt things were going to work out sooner or later.

The last twenty-four hours before the wedding were intense. We all managed to survive the preparations without running into each other with a knife or some other dangerous tool. Coco said goodbye and left to go to the tailors to get dressed in his new tuxedo and I hurried to get the girls and myself ready.

Luisa and Antonia remained in the house, making sure all the workers were gone in time and they too could get ready.

The religious ceremony was taking place at the cathedral and the reception at the house.

The church was full of people. We couldn't have fit a needle in it. People were standing in the alleys and blocking every entrance to the altar. We had to force them to move to let the bride come into the church. Elsa looked amazing. Her dress was pearl-white, embroidered by Antonia with golden flowers and a long train. Coco was waiting for her at the altar with a smile on his face and a look of happiness I had never seen on him before. Luisa and Antonia were standing next to him and on the other side was Elsa's family. Her brother was giving her away.

Everyone looked radiant. I hadn't felt this way in a long time. The girls were standing next to me, mesmerized by all that was happening around them. We would surely remember this day for the rest of our lives.

I kept looking for Hans' face in the crowd, hoping that he had changed his mind at the last minute and come anyway. But he was nowhere. I tried to imagine where he was at this moment and sent him my thoughts. I always liked to believe that people who loved each other could communicate telepathically and know exactly the other person's feelings and thoughts without being in the same place. But I shook my head and told myself to stop being a fool.

The one-hour ceremony was quickly over, and we all headed to the house. I told the girls we were going to walk because it was mango season, and I loved walking down the streets of Asuncion and smelling the mangoes' aroma in the air. The weather couldn't have been better. The air was fresh, the sunset turned the sky bright orange, and a smooth breeze lifted our skirts and made us laugh.

By the time we reached the house, the party had already started. There was a band playing and the waiters were making sure everyone had a drink in their hands. The girls left me and went on to play with their cousins. Suddenly I felt very lonely in the middle of a room full of people. I started looking for Coco—I needed to congratulate him and give him a big hug. I went from room to room, trying not to step on anyone's new shoes, but it was hard to avoid the crowd that filled every inch of the house.

I was about to give up and find a corner to sit in when I heard my name. I turned around and there he was, Hans. I ran to him and embraced him.

"I thought you were not coming," I finally said, hiding my choking voice.

"You know I hate going to church. But I can't pass up a good party," he replied in his thick German accent.

I was happy to see him but confused by his sudden appearance. After all, he made me feel terribly guilty before I left.

"Let me get us a glass of wine," he said, adding, "I hope they have some iced coffee."

I sat on a chair not completely believing what just had happened. Every time I thought I had learned to live with his disappointments, he always managed to surprise me and bring me back to him. He knew how to seduce me and draw me back into his intoxicating web of love, lies, and sorrow. I felt weak and powerless, but I knew I couldn't live without him. He had my life in his hands, and I couldn't break free. At least, not now.

I was deep in my thoughts when I saw Coco coming toward me.

"There you are! I've been looking for you all evening. I need a hug from my favorite aunt!" he said, and without giving me a chance to stand up, he grabbed me with both arms.

"Let me breathe first," I exclaimed. "I also have been looking for you. You look amazing and so handsome. I can't believe this day has come. You will make Elsa the happiest woman in the world."

"I can't believe it either. I'm a little scared though. Do you think I will be a good husband?" he asked.

"Not a good one, but the best one," I said, pulling his face toward mine and kissing him on both cheeks.

Hans joined us a few minutes later and gave Coco a big pat in the back.

"Here is to many happy years together," he said, lifting the glasses he had brought for us. "I hope you have fun tonight with your new bride," he added with a naughty look on his face.

Coco turned red in an instant, and I gave Hans a look he'd never forget.

"Don't be embarrassed, brother," said Hans. "The wedding night is always the best sex. After that, women always find an excuse to avoid you. Enjoy it while you can," he added, laughing out loud.

"Enough, Hans. Coco doesn't want to hear your opinion on that matter right now. Let him go socialize with his guests," I said, trying to prevent any further embarrassment.

"Chola, relax! It's just a little joke on the wedding day. Besides, I always had my doubts about Coco and women. I thought he didn't like them after all."

I was grateful that Coco had already left us and didn't hear such a hurtful comment from Hans.

"Well, I guess this wouldn't be the first time that you are wrong. Elsa is a lovely woman and will make Coco a very happy man," I said.

"Why do you have to make a big thing out of everything? He's almost thirty years old and we all thought he would never marry. The man never had a girlfriend in his life. That's why I thought maybe he preferred a boyfriend," he added.

"That's it! Not another word out of you if you still want to end this night in peace," I exclaimed, my blood boiling, my anger coming up to my face.

"All right, Chola, you win. He will be a wonderful husband." He turned around and left after a tray of food. The joy of seeing him here disappeared, and he stayed away from me for the rest of the evening.

His words kept going around in my head. He did have a point, but he was so wrong. Coco never had a chance to meet anybody because of Luisa. She always kept his potential girlfriends away from him, making sure he never developed a serious relationship. But this time was going to be different. This was matrimony. Luisa was supposed to stay out of it. She would have no other choice but to keep her mouth shut and let them live their life the way they saw fit.

The party lasted all night. We made sure we had some fresh coffee brewed to sober up some of our guests before we sent them home. Coco and Elsa left around midnight and spent their first night together at a very elegant downtown hotel. The day after, they were going to Brazil for their honeymoon.

I was completely exhausted. I helped Luisa pick up a few things before a crew of cleaners arrived, and soon after that I left to try to sleep for a few hours. When I arrived at Josefina's, the girls were sound sleep and Hans was nowhere to be found. I concluded he probably left with one of my brothers and that I would soon hear from him. All I could do was take my shoes off before I fell on the bed and passed out from exhaustion and excitement.

By the time I woke up, Josefina was getting ready to start making dinner. The girls were having fun playing with her three daughters. All of them were around the same ages and saw each other only a few times a year, so they enjoyed every minute they spent together. Josefina's husband, Cesar, a charming, high-ranking military man, stole her heart away and married her a few months after dating her, despite my father's objections. I guess this was the only time my bitter father knew what he was saying. Cesar turned out to be violent and abusive and hit Josefina regularly. We all knew about it, but she begged us not to say a word for the children's sake. They had three daughters and one son, his favorite. Cesar was a tyrant at home but a very beloved general in the military. He frequently visited the Indian communities around Asuncion, and many years later we found out that he had a second wife and children in one of the tribes. Josefina never left him. She died like a loyal wife by his side.

Every time I saw her, I reminded myself that my life could have turned out to be much worse, that I had no reason to complain, that things would change. Lying to myself was my favorite survival technique.

I asked around the house if anybody knew where Hans had slept the night before, and nobody answered. Josefina gave me a strange look and told me to meet her in the kitchen.

"We saw him leave with a woman last night, but we don't know who she was," she said.

"What do you mean? That's impossible. He came all this way to be with me, with us. I'm sure you are mistaken. He is probably with one of our brothers." I wished my words were true.

"You are probably right, Chola. Don't worry about it. He'll soon be back," she said, obviously sorry that she had even mentioned it to me.

I spent the rest of the afternoon quietly waiting and wondering. Dinner time came and went, and when we were ready to call the night off, he arrived radiant and smiling.

"About time you came home." I tried hard not to yell.

"I know. I lost track of time. I fell asleep and woke up just a few hours ago. You know I'm not used to drinking, so the wine just killed me," he replied.

"I'm not interested in the details. How dare you show up like this? You smell like cheap sex, so don't bother explaining. I want you out of my sister's house now. I can't believe you came all the way to do this, to humiliate me like this. You have no shame, no decency. The girls and I won't drive back with you. We'll see you back at home in a few days and we'll talk again," I said and walked away from him.

He left, too embarrassed to say anything else. My heart broke again, but I stood my ground and was proud of it. I wanted to stay in Asuncion and never look back. But I had invested already too much in this life. I had to come up with a solution or face the consequences. But the shame was intolerable. Staying in Asuncion would mean facing the hurtful gossip and people's judgments. I had to start from scratch.

The day of our departure, Josefina helped me pack our things and we left for home. I was very silent all the way, but luckily the girls didn't notice. They were happily exchanging stories about the wedding—their favorite gowns and the fun games with their cousins.

I was glad my sorrow didn't affect them. Not yet.

Chapter Eleven

My obsession for the next few months was to save as much money as possible. I was determined to change my life and find a way out of this misery.

When we arrived home after Coco's wedding, Felipe was waiting for us at the truck station and took us home. We barely talked but I knew exactly the reason he was there.

His best friend was in trouble and he was there to mediate between us.

I was glad to be back at home. It gave me a very much-needed sense of security, as if I was stepping on solid ground for the first time in a long while.

"He wants your forgiveness," Felipe finally said.

"If he wants forgiveness, he should go see a priest," I replied coldly.

"You know what I mean. He wants to come back home to you and the girls. He's very sorry for what he's done and wants to make it up to you."

"The only way I will let him come back is if he agrees to move away, as far away as we can," I said.

"But that's crazy!" he exclaimed. "His business is here. Besides, where would you go?"

"Where nobody knows us, where I can be anonymous and he can't cheat on me anymore. I want to move to Buenos Aires," I said firmly, as if I already had made my mind and wasn't willing to negotiate.

"Chola, you don't know what you're asking. Buenos Aires is a giant city. You have no family or friends there. You'll be terribly lonely," he insisted, trying to talk some sense in me.

"Since my mother passed away, nothing holds me here. Look around you. I live in a dump, full of dust and dirt, in a place where my daughters have no future. I don't want them to live my life. I'm not an educated woman, but I know this place is not right for them. I want to give them what I never had."

"I know what you mean, but we can help you here. Besides, Chola, you would break my heart if you go," he said quietly.

"Felipe, you have more important things to think about than me. The only way I can work on my marriage and try to save whatever is left of it, is if I'm away from this place. I hated it from the first day I arrived. The only good thing that happened here was you. I will never forget you." I took his hand.

"You are a brave woman, Chola. You do what's best for you and your family. I won't stop you. I will talk to Hans about it," he promised.

He kissed me goodbye, and I could see his eyes watering up as he walked away quickly to avoid showing me his pain.

I felt sad for him. He meant a lot to me, but I was finally taking charge of my life. This was an opportunity I couldn't pass up—my marriage and the rest of my life depended on it.

Convincing Hans wasn't easy. As a stubborn northern European he fought me tooth and nail, but I didn't give in. He slept at Felipe's house for more than a month before he finally agreed to come to terms with me.

In the meantime I started getting everything organized. We didn't have many possessions, so the ones that were closer to my heart—which were not that many—were put in boxes; the rest I either sold or gave away to people who were worse off than we were. Our house was small and it didn't take much time to empty it. By the time Hans was ready to sit down and talk about our move, most everything we owned was either gone or in a box.

I think it shocked him to see how determined I was to move forward with my plans and a little scared that I was doing it with or without him. He probably never imagined that I would have the courage to make such a decision on my own, that I would actually follow through with it, and worst of all, that I didn't care what he thought.

My biggest worry wasn't him or his business, but the families of the drivers that worked for him. They had children of their own, and I felt responsible for their well-being.

I had become very attached to them these past few years, always keeping an eye on their families when they were away, helping to feed them when they were working, or listening to their struggles when they needed to vent.

Then there were our children. They had made a life of their own in this sleepy, small town. They had friends, and they loved their school. They were going to miss our frequent trips to Asuncion inside the dirty truck cabins, listening to Paraguayan folkloric music on their way, watching children play on the side of the road with their faces covered in red dust, and most importantly, visiting their favorite cousins.

In Buenos Aires, a big metropolis, a life of uncertainty awaited us. Everything familiar to us would be gone. But that was exactly what

I needed. No familiar faces, no guilty looks, no destructive gossip. Hans' affairs had become public knowledge in our small town. Husbands gave me hateful looks on the streets, and women would sanctify themselves when they crossed my way. I always wanted to shout at them: It's not me! It's him! He does it! He's the one to blame!

But I knew I was partially responsible. I was his wife; I was supposed to keep him home every night, to please him sexually. But his sexual appetite was insatiable. He would have been happiest in the middle of the desert with his own harem. For a brief period of our marriage, I thought I could satisfy him, but I was never enough for him. Sex with me was part of his duties and obligations as a husband. He was always a gentle lover, never forcing me or hurting me. It pains me to admit it, but I was never completely comfortable with my own sexuality. Years of Catholic guilt were almost impossible to erase, and though I tried very hard to connect with him intimately, we rarely did.

On the other hand, he just loved the thrill of the hunt. The process of catching a new prey, to lure her and finally bring her to his bed was extremely exciting to him. It was like a drug, like an uncontrollable addiction.

Again and again I tried to understand in my head what drove him inside. I kept telling myself that if I could just overlook his worst weakness, I would be able to accept him and love him as he was. But adultery wasn't an easy pill to swallow.

Memories of my mother's sufferings and struggles made me always think that my life wasn't that bad. She never complained, never said a negative word about my father. She stood by him until the day he died, always forgiving him, always loving him. But if she could forgive him, why couldn't I forgive Hans? I was giving him one more chance to redeem himself by moving away and starting from zero. I wanted to give him the opportunity to be a better husband and father and show us that he loved us above all.

His actions had hurt me in a deeper way than I ever expected. The damage was done and I was afraid there was no redemption possible.

The only way I could survive another day by his side was moving away. In my heart I knew I was strong. If I'd just follow my heart, I would be able to overcome even the worst situations.

After a few weeks in the market, Hans' trucks were not selling and I started to get nervous. We decided I was going to move with the girls to Buenos Aires and start getting settled until Hans could join us. Since her husband's death, my mother-in-law lived very comfortably in a home for the elderly outside the city, and we were able to rent a small house through one of her friends.

We finally managed to sell the hut I had called home for the last few years, and with the little money we got for it, we were able to finance our move and pay the first few months of rent in the city.

Before I shut the door on one of the most painful stages of my life, I stood in the middle of my empty living room trying to take with me at least one happy memory. I tried very hard to remember, but all I could think about was the loneliness and desperation of all these years. I decided to sweep my floors one last time, when Felipe walked in.

"I was hoping to find you here," he said.

"I'm just saying goodbye to this phase of my life," I answered, continuing to sweep.

"I hope it was a good one—it was for me," he said and walked around me to avoid my broom.

"Meeting you and your wife was the nicest thing that happened to us here. I will never forget you."

He started to cry and hid his face against my shoulder.

"Chola, I love you. I always have, since the first day I met you," he confessed.

"I know, Felipe, I know. You were never very good at hiding it."

"I need to be with you before you leave. I want you to meet me and—"

"Don't, don't ask me that," I interrupted him, putting my fingers gently on his lips. "I can't be with you. Then I would be just like him. I don't want to use you as my revenge. I would never do that to you. I will take your love with me for the rest of my life. You are a good man and a good husband, Felipe. I will never forget you."

We embraced, and he kissed me for a long time. It was beautiful to feel loved and to taste it in someone's kiss. His lips brought back all the memories of love that I had forgotten. They reminded me how little we need to be happy in life and how hard it can be to get it. I felt lost in his embrace, safe from this world, happy for a brief but unforgettable moment.

Chapter Twelve

Life in the big city was nothing like I had imagined, but it wasn't bad either.

We rented a small house in a working-class neighborhood called Lanus. My mother-in-law's roommate had a wealthy son who made his fortune in real estate, and she asked him to find us a place to live in a safe area, but not too far from the city center, where Hans would most probably end up finding work. We had the upper level, while another family lived downstairs from us. It had two bedrooms, a bathroom, and a small kitchen/family room. It was just what we needed. It was painted white inside and outside and had real ceramic floors that I could wash with soap and water.

Our street was always busy. There were people and shops everywhere, always loud and crazy. That was one of the hardest things to get used to: the noise of the buses driving by and their exhaust fumes. The buses in Buenos Aires were unlike any others I'd seen. They had their own transit rules, which basically boiled down to: they owned the road and you just moved out of their way. They never fully stopped. You had to be fast to get in and out before they'd leave you behind, and the drivers would yell at you if you took longer to get in than they could afford. The drivers were always counting handfuls of bills and change, all while driving, talking to some passenger about the next stop, or screaming at people to move back and make room for more passengers. Every so often, controllers would get on their buses to make sure that the drivers were not stealing any money. They had forms to write down the amounts they made every hour. It was a brutal job, but they seemed to manage it well. The drivers covered the windshields with the colors of their favorite soccer teams, pictures of their most beloved saints and all kinds of paraphernalia that obstructed the view, making the cabin look like their own private sanctuary—or a circus tent.

I was so terrified of getting on a bus that for months I only went as far as my feet could take me. We could not afford taxis, so we walked everywhere until my daughters refused to do it anymore. One day they forced me to get into one of those devilish machines, and once I realized I could actually survive the ride, it became second nature.

That was the way I found my first job. As I was getting ready to step out of a bus, a man right behind me stepped on my skirt as I was going out the exit door. It ripped completely in the back, almost showing my entire behind. I was mortified, but he was even more embarrassed. He kept apologizing to me and begged me to let him pay for the tailor to fix it. He even took me to the nearest tailor and waited outside until my skirt was as good as new. I had no choice because I was a long way from home and didn't want to have to walk showing off my underwear. While I was waiting for my skirt, the tailor's wife offered me a cup of tea and complained that her husband had way too much work in his shop. His only employee had left him recently and he couldn't find anybody to replace him.

I explained that I was good with a sewing machine and that I would be very happy to work for them if they were interested. They told me they were willing to test my abilities and gave me a few pieces of clothing that needed alterations. I was supposed to bring them back in two days, and if they were happy with the results, they would give me more. I was overjoyed with my first job. I could not believe it. I could not wait to tell the girls about it.

We celebrated by cooking their favorite Paraguayan dish, *sopa paraguaya*, made with corn flour, onions, and cheese and baked in the oven.

I started daydreaming about all the things I would do with the money I would earn. First, I would find the best music teacher for Matilde. Then I would start saving to buy her a new piano –it had been too expensive to transport our old one. How exciting! For the first time in a long time, things were finally starting to go my way.

I went back to the tailor a few days later with the finished products and thus began a long and fruitful relationship.

It took Hans a few months to sell his trucks, which were so old and run down that he didn't get as much as we had expected originally. But nevertheless they sold, and he finally joined us in Buenos Aires. He was glad to be with us again, maybe more out of habit than love, but we were all happy to be reunited and together again. His job search started immediately because we could not afford one day without pay. Life in the city was expensive, and I wasn't able to raise chickens or plant a garden to help ends meet.

But we all adapted very well. The girls started their new school shortly after we arrived and made a few new friends. I was shy and insecure and had a very hard time meeting other women or making any friends. My home was my own little world; it made me feel safe and I didn't feel the need to invite any stranger in. Besides, in a big city, you can't trust anyone. My job kept me occupied, and it was our only source of income as Hans was having a hard time finding work.

We were running out of our savings when one of our neighbors, noticing Hans' accent, recommended him to the only German businessman in the area. He was a Jew who settled in Buenos Aires after surviving the concentration camps. He was a small man, wore thick glasses, and barely spoke any Spanish. His children were his translators, but when it came to business, he didn't need anyone. His store sold men's ties and socks. It was small and unorganized, with boxes everywhere. He knew his shop so well and didn't bother putting labels on anything. He knew exactly where the blue ties or the black socks were. He could have been blind and run the place effortlessly. His name was Samuel.

I went with Hans the first time they met. Samuel welcomed Hans as if he was a long lost friend. They hugged and sat down in the back of the store. I waited patiently for their meeting to end, wondering what they were talking about. I couldn't understand a word they said and that irritated me. I wished I could understand my husband—maybe behind all those words was the secret to his soul. Maybe that was the only way to get to his very core, through his childhood language.

After a little more than an hour, both men came out, shook hands, and smiled at each other. Samuel turned to me and said in a thick accent I could barely understand, "Hans, a good man. He work with me and take care of you and children. No worry, no worry."

I smiled politely and extended my hand to shake his. He pushed me closer to him and hugged me with both his arms. I felt his warm embrace and knew he was a kind soul. He had arrived in our lives for a reason and was there to stay. Hans started working for Samuel immediately, doing anything and everything he needed: sorting the merchandise, organizing the store, helping with the books, and even cleaning when needed.

After six months of struggling, we could finally call this new place home.

Hans and I never talked again about the episode at Coco's wedding. We both understood we had to put it behind us to be able to start again. I was willing to give him another chance, hoping that a change as dramatic as this would make him appreciate us more. And he did, for a while.

Being poor had its advantages. There was no money for gambling and there was no money for parties. Every penny we made went to pay rent and to our daughters' education.

I found an excellent music teacher for Matilde, and Baby was attending the best Catholic school in the area.

They were both growing so fast; it was very hard for me to keep up with them. I was always very nervous and afraid that something bad would happen to them in this big city. I was strict with them and didn't give them too much freedom. I had never felt this way before. Until then I had always been in control. They were either with me, or I knew exactly where they were or with whom. In Buenos Aires, they were going to be exposed to so many strange and dangerous things that I was always terrified of what could happen to them at any given moment.

Hans wasn't as preoccupied as I was. He grew up in a big city and felt comfortable with our new life. He was always mediating for the girls if they wanted to stay later in school or wanted to go to the movies with their new friends. I trusted my daughters, but I didn't trust the new world around them. Matilde was only ten years old when we moved. She was still a child, but Baby was fifteen, and she no longer looked like a little girl. She grew more and more beautiful every year, and everybody noticed her.

She was always shy and reserved, like me. She wasn't interested in socializing with boys her age, and that gave me some peace of mind. But that didn't help when it came to the rest of the world. Older boys constantly asked her out, and she felt pressure from her peers. Her school was an all-girl facility run by a Spanish order of nuns called *Patrocinio de San Jose*. The headmistress was the strictest and meanest of them all and I loved her. The meaner the better. Someone had to control this new generation of crazy girls who wore short skirts, loved loud music, and didn't respect their parents.

Baby was never like that. She loved to stay home with me, studying for her next test, reading her favorite book, or helping me with work.

One day, without any announcement, Hans brought home a yellow canary bird. The girls named him Toto. It was our first real pet. Our chickens were not pets, and the dogs that came to eat at our house were all homeless mutts.

Toto could sing like an angel. Every morning, he woke us up with the most heartfelt melodies, and because we all loved music so much, it was the perfect fit for our family.

The girls tried to imitate him, but his voice was so unique that not even the most gifted singer could have competed with him.

Toto was the best company I had and the closest thing to a friend. He would sit on my shoulder for hours while I sat in front of the sewing machine until the girls came home from school. We used to let him fly free around the house until it was time for his meal. At that point, he would fly to his cage, and we would close its gate for the rest of the evening. After that I would open my windows to let the fresh air in. He would stay there until it was time to sing us good night. We would all sit around his cage and enjoy his voice. When it was done, I would put a blanket on the cage, say good night, and go over to the kitchen to finish doing dishes.

This was our nightly routine for the ten months he was part of our family. One day, after I opened our windows, I didn't notice the neighbor's cat entering our living room. It sat patiently until the girls came home and opened the cage to let the bird out to play. With one precise jump, the cat caught the bird in his mouth. We all screamed and pulled our beloved pet out of the feline's teeth, but it was too late. His broken body could not move and his voice was forever silenced.

We were all devastated, and even Hans cried with us. The girls lost their favorite pet. I lost my only friend.

Every Saturday morning I walked five blocks from our house to the local pharmacy, the only place in the area with a pay phone. From there I could call Asuncion and talk to my sisters. It became my special routine and I used it to escape my daily chores. The girls always stayed to have breakfast with their father, whom they hardly saw during the week. So I looked forward to my Saturday morning walk and my conversations with Luisa over the phone. They didn't have a phone either, so she waited at a neighbor's house for my call. I knew I always had to be on time because Luisa didn't like to sit too long making small talk with her neighbor's wife, an 80-year-old lady who could hardly hear.

It was nice to catch up and listen to her talk about the rest of the family and the latest gossip in Asuncion. It was much better than the telegrams or the letters that took forever to arrive.

I knew things had been hard for her since Coco's wedding, but I hoped it would improve with time. The marriage was too new and after many years controlling her son's life and destiny, it was time for her to let go.

She didn't like to talk about Elsa. She avoided the subject and limited herself to more mundane things. Antonia was getting old, she complained, and her lack of exercise was making her arthritis worse. Josefina was getting heavier and used food as comfort to forget about the pain her husband caused her. Choli was expecting her first child and was doing great, and so the list went on and on about every member of the family.

Our conversations reminded me of the time when we all lived under one roof together and spent long hours talking about our lives. She always reminded me of who I really was.

Many times I asked myself what my life would have been like if I had never married. What an irony if the oldest and the youngest of us would have stayed together, unmarried, living happily but alone. No man to take care of, no man to hate.

But today I was just happy to listen to my sister's news.

"But I haven't told you the best yet," Luisa said with anticipation.

"I'm all ears," I responded.

"Coco went to one of his powerful friends and requested a telephone line to be installed at our house," she said almost screaming with joy.

"That's fantastic!" I replied. "When is it happening?"

"They are coming next week, so if we are lucky, we will have a telephone by next Friday."

"But how will I know your new number?"

"I will give it to our neighbor as soon as I know it. When you call them, they will be able to tell you how to reach us directly. You will be making two phone calls. I'm so sorry you will have to pay for that. I know how tight things are for you right now."

"Don't worry about it, sister, I'm so happy for you. I can't believe I will be able to call you any day of the week," I said.

We said good bye and wished each other a good week.

Phone lines were very hard to come by in Buenos Aires as well. You had to go to the government-run telephone company and put your name on a long waiting list. With luck, you would get a line in the next ten years. Unless, of course, you knew somebody in the right places to help you get it faster. But we were new in town and our chances of getting a phone line sooner were as good as none.

The following week, I walked faster than usual, almost jumping with excitement. I had to wait a few minutes until a man finished using the pay phone, and then it was my turn. I called the neighbor first, and then I dialed Luisa's number.

"Hello?" a voice I didn't recognize said on the other end.

"Luisa, is that you?" I asked.

"No, it's Elsa. Is that Chola, from Buenos Aires?"

"Yes, it's me, I can't believe I'm talking to you."

"It's been too long, Chola! How nice to hear your voice! Your sisters miss you very much. They think about you and the girls all the time," she told me.

"Well, I miss them too, but I'm so excited we will be able to communicate more often now that you have a phone."

"You sure will, and it will be nice for Luisa to have someone to talk to," she added.

Something in her voice wasn't right.

"What do you mean? We talk regularly and she seems fine," I said wondering what was really going on.

"Things are not well around here. She didn't tell you?" She seemed surprised.

"Tell me what?" I said, holding my breath for a second.

"She didn't tell you she wouldn't let Coco and me sleep in the same room? She has made my life a living hell since we came back from our honeymoon, and she forced Coco to move out of our bedroom. We have separate beds, Chola. You didn't know?" Her voice started to break down in sobs.

"Of course I didn't know. That's absolutely crazy. How can you tolerate this? This is your house now. How about Coco? What did he say?"

"He has no control over her. He is afraid of her. Every time he tries to talk to her, she cries and tells him he doesn't love her, and she will die if he asks her to move out. I've tried everything, Chola, but his mother has so much power over him. It will be impossible to change that," she explained.

"I'm so sorry to hear about this. Maybe I should invite her to come visit us. It's been a long time since we saw each other, so maybe she will say yes."

"That would be wonderful, Chola. I will be forever grateful. But please don't tell her I spoke with you. She should be back shortly. She was waiting for your call, but since it took you longer, she went to the neighbor's house to find out if you called. I guess she is not used to the phone yet. She decided to go and ask in person."

"Listen, I don't think I have enough money for another call but I will try again tomorrow. Elsa, don't worry, I will do everything I can to help you," I promised.

"Thank you, Chola. You are so kind to me." I could hear the sadness in her voice.

"Don't mention it. Oh, and say hello to Coco and Antonia from me."

"I will. Kiss the girls from us. Good bye."

I was speechless. Just the thought of what Luisa was doing to Coco and Elsa made me sick to my stomach. She never mentioned a word to me. I guess she knew very well what my opinion would have been. All these months thinking that Luisa was actually behaving and letting them have a life. How silly of me to think that she was actually capable of letting go of her son. Elsa would never be able to have a married life living under the same roof as her mother-in-law. I just couldn't understand why Coco didn't face his own mother and put an end to this crazy nightmare. His wife should come first, especially after so many years waiting to find the right woman. Besides, if he ever dreamed of having a child of his own, it would never happen under these circumstances.

On my walk home, I decided I was the only one who could help Elsa by convincing Luisa to step back. But I had to be very careful not to make her mad and make things worse. It had to look like a harmless visit to see her nieces and her little sister. Luisa could be very stubborn, and if she knew that I was trying to help Elsa, she might never want to speak to me or see me again. I adored my older sister, but I knew her too well. All these years obsessing with her only child had turned her into a monster capable of anything to keep him under her wing. But maybe the thought of having a grandchild could soften her a little. Having a baby in your life could work miracles. It would remind her of how wonderful it was to have a child to love and take care of, and it would divert her attention to somebody other than Coco. But if she forced them to sleep in separate bedrooms, there was no way in the world that Elsa would get pregnant.

Still, I was very hopeful. I just wanted Hans' blessing before I invited Luisa to stay with us for a few months. He always liked her and respected her, but I needed to be sure that he would be fine with it. Our new house was very small, and we were on a tight budget, but if Luisa came, she could help me with my job and I could work on more pieces faster.

That would help raise my income and offset the cost of having one more person living with us.

Besides, the girls adored Luisa, and she loved them dearly. So spending time with them would probably keep her mind occupied.

I walked faster than usual, excited with the possibility of having my sister soon with us.

Hans and the girls were finishing breakfast as I walked in.

"Good thing you're all here. I have something I need to ask you," I said looking at the surprised expression on their faces.

"I wanted to know how you would feel about Luisa coming to visit and staying with us for a few months." I waited anxiously for their reaction.

Even before I finished my last words, the girls jumped for joy and started screaming in approval. Hans looked at me and smiled.

"Of course she's welcome to stay with us. Did you talk to her about it?" he asked.

"Not yet. I wanted to have your blessing before I invited her to stay. Besides she could help me with my job, and this way she won't feel she's a burden to us," I explained, trying to make his decision easier.

"I don't think that's a problem, Chola. But I thought she was very busy in Asuncion taking care of Coco's every need." I noticed a hint of irony in his voice.

By now the girls had moved on and were busy playing in their room.

"That's exactly the reason I want her to come. She has forced Coco and Elsa to sleep in separate rooms. She can't stand the idea of them sharing a bed together," I explained, embarrassed by the truth.

"That's the most ridiculous thing I ever heard," he complained. "How in the world would Coco let this happen? What kind of a man lets his mother rule his life this way? See, I told you there was something strange about your nephew. No real man could stand sleeping in another room away from his wife—not a chance that would ever happen if you were normal!"

"Don't exaggerate, Hans. I know it all seems crazy, but maybe there is a good reason for this situation."

"How can you even justify such madness? Coco is not a real man. He doesn't have a pair of balls," he said, yelling by now.

"You are in no position to judge or criticize anyone. Last time I checked you were not the perfect husband either. So before you jump to conclusions, I think you should just keep your opinions to yourself, especially if they are offensive. The best thing we can do for them is to get Luisa away and keep her here as long as we can. So, are you fine with that?" I was irritated with his attitude.

"Yes, I'm fine with that. But I still think there is something wrong with your nephew." He walked away from the room and left me alone with my thoughts.

That night I didn't sleep, thinking of a way to convince Luisa to come. I tried to remember the long conversations we used to have before bedtime growing up. Luisa or Antonia always kept an eye on me and made sure I went to bed on time. They would sit next to me and tell me all kinds of stories. They were both like mothers to me.

Many years later, I found out that the stories they told me were based on the films that they saw at the local cinema. I actually didn't care and, in fact, I passed on this tradition to my own children. Because I didn't have time to read much, I needed to find a source of inspiration, and the movies were the perfect place for that. It was the only thing I liked doing with Hans when we had the money and the time to go out together. The movies were the cheapest form of entertainment, and it remained that way for many years until we were finally able to buy a television.

I couldn't tell Luisa the real reason for my invitation, so I had to try to convince her of how much I needed her with me. Just as much as I needed her growing up, I needed her with us right now. She could fill the void that my mother left after she died, and she could grow closer to my daughters. Maybe being with the children, like a grandmother, would awaken a need in her heart to have her own grandchild. That feeling should be more powerful than anything else; at least that was what I thought.

On Sunday morning I got up early, made breakfast, and got ready for church. I liked going to the early mass, but the girls preferred to sleep, so we all went a little later. Today, however, it was different. I needed to make that phone call, so I woke the girls up and asked them to get ready for mass. Hans never came with us. He hated priests. He found them shallow, empty, and boring. For him, a man who couldn't sleep with a woman was not a real man. It would take years for me to understand his philosophy. But I never agreed with him. For me, church was a safe haven. I felt comfortable inside its walls, as if they were protecting me from all evil. Nothing could go wrong as long as I believed. And this morning I had a big favor to ask God.

After Mass, we walked home and stopped at the pharmacy to call Luisa. She picked up the phone after the first ring.

"Chola, is that you?" she asked with an anxious tone in her voice.

"Yes Luisa, I tried you yesterday but you were out."

"You were late and I thought you didn't have the right number. Isn't this amazing? I can't believe we are talking like this. It's just incredible," she exclaimed, happy to hear my voice loud and clear.

"I know. I'm so happy I can reach you any time I want. But it's still not the same as talking in person."

"You are right. We miss you and the girls terribly. When are you planning on coming to visit us?"

"Well, that was exactly what I wanted to talk to you about. I can't afford to come right now, and the girls are in the middle of the school year. But I can't wait to see you, I have so much to share with you," I replied.

"I understand. For you it's a lot of money to buy three bus tickets, but if I come to you, it's only one. And I love Buenos Aires!" she said with excitement.

"Would you do that?" I asked, not sure if what I was hearing was actually happening.

"Of course I would. Things are well here, Coco's business is doing great, and Antonia can help him keep the house in order. You know Elsa is not much of a housekeeper."

"Well then, I will have Hans look into it. You just tell me when you want to come and we will buy the ticket for you," I said.

"Absolutely not! Coco can do that for me. I haven't had a vacation in years, and he's been telling me I need to get away and relax."

"I'm glad he's taking care of you for a change. You can't be always responsible for everybody."

"You know I can't help it—that's just who I am. But I can't wait to see you and the children. Tell Hans I'm very grateful he is letting me stay with you."

"Of course, he's also looking forward to your visit," I said.

"I will let you know next week about possible dates. Now I'll let you go before this call becomes too expensive," she replied and said goodbye in a hurry.

I sat inside the telephone booth for a few minutes trying to understand what had just happened. It was very strange that she went with it so fast. She was obviously hiding something from me or the situation at home had turned unbearable. One way or the other, the best solution for now was to get her out of there.

I went home and started making plans for her visit. She would be a great help to me and the children. Life in the city was busy and

I felt lonely. Her company would lift up my spirits and help me get through my days.

Since our move to Buenos Aires, Hans and I hadn't been close. We only talked about our work, the girls, or the bills. Our only get-away was to the movies or to visit his mother, which was the only chance I had to be somewhere different. But I could still feel resentment in my heart. I tried hard to forgive him and move on with our lives, but I found it almost impossible to trust him again. I knew he made sure the girls and I had everything we needed, but he had stopped being my partner a long time ago.

Our conversations were short, never more than a few sentences. He came home every day and told me about his day, but he never gave me too many details. He stopped going out in the evenings and somehow lost the joy that everyone loved him for. His personality became darker, as if he had lost the spark that kept him alive. Often I visited the shop where he worked to say hello to Samuel and make sure that he was there. His boss was a fair man who was kind to us and paid Hans well. His income was enough to pay the rent, and my little salary took care of the food and any unexpected extras. I still loved him, but I wasn't in love with him. I didn't let him touch me again after the wedding episode, and he knew I was punishing him for it. He kept silent as if he admitted his guilt and accepted his sentence. He acted as if he was on death row. We shared the same bed but I was ice cold. I had lost my desire for him, as if I was sleeping with a complete stranger. Sometimes I remembered what it was like when we shared the same passion, when the smell of his skin would awaken all my senses and the touch of his lips transported me to another world. It pained me to remember that we were happy once, that we shared the same dreams. And with those memories came the pain and disappointment of all his weaknesses and mistakes.

One night his fingers started looking for my skin under the sheets, and I jumped out of the bed as if he had poked me with a sharp knife.

"How much longer are you going to punish me?" he asked, sitting straight up in the bed.

"As long as it takes me to trust you again." I buttoned up my night-gown.

"I've done all I can to show you how committed I am to you, to our family. But you show me nothing in return. You refuse to be a wife to me, so why should I remain faithful to you?" I could hear the frustration in his voice.

"I'll be a wife to you when you truly become a husband to me," I said firmly. "I don't understand you, Hans. I don't know you anymore. Maybe I will never be able to give you what you need. But as long as we are together, you will respect me. That's the least I can ask from you."

"I can't respect you when I feel rejected. I know you resent me for what I've done, but I told you many times those women don't mean anything to me. I love you."

His words had no power on me anymore. The thought of him being intimate with other women, strangers, infuriated me to the point of madness, but I had to let go. I couldn't torture myself anymore.

"I'm willing to give you another chance," I finally said, "but you will have to show me more than that. You will have to change for me or you will lose me forever," I added, trying to hold back the tears.

I came back to bed and he sat next to me. He cried in my arms like a child. I felt pity for him, for being so small, for being so weak, for not being able to be the man I needed him to be.

Chapter Thirteen

Luisa arrived in Buenos Aires five weeks after I invited her. She had changed a lot these last few years. Her hair had turned gray and the first signs of wrinkles had started to show up under her blue eyes. But she was still breathtaking. Her face was radiant, her smile bright. Her eyes still shone as they did decades ago, when every man in Asuncion dreamed about having her.

The years had turned her into a mature, beautiful woman. She still walked tall and got everyone's attention.

I was the person who knew her best. We were connected by an indescribable bond that lasted through the years and stayed with us until her death.

Although obviously tired, she seemed happy when she stepped out of the bus and showered the girls with hugs and kisses. But when she came to me, she held me in her arms a little longer than usual. It was as if she was trying to speak to me. I took just one look at her, and I saw her sorrow.

We went to the house where we all had lunch together, and we left her alone to have some rest after the twenty-six-hour bus ride. Traveling by bus was arduous, but it was the only transportation available to us. Flying was out of the question—it was much too expensive. The roads were in bad shape and the buses made several stops along the way. It was a trip that seemed to last forever.

I was anxious to have an hour alone with her, but I needed to wait until the children were in school and Hans was out of the house.

The weekend went by quickly with the excitement of our new guest and preparations for the week ahead. Luisa shared the same room where the girls slept and insisted she was comfortable sleeping on a mattress on the floor. I wondered how long she would last under these crowded conditions, but there was nothing better I could offer her. Baby tried many times to convince her to take her bed, but Luisa refused. Eventually, when her bones start aching she will give in and take the bed, I thought.

She didn't have a return ticket. I was hoping that she would stay with us for a considerable amount of time, but I had my doubts about how Hans would feel about a prolonged visit. This was my house as much as it was his and I needed Luisa to stay.

It was such a joy to have my beloved sister with me. I still could not believe that she was actually in my home. So much had happened since we saw each other last. Our phone conversations were short and I limited myself to the most important news. Now that I had her sitting at my kitchen table, we would be able to talk until we had nothing else to say. But first I wanted to hear from her. If I knew one thing about Luisa, it was not to ask her anything directly. I just had to wait patiently until she was ready to tell me what was in her heart. I had the feeling, though, that it wouldn't take too long until she was ready.

On Monday, after the girls left for school and Hans went to work, we sat together for a cup of tea.

"I am so happy you came." I embraced her one more time, as if I needed to make sure she was really standing in front of me, and she wasn't just a product of my imagination.

"I am very happy too," she replied. "This is the first time in a long time that I feel content." Her voice didn't sound well. She took a cup of tea in her hands and looked down on it.

"But I thought things were working out fine in Asuncion," I continued, wondering what was really going on and what she was hiding from me.

"Oh, Chola, it's been hell. Elsa is not the right woman for Coco. She doesn't cook, and she cleans badly. She doesn't know how Coco like his shirts pressed. She is a mess and there is nothing I can do about it," she exclaimed, now letting her frustration show.

"Luisa, those things can take years to learn. It took me a long time to get to know Hans better, and even now I don't think I know him at all." I tried to reason with her.

"But you are different. You are trying so hard. She doesn't want to try. She's only interested in convincing Coco to get rid of me. She wants me out of the house."

"Well, it's her home now," I said carefully. "She was very kind to let you and Antonia move in with them. You should be thankful and give them their space. Think about what the other option could be. She could simply ask you to move out, and of course, you don't want to get to that extreme, do you?"

"Coco would never do that to me!" she exclaimed. "They couldn't survive without us. She is useless. I run Coco's business—without me, he would make no money. I'm the only one who knows who his clients are, his deadlines, how much money he makes. He'd be lost if I left," she repeated, as if she was actually trying to convince herself.

"Luisa, you may be right, but it's not your job anymore to take care of him. Coco is a grown, married man. You should teach his wife the business and let her help him, that way you can start living your own life. Don't you ever think about yourself?"

"How can you say that? She could never do my job. She could never replace me!" she exclaimed as she stood up. I could see her bad temper coming out and her face becoming red. She was shaking and didn't notice when some of her tea spilled on the table.

I realized it was going to take a lot more than one cup of tea to talk Luisa into her senses. It was going to be a long road until I could convince her to set her son free. So I let it be for now because no one was going to give in that day. It was useless to have an argument with her about Coco. Maybe time and distance would give her some perspective, and would make her see that things could actually be different. Change is not always a bad thing. I had learned that lesson myself.

Luisa adapted fast to our routine and became a member of our household before we even noticed. She helped the girls get ready in the morning and worked with me in the afternoons.

Every Saturday she walked the five blocks to the pharmacy to call Asuncion and find out from Antonia how things were going. She never told me much about her conversations, but her facial expression would reveal to me how good or bad things were. I never asked—I just waited patiently until she was willing to talk.

Sometimes it took longer than I hoped, but surely she managed to paint the situation for me. Of course, she didn't know I had spoken with Elsa and was aware of what was going on. Luisa's version of the story was never the complete truth. She managed to fabricate a different version every time we spoke and manipulated every situation in her favor. For the time being, I decided to just let her believe what she wanted.

She told me that Coco had suffered insomnia the past few years and needed his rest. Sleeping with somebody else in the same bed would only make his ailment worse. He needed to feel rested in the morning to be able to work on his projects. Of course, his long afternoon naps had nothing to do with his sleeplessness at night.

Another version, which I loved, was that Elsa had a bad gas problem that occurred only during the night. She could not help it and passed gas while asleep and stunk up the whole bedroom. Therefore Coco could not sleep well next to her.

I have to admit she was very creative in her quest to deny the simple but painful truth: she could not tolerate her son being intimate with a woman.

But as long as she was visiting with us, Elsa and Coco would have a chance to work on their marriage. At least, that was my hope.

Having Luisa around made us all so happy, even Hans. He liked her company and was always glad to see her. They seemed to connect, and many times I found them having deep conversations at the dinner table long after the rest of us had gone to bed.

The girls adored her and adopted her like a grandmother as her presence reminded us so much of my own mother. She took them to the movies, helped them with their homework, and was always available to listen. Having her around also gave me a chance to have more time for myself. At the beginning I didn't know what to do with myself. I had no friends. I had no hobbies. I just worked all the time, and when I didn't, I had to take care of my daily responsibilities. Until Luisa came, I had never even given it a thought, but suddenly I felt I needed some time for myself.

Music and movies were the only other passion I had in my life, besides my children. I was already paying for Matilde's music lessons and saving to buy her a piano, so I had nothing left for myself. But I still managed to escape to the movies once a month. I would catch the afternoon matinee and be home just in time for dinner. My favorites were Doris Day's romantic comedies. I was secretly in love with Rock Hudson and had a crush on Tyrone Power. Life was always simple and predictable on the big screen, and it gave me a chance to escape. Many afternoons I would find myself walking back home, dreaming of the many different possible directions my destiny could have taken if I had never met Hans. But time and again I would arrive at the same conclusion: without him I would never have had my beautiful daughters, and life seemed pointless without them, even if Tyrone Power was the man waking up next to me every morning.

Luisa also liked having time for herself. Her help with the clothes allowed me to increase my work load substantially and make some extra money. We shared the profits and even though she insisted on spending some of her money on food and supplies for the family, she had some extra cash to spend on herself. Once a week, she would get dressed up and take the trolley downtown. She had a little routine that she liked to keep, starting in the heart of town: she would get off at the corner of Avenida Corrientes and 9 de Julio, where a magnificent white obelisk rises in the middle of the two most famous avenues in Buenos Aires. From there, she would walk up to the theater district, on Avenida Corrientes, all the way to Callao. There she would turn right and head over to Recoleta, her favorite place for afternoon tea. She would walk around and visit some of the most exclusive boutiques on Avenida Quintana, searching for an inspiration for the girls' next dress. With her perfect face, her deep blue eyes, and her aristocratic air, she blended pretty well amongst the wealthiest Argentineans. She had this wonderful gift that made her as comfortable with the neediest of people, as well as with the richest. She made everyone feel special, no matter where they came from or who they were.

She would sit in one of the many coffee houses overlooking the park in Recoleta and watch people go by. Her favorite was Café de la Paix. Sometimes she would head to the art museum to see their latest exhibition or visit some of the art galleries in the area. Her passion for art, and especially paintings, was undeniable, and I could tell how much she missed Coco every time she would talk about his paintings. She also enjoyed stopping at the small church next to Recoleta's cemetery, built originally in colonial times. Its interior was simple and peaceful, not opulent or overdone like many other Catholic cathedrals in Latin America. Right next to it was the entrance to the cemetery, where the most powerful and influential families of Argentina had their mausoleums. The whole place was like an outdoor museum, a small city where history came to life through the names of its inhabitants. Many narrow streets crossed it in every possible direction, creating a labyrinth of short buildings, topped by statues of angels looking peacefully down upon its visitors. The most amazing thing about this place was its ability to transport whoever crossed its gates to a parallel universe where time stood still and life was just an illusion.

Luisa liked to get lost in this labyrinth of history as if she could transport herself to another place in time. It was hard not to search your soul in a place like this. She probably found herself thinking about the many unexpected turns her life had experienced and of all the choices she made that brought her to this day. Of all the years I knew my beloved sister, I never saw an ounce of regret in her face. She had made peace with who she was a long time ago. The day she conceived, she found a purpose in her life stronger than anything else that could exist. She was a survivor. We both were.

Weeks turned into months and months into a year. I kept wondering when she would tell me that it was finally time to go. But I was happy with her around. I was selfish. She always made me feel that she was taking care of me. And I loved feeling that way.

For a long time, I took care of my husband, his parents and sister, my daughters, my house. But who was taking care of me? Who was thinking about what I needed? Who cared enough about me to even wonder what I was feeling or thinking?

I was used to thinking that person just didn't exist. After my mother's death, the only person who truly loved me and cared about me was gone, and no one would ever take her place. But Luisa reminded me of her, and her presence around me made me think of how much I missed my own mother.

I wasn't in a hurry to make her leave and because Hans didn't mind having Luisa around either, I wasn't going to push her away.

On the other hand, my quest to save Coco's marriage wasn't over. I knew the moment she went back to Asuncion, she would make their marriage miserable. Luisa had to stay with us as long as possible.

One morning, I decided to ask her about her plans, just to know what to expect. I had to prepare myself mentally for when the moment of her departure came, whenever that may be. I waited to be alone with her. It was the afternoon, and we were sitting at the kitchen table, tailoring some clothes. Outside it was raining hard, and that gave me a good excuse to make some hot tea.

"Luisa, you know we love to have you here with us, but I'm wondering what your plans are," I said while I put the tea kettle on the stove.

"I don't know, Chola. I've been thinking about it a lot, but I don't know if I should go back yet," she replied, her eyes focused on her work.

"What do you mean?" I wondered if she was referring to Coco.

"Chola, you need me here. The girls are fine, but I'm afraid to leave you alone." She stopped what she was doing to see my reaction.

Her answer sent a wave of shock under my skin. Was I that transparent? Did she realize how much I needed her?

"I know you're not happy with Hans—I can sense it. I watch you both interact and you seem like two strangers trying not to bother one another. I can see you haven't forgiven him yet and it's killing you inside." She had found an open window to my soul.

"I did forgive him. I just can't forget," I whispered so low I thought she probably didn't hear me.

"The minute you decided to stay with him, you knew you had to find the strength to forgive and forget. Every day you live this way will kill you inside," she said, holding my face between her hands. "That is why you need me here. I can't leave you like this. You need my support."

All this time I thought I was the one helping her deal with her situation, that I was the one trying hard to make her come to terms with her son's choice of life. I never realized that I was the one needing her help the most. Because she couldn't change Coco's destiny, Luisa took my life and turned it into her new obsession. She felt she needed to rescue me and fix what was wrong in my marriage. The question was if any rescue was even possible.

"If you are so unhappy, why don't you leave him?" Her question pierced my heart like a sharp arrow.

"I can't. I thought about it many times, but I can't. It would be devastating for the girls. He is their father after all," I said, trying to convince myself that there was a reason strong enough for me to stay, and that it wasn't simply my own cowardice that was stopping me from leaving him.

"Your daughters are growing. Do you truly think they don't know what he's done to you? They can see you suffer—they are not blind. And besides, they love you dearly. They would never want to see you suffer for their sake."

"Luisa, I married for life. I chose him and I was wrong, but not because I didn't love him. I still do. I just can't imagine the shame that it would bring us if I ever decide to leave him. Think about how much pain this would bring to the girls' lives. They will be outcasts. Their friends will stop talking to them. Baby won't be able to attend a Catholic school anymore."

I stopped talking because I couldn't bear the thought of the consequences of a separation as divorce was illegal in Argentina at the time. A separation could be the only possible route and it would stigmatize our children forever.

Perhaps even more importantly, I could not go against my own religious beliefs. My spiritual life was a big part of who I was, and I strongly believed that our marriage bond was unbreakable. Even if we separated physically, we would always be connected through our daughters. I knew the Catholic Church accepted a separation under special circumstances, but infidelity wasn't one of them. Besides, I didn't have the money or connections to get an annulment and I could not bear the idea of being excommunicated.

"Baby is turning seventeen," said Luisa. "She will be graduating soon and Matilde is in public school. As for what the others say or think, screw them! It's your happiness that's on the line. You have only one life. Are you going to waste it with a man who doesn't love you? Maybe there is someone out there waiting for you, wanting to take care of you," she added.

"What man would ever want a divorced woman? He would see me with pity. He would consider me dirty, a parasite of society, a pariah. But for Hans, on the other hand, it would be so easy. He would move on to another woman while I suffered the consequences alone. How fair is that? He is the one cheating and breaking our family apart, and I'm the only one paying for it. In what world do you see me happy? There is no happiness possible for me in this world or any other world as far as I know. Do you really think I should leave him? Do you truly believe that's the solution to my troubles?" I looked intently into her eyes.

"I understand, but you are the only one who can answer that. I know what it means to be loved and you deserve to have that too. My experience was brief but it marked me to my core. I was never the same again. I was so fortunate to be loved that way. Why couldn't you have the same? I know it would be hard, but you're still young and beautiful. You should give yourself a second chance in life."

"I was once loved too, or so I thought," I replied.

Every one of her words cut me like a knife. It had been several years since the wedding episode, yet my wounds were still fresh. I realized that the only way not to fall apart had been not to talk about it, or think about it, or mention it. But the pain was still there. I wasn't going to fool myself. And obviously, I couldn't fool Luisa either.

"When we moved to Buenos Aires, I decided to give him another chance," I continued. "That's what I'm doing. He's trying hard to be a good husband. I can see that. I just have to learn to live with what I have, not with what I wished I had."

"If that's how you feel, then try to make the most of it and don't keep punishing him. Make him feel like you are truly giving him a second chance," she said.

"I can only try. Having you around gives me the confidence I need to move forward. I'm so glad you are here with me."

"I won't leave you until I know you are okay. You can be sure of that."

"Thank you, Luisa. I love you."

"I love you too," she replied.

We spent the rest of the afternoon sitting across from each other, concentrating on our work, both our minds wondering what the future might bring.

That night I made sure I cleaned the kitchen early after dinner and decided to open up my heart one more time. I was afraid of being hurt again, of letting my guard down, but I refused to keep living my life this way, numbed and in fear.

I waited for Hans to finish reading the newspaper and asked him to come with me to the bedroom. I stood in front of him silently, looking straight into his eyes, wondering what he was thinking at that precise moment. I took his hands and slowly guided them to the top of my shirt. He stood very still, waiting for me to pull back or turn around. I didn't. I waited for him to finish opening my blouse. After that, he unzipped my skirt and it fell on the floor. I walked slowly and climbed into our bed. He followed.

I made love to him for the first time in more than two years. I didn't hold back. I did it with no regrets. I was a fighter, and I was going to fight for this marriage no matter how long it took. He was surprised and silent. He went along but I could tell he was more afraid than I was. We lay next to each other silently, both wondering what the other was thinking. Maybe this could be a new beginning, I hoped.

The next few weeks I took Luisa's advice and I concentrated on being happy. Hans was kind to me, but we kept our conversations short. I could tell by the way he behaved that he still felt guilty, but I knew he was grateful for a second chance.

His job situation was stable, and he was content working for Samuel. He did anything that was needed at the store. He even sold ties on the streets when they had a slow day. The money he made was enough to cover our basic needs, and we managed for a long time to stay afloat. Nevertheless, he was never completely satisfied, and his business instincts remained strong. He was constantly asking around and looking for new opportunities. He joined the local German Club where he could network with other successful German immigrants. He made a few new friends and socialized there on a regular basis. We rarely joined him because none of us could speak the language, something the girls resented. Both of them wished they could understand their father's language, but he never had the patience or the interest to teach them. Baby and Matilde loved their grandmother but they had a hard time communicating with her, especially in her old age. Between her hard hearing and her bad Spanish, our afternoons with her went very slowly, though we all made an effort.

Around that time, Hans came home with the news that he was talking to a contact to see if he could represent a German company in Argentina. After the war, it took a few years for German companies to get back on their feet, and once they did, they tried to find markets for their products all over the world. Hans told me that the biggest manufacturer of car lamps was looking for a sales representative in Buenos Aires and that he applied for the job. They wanted someone with experience who was fluent in German, understood their business philosophy, and had a good work ethic. That was probably the only kind of ethic Hans knew about.

We waited a few weeks to hear back from them and the letter with the job offer came soon enough. The first step was to break the news to Samuel. He had become an extension of our family. He helped us get on our feet when we needed it most, and we would never forget that. He had treated Hans like his own son and always made sure we had enough money to survive, even when his own business was hurting. We all knew this was a necessary step forward, but we felt we owed a big debt to Samuel.

We didn't know much about his past. He never wanted to talk about the concentration camps, but his wife told us that he had barely survived. An American soldier found him almost dead, hidden in one of the barracks after his battalion invaded Auschwitz looking for survivors. It took months to nurse him back to health and he still suffered a few ailments that dated back from those days. He left Germany and never looked back, just like Hans. They both had that strong connection with each other. Neither of them wanted to return to the country of their birth.

But Hans understood his job with Samuel was a temporary one. He needed to take care of us, and that was his priority. So he sat down with his old boss and explained the situation. Samuel was overjoyed with the news, hugged him, and wished him the best of luck. He then turned and walked away, hiding his tears. Hans continued to visit him every month until he passed away a few years later.

After signing a contract with the German manufacturer Osram, Hans started looking for office space in the downtown area. He opened a bank account and registered with the customs authorities to start importing the lamps. This process took a long time and Hans was away most of the day, but his excitement was contagious. We hadn't seen him so happy in a while. He started talking about buying our first car, moving out of our rental into our own apartment, and taking a vacation to the shore.

I could see his eyes light up at the idea of making enough money to pay for more than just the basics, and I let myself hope for the first time in recent years that it might actually be possible.

Suddenly we were not just surviving, we were living. I had a hard time thinking that I deserved any kind of happiness, so I tried hard not to be a pessimist and enjoy what we were experiencing.

The first thing I bought when we saved enough money was a piano for Matilde.

We gave it to her on her thirteenth birthday. She had been taking lessons since we arrived in Buenos Aires, and Luisa had taken her to a few concerts at the Teatro Colon. After her first concert, she came home in a kind of ecstasy. She could not stop talking about the experience, and she made her teacher show her how to play the piece she heard that time. Her passion for music was a joy to me. I lived it through her; I could feel it every time her eyes lit up and her smile was bigger than her face.

Luisa always set some of her own money aside to buy concert tickets for Matilde. It brought her so much joy to be able to take her and expose her to this new and amazing world.

I wasn't sure of many things, but I knew that music would always be a driving force in Matilde's life.

Next was Baby's graduation. She was the first one in her class and graduated as an honor student. My daughter, an honor student! I didn't finish school, and here I was with a daughter who was the smartest in her class. What else could I ask for? She was kind, thoughtful, and all mine. I was so proud of her achievements, and I had such high hopes for her. Her dream was to become a doctor. She wanted to go to medical school and become a pediatrician. She was focused and willing to do everything to get there. I admired that quality in her. She reminded me of my sister Sara and her passion to help others. Stubborn and persistent women were the norm in my family.

As a graduation present, Hans decided to treat us to a vacation at a very popular shore destination called Mar del Plata, five hours south of Buenos Aires on the Atlantic Ocean. Neither the girls nor I had ever seen the ocean and the possibility excited us all. Luisa would come with us as well. One thing worried me though. This vacation spot was famous for its casino.

Baby graduated with honors at the beginning of December. The weather was unbearably hot. Every summer, Buenos Aires turned into a humid inferno that burned without a break until late March. In January and February, the entire city became a skeleton of empty buildings. Every government office closed its doors until March, while businesses opened a few hours in the morning and a few in the evening, once the temperature was down. My favorite part of the summers, though, was the sudden disappearance of the traffic. The masses of cars transported themselves to other places, usually down the Atlantic coast, looking for some fresh sea breeze. Only the poor stayed in the city and survived, only barely, the asphyxiating heat irradiating from the asphalt and concrete that made up this metropolis of eleven million people.

Despite the heat, the coming of the holidays kept us busy. We missed our Christmas celebrations in Asuncion when most homes opened their doors and welcomed strangers with cold drinks and snacks and showed them their nativity scenes. Nothing like that happened in Buenos Aires. Every door remained closed; every family kept to itself.

Since our arrival, we started our own Christmas tradition, setting our dinner table on the terrace of our small building and sharing our supper with our neighbors from the ground floor. Luisa's presence made it a happier event and our upcoming trip gave us all a reason to celebrate more than usual.

Money had always been scarce in our household so we focused on the religious aspect of the holiday and skipped the buying frenzies that would take over the month of December. Luisa and I cooked a light but delicious summer meal—you couldn't eat anything heavy when the temperature was above 90 degrees at midnight—and we had everything ready before we went to church. Hans never came with us and preferred to wait in the hot apartment, snacking on food to avoid losing his temper because of the lack of nourishment. This made me laugh out loud because I knew how difficult it was for him to eat past seven o'clock.

Every night, the food had to be on the table at the exact same time. It didn't matter who was sitting with him at the table, he would not wait for anyone. His supper was like a sacred ceremony, and the biggest offense to him was for it not to be ready on time. Punctuality was a must. Once the food was on the table—at seven sharp—he would start eating immediately and not stop until his plate was empty. He wouldn't talk or interact with anybody until his entire meal had been devoured. Once he was finished, he drank a glass of Coca-Cola. Usually, by the time I was ready to start, he had already finished. So our meals were never very interesting; they never represented a moment to share our day or to talk about our life. They were simply a brief encounter before we moved on to other matters—me washing the dishes, him sitting down with the newspaper or listening to the evening news on the radio.

But for me, Christmas represented a rare occasion when I was in charge of the schedule. Even if it was only once a year, he had to wait for me to come home from mass to be fed. Besides, he was so useless in the kitchen that even with a refrigerator full of food he would have probably starved to death. Chocolate was the only thing he knew how to find. I always kept it in the same place, where he would get it every night after dinner. Nothing could stand between him and his dessert. I was so happy I was never like that, though I had my own weaknesses—like a good glass of wine. Self-control was not his strong suit. I had too much of it. He had none.

I knew we had to get our bus tickets and accommodations early because January was the peak of the summer season. I had everything organized and ready before we celebrated the holidays. We were leaving the first week after the New Year, for fifteen days. This was our first family vacation, and I wanted it to be perfect. I found a little hotel a few blocks from the beach, recommended by the tailor I worked for. He told me he could help us get a good deal through his worker's union. Argentina's populist government had strong ties with the unions, which in return made sure they got their members' votes.

Our departure day arrived, and we took the trolley to the bus terminal. The six-hour bus ride to Mar del Plata wasn't so bad. I was used to our long trips on noisy, dirty trucks, so sitting in a comfortable bus seemed like a luxury to me. While the girls played cards or took a nap, I let my imagination go wild. Mar del Plata was famous for its casino, night life and shows, good restaurants, and long beaches. Celebrities had their summer homes on its shores with magnificent views of the ocean while politicians and show business people made it their playground. New, hot affairs started and ended in only a few short weeks. There were no rules in summer. Everyone left their inhibitions at home, back in the city. The beach was the perfect place to strip down to the bare skin; it was the place where everyone was equal. The ocean didn't have any preferences. We could all enjoy it the same way. Its waves didn't stop for anybody, no matter how important, or rich, or famous you were.

The city life was centered on the casino. Two massive stone sea lions guarded its gates while marble stairs led you into its walls. It was a sight to see. Beautifully dressed people came in and out, some of them with a winner's look on their faces. Others simply observed from a distance, savoring a forbidden fruit. How easy it was to dream of a fortune and all the things you would do with it!

I could see now what was so attractive about gambling. It was not the thrill of the game, but the whole experience of it. It was about the crowd, the dream, the infinite possibilities, all waiting for you to unravel. But only if you were the lucky one that night. And I knew that would never be me.

Once we arrived, I made sure we paid the hotel in advance and bought our return bus tickets home immediately. I knew my husband too well and could not trust him with our money. If he lost all we had at the casino, at least we were going to be able to go back home.

We booked two rooms, one for Luisa and the girls, another one for Hans and me. The first thing we did after dropping our bags off at the front desk was to go see the ocean. Nothing I ever experienced before in my life was so powerful. I sat on the beach, mesmerized under its spell, while the girls and Hans ran into the water. The immensity of it reminded me of the infinite sky in northern Argentina, the sky I used to admire on my long trips to Asuncion. Luisa sat next to me, and we both admired the view in silence until it was time to get ready for dinner. I had bought my first bathing suit for the occasion, but I didn't want to waste any time unpacking our first day. I needed to see the ocean first.

Every day we went to the beach. Because I had never learned how to swim, I was content to sit on the sand under the umbrella, and watch from the distance as everyone enjoyed playing in the waves. That was good enough for me. My mother had always been afraid of the water since our neighbor's child drowned in the river. I didn't mind, though. I was happy getting my feet wet on the shore and watching the children having fun.

We all got along and liked sharing time together as a family. I couldn't remember the last time we had felt this way.

Every evening after dinner, Hans went to the casino, but not before promising me that he would quit before he lost it all. Of course, I knew better and hid some cash with my underwear just in case. Luisa and I went to the theatre once and took the girls out daily for long strolls along the board walk.

The last night before our departure, I told Hans I wanted to go with him to the casino. I wanted to experience it for myself. I was intrigued and needed to see it at least once. He made a face but agreed to take me.

I wore my best dress, and we both left the hotel looking radiant. He offered me his arm, which I gladly accepted. Even after all these years, he looked devastatingly handsome to me. He had lost some of his blond hair and gained some weight, but he was tall and had an aristocratic air that made him stand out in any crowd.

We walked the few blocks between the hotel and the ocean.

"You look beautiful tonight, Chola," he said, looking straight ahead.

"*Gracias*, you are very handsome too. This was a good idea." I tried hard not to get sentimental. I knew how much he hated to talk about his feelings, and I didn't want to ruin the evening.

Once we were closer to the beach, we started to feel the fresh ocean breeze. The casino sat right next to the ocean, with an over-sized terrace looking over the water. Tables were set up outside, but most of them were empty because the evening breeze was cooling down quickly. I never realized how quickly temperatures could change next to the ocean. Days were hot and nights could be freezing cold. I hadn't packed any coats and my light summer sweater wasn't enough to keep me warm. Hans noticed my shivering, took off his sports jacket, and put it on my shoulders. This small gesture made me wonder if we were possibly reconnecting. I gave him a smile of gratitude as we sped up our walk and went inside the casino.

The place was enormous. The entrance of the building was shaped like a circle and had Greek inspired columns in every corner. The marble floors were shiny and reflected the light from a gigantic crystal chandelier. I had never seen anything like it before.

Everyone seemed sophisticated and elegant. Hans noticed my nervousness and held my arm tightly. For him, this place was probably nothing special. He had been a regular at the most exclusive casinos in Europe, including Monte Carlo. This was just one more place for him—but not for me. The minute I walked past the foyer, I was transported into another universe.

The main room was dedicated to the roulette tables. In the center of the room was a bar from which attractive waitresses came in and out with drinks on their trays. Toward the back, there were smaller areas where the poker players had their tables. I could not tell what the other games were, but everyone seemed to be having a good time.

The smoke in the air made me a little dizzy, and I told Hans I needed to sit down somewhere. He chose a small table to the side, close to an open window where I could get some fresh air.

I was obviously out of my element and couldn't hide it, so I told him to go ahead without me and come back for me later. He kissed my hand and left for the poker tables. I ordered a glass of wine from one of the waitresses and sat there for the next few hours, people-watching.

What a fascinating crowd! Some people fit right in, but others looked like they couldn't afford to lose a penny. Women seemed hypnotized by the game of roulette, cheering and screaming when their lucky number was called. I always thought gambling was a men's passion, but I was so wrong. Women were the worst kind. They sat next to the tables, with their drinks and cigarettes, their eyes focused on the little ball rolling until it sat on a number. Their hands were quick to pick up the chips they won and place them again on the board. It looked all so scary and mechanical, as if there was no real thinking involved.

Hans came back after an hour and said he was having a good night. He lost some; he won some. He offered to give me a few chips to try my beginner's luck. I was definitely going for the roulette. I had to give it a try.

I walked the room a few times until I made up my mind where to sit. It wasn't a crowded table and the croupier looked friendly. I smiled at him and gave him my chips. He assigned me a seat. I told him it was my first time and he gave me a few tips quickly. All I could understand from looking at others play was very simple: pick a number and make your bet.

I chose carefully and decided I would start with my children's birthdays. When those didn't work, I moved on to all the important dates of my life. Finally, my mother's death anniversary was the lucky winner. By then I had only one chip left. I jumped out of my seat with excitement. It was not much money, but I felt like a winner for the first time in my life.

I took my money and went looking for Hans. I was so excited. I had to tell him I had won.

It took me a while, but I found him at one of the poker tables in the back room.

He was focused and concentrated. A small mountain of chips sat in front of him. I touched his shoulder to let him know I was there. He gave me a quick look and a smile. I decided to wait until the hand was over to tell him I won. The game was slow and the men sitting around the table didn't look very friendly. The smoke was thick, and it was hard for me to breath. Suddenly the game was over. Hans stood up, took his chips, and turned around to face me.

He hugged me tightly against his chest and kissed me long on the lips.

"We won, Chola. *Ganamos*," he said in my ear.

"I won too," I responded, showing him my few chips.

He laughed hard.

"Not bad for a beginner. You brought us both luck tonight. If I had known, I would have brought you with me the first night, not the last," he said, still laughing and gasping for air.

"I'm glad you had a good night. Maybe it's time to go back to the hotel." I was concerned that he wouldn't know when to quit.

"I'll do it for you, Chola. We'll go, but we must come back soon."

We walked back and I told him all about my experience at the roulette table and how much fun I had. I spoke the entire way home. When we reached the hotel, he said, "Chola, I won a small fortune tonight. Our lives are about to change."

"What are you talking about? How much money did you win?" I didn't fully trust what he was saying.

"A lot. Enough to buy a car or more."

"Please don't joke with me." I was getting angry and felt the joke was on me.

"I am not joking. Take me seriously for once. If you weren't with me tonight, I would have probably stayed and lost it all again. But you made me walk away on time. You were my saving grace." He kissed me again.

We walked into our room and he took my clothes off, kissing me passionately. The night had been intoxicating for both of us. He was different—he was back. I felt as if we were back in the days when we couldn't get enough of each other. When he had eyes only for me and I was his whole world. It was too much to take in one night. I couldn't sleep. My mind was racing. I tried to convince myself this was not a dream. I closed my eyes and before giving in to a deep sleep, I wondered if a dream could actually feel this good.

Chapter Fourteen

We came back home sunburned and tired, but happy. Luisa and Baby were as red as lobsters, but Matilde and I had a nice tan after the redness was gone. Hans avoided the sun as much as he could. His skin was pale white and highly sensitive and he could burn easily. For that reason he preferred to stay under the umbrella or indoors. He was the only one who didn't suffer any unpleasant burns during our trip.

To our surprise, we found out after our arrival that we had new neighbors. The family that lived downstairs from us had moved suddenly and without notice. We were surprised by the sudden move because we didn't know much about them. They were a family of five with two boys and one girl. They seemed nice but always kept to themselves. We had invited them over a few times for dinner to get to know them better. She was a housewife like me, and he worked for the railroad union. The political situation in Argentina was very volatile in those years, and we tried to stay away from it as much as possible. Hans never liked politics, and he particularly hated the government of President Juan Domingo Peron for its sympathy towards fascists like the Italian dictator Benito Mussolini, one of Hitler's allies. In fact, Argentina declared war against Hitler's Germany at the very end of the conflict when it was obvious that he was about to lose. Peron, a former member of the military, used the powerful unions to gain political control of the country. In those days, you could not find work if you didn't join his party or were not a member of the union. There were riots, protests, and strikes almost weekly. The tension between political factions was extreme, and his followers could turn violent at any event.

We didn't know exactly what our former neighbor did for the union, but our imagination ran wild, and their sudden move fueled it even more. We speculated about a few possibilities, and we knew that soon enough we would hear about it through our local gossip network. I was sure to get the full story the next time I visited the market.

A few weeks after their move, we found out that he had been promoted to a more powerful leadership role, and they moved to a more affluent area—not as juicy as we envisioned.

The lower unit stayed vacant for a long time. Eventually a couple with no children—Marta and Julio Fernandez—moved in. She was a nurse, and he was a former police officer, who, after a bullet wound left him with a limp, had to partially retire to a desk job. Both of them were polite neighbors and seemed eager to make new friends.

Because we lived in the same house, it was almost impossible for me to avoid them, especially Marta. She worked four days a week at a local hospital but was around the rest of the time.

Luisa was curious about them and insisted that we invite them over for dinner. I was uncomfortable making new friends. I hardly had time for myself and didn't want to feel the pressure of having to find time for someone else. But I knew that Luisa would leave eventually and I was going to feel very lonely once she was gone. Maybe a new friend wasn't such a bad idea.

I talked to Hans, and we both agreed it was the right thing to do. It would be just a simple welcome dinner.

They came on a Saturday night. Luisa and I cooked a few Paraguayan dishes and meat empanadas, Hans' favorite.

Marta and Julio brought wine and dessert. They dressed up nicely to dine with us. She was not particularly pretty but there was something very attractive about her. Her long black hair was always perfectly combed in a bun and she used a little too much makeup for my taste. Her dark eyes were always accentuated with strong black eyeliner, and her lips were an intense red. She reminded me of a flamenco dancer. She was a rather tall woman, with typical Latin curves—a small waist and generous hips. She walked elegantly on her high heels and seemed very put together. Only a woman without kids can look like this, I thought. Children have a way of destroying your vanity. You could consider yourself lucky the day you were able to put on some lipstick before leaving the house.

But Marta had all the time in the world to look perfect. It didn't matter that she wasn't a beauty; she exploited every one of her features masterfully.

Her husband was much older than she. He had probably been handsome in his youth but now he had a full head of gray hair and bad teeth. He was a little taller than she but not by much. Her high heels made her as tall as he. His limp made him walk with difficulty, and I felt bad that he had to come up the stairs to reach our apartment. He seemed kind and treated her with adoration. He had eyes only for her. To see him so in love with his wife moved me deeply, but it also made me feel a little envious of their relationship. Once someone felt that way about me, I thought.

They arrived on time. Marta walked in first, followed slowly by her husband. "Thank you for having us," Marta said. "I love your home."

"Welcome to our neighborhood. We are glad to have you as our neighbors," I replied, ever the skilled diplomat.

She introduced her husband, Julio, and we shook hands. She brought me flowers, a gesture I didn't expect. Luisa and the girls greeted them warmly and Hans shook their hands.

The evening went smoothly. We talked about the neighborhood, where to get the freshest meats, and which bakeries had the best desserts. I was dying to find out more about his accident, but didn't know how to bring it up. Marta was the one who broached the subject.

"We were glad to find a ground floor unit since Julio can't do stairs," she explained.

"I'm so sorry you had to come up the stairs for dinner," I immediately apologized. "We could have brought the food down, if that would have been easier for you." I tried to be polite.

"Chola, it's no trouble at all. I can do it. I just wouldn't want to do it every day. That means I won't be crashing for dinner very often," he said, defusing the situation.

"Julio has been so positive about the accident and has adapted well to his new routine. He's a fighter." Marta gave him a sweet look.

"I could only survive because of you, my dear," he answered her. "I spent many months at the hospital after I was shot. If it wasn't for Marta, I would have died."

"No, you wouldn't!" she laughed. "Julio likes to dramatize the whole thing."

"Why don't you tell us what happened?" interrupted Hans without any sense of diplomacy.

"You don't have to tell us if it makes you feel uncomfortable," I added quickly to avoid any embarrassment.

"It's no big deal," said Julio. "I was ordered to go join the anti-riot unit to control a protest taking place across the street from the Congress. It was my day off, but you can never disobey an order when you're a policeman." He reached for his wife's hand.

"It happened very fast. The crowd went out of control, and we heard a few gunshots. The bullet came out of nowhere. We still don't know who fired it. It hit me in the back and threw me to the ground. My colleagues put me in a car and took me to the hospital. I guess I was lucky they were able to drive out of that mess and get me to the emergency room. I don't remember much after that."

"It could have been a lot worse," Marta interrupted. "He could have ended up in a wheelchair or worse," she said, not finishing her thoughts.

"I'm so sorry this happened to you, Julio," I said, feeling sorry for him.

"I work at the police station now. I have a desk job and I don't mind it. With all the strikes and riots out there and a government that doesn't want to do anything about it, I'm better off where I am now. " I could tell he was justifying a situation he could not change.

"I think you are very brave," I said. "It must be hard to overcome such difficulties with so much grace."

"This country is going to explode one of these days," said Hans with irritation.

"I agree," answered Julio. "The Peronist Party is plagued with corruption, and if it keeps abusing its power, there will be a civil war."

"Let's not talk politics," interrupted Marta. "You know how it always ends, Julio. I think we should just enjoy our new friends' company and leave politics for another occasion," she added, keeping a forced smile on her face.

"I agree with Marta," I added quickly. "Let's have dessert now."

The rest of the evening went by smoothly and we kept the conversation light. It was soon time to say good night. I watched Marta leave, walking slowly next to her husband, taking him by the arm to make sure he walked straight and didn't trip. They looked perfect for each other.

After our guests left, Hans began to read the newspaper and Luisa and I took care of the dishes.

"They seem nice," I said to Luisa.

"I'm glad you have such nice neighbors. Maybe you and Marta could become friends in the future," she suggested with a smile on her face.

"I doubt it," I said without hesitation. "We are so different. Did you notice how much makeup she had on? And the way she moved? She looks very confident and secure with herself," I added with a hint of envy.

"Well, that's a good thing!" exclaimed Luisa. "Why? Does she intimidate you?"

"A little," I confessed, finally admitting to her and myself the way I felt all night.

"You shouldn't feel that way. Maybe you could learn from her."

"What do you mean? I don't want to be like her," I answered, irritated.

"I'm not saying that. All I say is that you should give her a chance to be your friend. It would make me feel a lot better if you have somebody when I leave," she added while she dried the dishes.

"But you said you'll be staying with us a while longer," I replied, stopping immediately what I was doing to look my sister in the eyes.

"Chola, I've been thinking it's time for me to go home. I miss Coco and Antonia a lot, and I've abused your hospitality for too long. You are now in a better place than before, and I can tell you are a little happier than when I arrived," she said now holding my hands in hers.

"You are the reason I'm happier," I exclaimed. "You bring so much joy to our lives. I don't want you to leave."

"I love being with you and your family, but it's time for me to return. You know it, and I know it. Please don't make it harder on me."

I could feel my eyes tearing up but I didn't want to cry. It would only make things worse and I didn't want Luisa to feel bad for me. She had helped me so much these past few months, and it wasn't fair to her that I was trying to hold her back. I knew I was being selfish. At first, I believed I was helping Coco save his marriage by keeping Luisa with me, but later I realized I was keeping her for my own personal reasons. I needed her more than she needed me. But she was right. It was time. She had to return to her life, and I had to return to mine. I needed to take charge of my own situation.

"You are right," I finally said. "We will miss you terribly, especially the girls, but you need to go home."

"*Gracias*, Chola, for everything. I promise you I'm going to try to be a better mother-in-law in the future," she said.

"About that, you have to promise me you won't interfere in Coco's marriage. At least not all the time."

"I promise you I will try. Are you happy now?"

"Yes, I know you can do it. Besides, if you leave them alone, you may become a grandmother soon!" I added.

"That would be wonderful!" she exclaimed and gave me a big hug.

The following week I helped Luisa get her things organized and went with her to buy a bus ticket to Asuncion. We spent the day together visiting her favorite places and enjoying each other's company one last time.

We walked around Recoleta and sat for tea at the Café de la Paix.

"I will miss this place," she said. "I wished we had a place like this in Asuncion. When I return, everything is going to look so provincial compared to Buenos Aires," she added with a nostalgic tone.

"I know what you mean. Asuncion is such a little town compared to the big city. But you will fit right in again. I'm sure you will keep busy going to parties and socializing with Paraguay's high society," I said, only half joking.

"You know I don't care about that!"

"Everyone will be delighted to have you back," I added, this time with a little bit of sadness.

"I will still miss you," she said, aware of my feelings. "Maybe next time you can come visit us."

"Of course. Now that Hans has a more stable job, I could take a few weeks off."

"There is something I promised Baby I would talk to you about before my departure," she added, putting down her cup of tea.

"What's that?"

"She met someone," she said, waiting for my reaction.

"You mean a boy?"

"A man," she replied.

"When? How?" I asked, feeling my blood heating up my face.

"Please calm down. It's nothing serious yet, but she wanted you to know she really likes him."

"Why didn't she tell me this herself?"

"She didn't know how you would react. It's her first love, so please try to be understanding. She's very shy, and she's afraid you will make her put an end to it."

"Of course I will, right now. How could she do that behind my back?" I was upset. I felt betrayed by my own daughter.

"Chola, this isn't about you. It just happened. She fell in love. Let her have her own experience in life. Remember how hard it was for us?" she asked, and I could not bear remembering the years under my father's tyrannical rule.

"I don't want to remember. But my daughter, she's so innocent. He will take advantage of her," I said, feeling very protective of my child.

"First of all, she's not a little girl anymore. She met him at the graduation party. He is only two years older than she is. He is a navy cadet. He only comes to the city one weekend a month. The rest of the time he's at the Naval Academy. He wants to be a naval pilot. He's a very nice young man."

"What? You met him already?" I was getting more upset by the minute. My heart was racing, and I wanted to scream.

"Please calm down and lower your voice," she said with an authority that reminded me that she was my older sister and I needed to watch my tone.

"I will calm down, but not until I meet this man." My thoughts ran wild.

We both remained silent for a few minutes. Once I noticed my breathing was normalized, I took a deep breath and said, "I will let her see him but under one condition: He needs to know that Baby comes from a decent family. She is not just any girl, and his intentions better be serious."

"Chola, don't be so tough. Baby will be eighteen soon. She's only one year younger than you were when you got married. This is her first love. Let her enjoy it without any guilt."

"It's so easy for you to say, she's not your daughter." The second the words were out of my mouth I regretted it.

"I know you think I wasn't fair to my own son, so how can I have an opinion about your child? But I know where I failed as a mother and I don't want you to do the same. Baby deserves to be happy, just don't forget that."

"I know, I'm sorry," I apologized. "I can see your good intentions. But this is so unexpected. I remember vividly when she was born, when she was just an infant, and now she's a woman. I haven't had a chance to absorb it all. Soon she'll be out of the house, going to medical school. She'll be out in the world where I can't protect her anymore."

"Your job will be done by then. She's a wonderful young lady. She will always respect you and your rules. She's not the rebellious kind. You should be proud of her," she added.

"I am. But she and Matilde are my life. I'm not ready to let them go," I insisted.

"You may never be ready. But if you see them happy, you will be happy. It will all work out fine—just trust them a little."

"Luisa, it sounds so easy. I just don't know if I can do it."

"Oh, you will. They will find their way and you will have to let them go."

"I know, I know," I said, and tried to concentrate on my breathing to avoid a panic attack.

We finished our tea and didn't talk anymore about Baby or her departure.

We arrived home rather late. Hans and the girls had finished dinner and were getting ready for bed. I waited until everyone was gone to speak to Hans alone.

"Baby has met someone," I finally said.

"I know," he responded, his eyes focused on the newspaper.

"You knew, and you didn't tell me!" I raised my voice.

"Keep it down. Everyone is sleeping."

"I can't believe you didn't tell me," I repeated.

"It's not such a big deal. She's almost eighteen. She's allowed to date if she wants." He was completely calm while I felt my rage boiling up inside me.

"I don't care how old she is—she's never asked for my permission."

"She asked me, and I said it was fine."

"And it didn't occurred to you that I might disagree," I said.

"I knew you would. That is why I didn't tell you. You are making a big deal out of nothing. He's a nice guy. There is nothing to worry about," he insisted.

"How can you be so calm about this? He could be a rapist for all we know. I want to meet him before I let this go any further," I replied firmly.

"If it makes you feel better, I asked a few people about his family, and he seems to be pretty decent. But I agree we should meet him and make it official," he continued. "Please calm down now. Baby is a woman now. You have to accept it," he added, "or will you do the same thing your sister did to her son?"

His last words hurt me deeply. Of course, I didn't want to be like Luisa, but I had to protect my own daughter.

"I will do what I think is right. She will not see him again until we have a chance to meet him. That's all I'm going to say for now."

I walked away and went straight to bed. I couldn't sleep all night. I was so sick with worry. My two daughters were my most valuable possessions. I wasn't going to just give them away.

I was already in the kitchen when the rest of the family finally woke up. One by one, they came in, and we sat down for breakfast. Because I was the last one to find out about the boyfriend situation, I figured I would include everyone in the conversation.

"Luisa told me yesterday about your new friend." I looked at Baby, who almost choked on a piece of toast.

"You know?" she asked, so quietly I almost didn't hear it.

"Yes, I know. And until we meet him, and he introduces himself officially, I won't let you see him," I said with authority.

"That's fine. He will be coming to town this weekend. Maybe you could meet him then," Baby answered in a timid voice.

"Okay then. We will have him over for dinner Saturday night," I replied coldly, and we didn't talk about the subject any further.

Everyone else, including Luisa, remained silent for the rest of the breakfast. Hans took off quickly without saying a word, and Matilde hurried to get to her music class. Baby had some reading to do before medical school started in the fall and excused herself.

Luisa and I stayed in the kitchen to do the dishes.

"I'm very proud of you," she finally said.

"Why? What's to be proud of?" I asked, finally letting go of some of the tension that had built up.

"I think you are handling everything so well. I know it's not easy for you, but you seem calmer this morning."

"I am, but that doesn't mean I will let her continue with this romance, or whatever it is." I cleared the last few items from the table.

"This is the first time for you and for her. Both of you need to be patient with each other. Everything will work out fine, you'll see. I have a very good feeling about this young man. I think he's right for her."

"Luisa, don't say that yet! You don't know him, and I don't know him. Let's not jump to conclusions," I added.

"I'm glad he'll come before I leave. I wouldn't want to miss it for the world," she said as if we were talking about the best spectacle in town.

The following days, I kept busy working on a few garments that were due that week. I didn't have much time to think about anything else so I let Luisa and Baby work on the details for the dinner.

His name was Hector. He had lost his father to cancer at a young age and was raised by his mother and an older sister. His family lived in a small town about thirty minutes away from where we lived. His lifelong dream had always been to become a pilot. He had applied to the Air Force first, but after being rejected, he was admitted at the Naval Academy. He was being trained to become an engineer, but hoped he could one day change careers and join the pilot's branch of the Navy. He was only in his second year as a cadet, which meant it would be a long time until he became an officer.

He had gone to the graduation of his best friend, who was in Baby's class. That's when he met her.

Hector arrived on time for dinner, with a bouquet of roses for me and chocolates for Hans. I was more nervous than Baby. Luisa was the first one to break the ice and welcome him to the house.

He was wearing a summer suit and tie. He looked groomed and polite.

He wasn't very tall nor terribly handsome, which made me happy. Good-looking men can be trouble. You could tell he was in the military because all his moves seemed perfectly coordinated, as if he was training for a military parade. But he looked confident and relaxed. He shook my hand first, obviously aware of whom he needed to impress. Hans was next. He kissed Luisa, Baby, and Matilde on the cheek with a relaxed familiarity. I realized then that the three of them had been partners in keeping the secret. Baby took his hand and led him to the sofa, where they sat next to each other. He looked at her with such love in his eyes that I had a hard time ignoring their nonverbal communication.

After five minutes of light conversation, which included among other things where he was from, where he went to school and who his mother was, I felt I needed to get the formalities out of the way so that we could have dinner without feeling uncomfortable.

"So, you are in love with my daughter," I simply said, causing a few coughs in my family members and a piercing look from Baby.

"Yes, I am. Since the moment I saw her," he replied with conviction and determination as if he was accepting a dangerous mission. His answer was short and to the point. I liked it.

"The main reason we wanted to meet you is to know what your intentions are." I tried to avoid any eye contact with Baby or Hans.

"My intentions are the best. I still have a few years at the academy, but if Baby is willing to wait until I graduate, nothing would make me happier than to marry her," he said as he held her hand.

"We'll see about that," I replied. "Baby is going to medical school to become a doctor. She will be very busy with her studies. A lot can happen in the next few years."

"I'm well aware of that. She's free to choose her own path, but if she loves me and wants to be with me, I promise you I will do everything in my power to make her happy. Her happiness will always come first for me."

His words sounded honest, but I knew better. I had heard words like that before. At least now everything was out in the open. If he didn't keep his word, if he disappointed her, if he hurt her feelings, I would remind him of this evening.

He said what we all wanted to hear. He was a very smart young man and he handled the situation with skill. I decided I was going to give him the benefit of the doubt and let him show us what kind of person he truly was.

Besides, I was sure once Baby went to medical school she would meet other people and maybe fall in love with somebody else—like a real doctor. But I couldn't ignore their connection. They couldn't stop looking at each other, and she was focused on his every move. He had eyes only for her and didn't let go of her hand all night, which I thought was highly inappropriate.

Matilde seemed to be having fun with the whole situation while Luisa and Hans looked very satisfied with our visitor.

The only one who had doubts was me. There is a saying that goes: "When you burn yourself with milk, you see a cow and cry." I had been burnt by a man and since then I had a hard time trusting any member of the opposite sex, especially someone who wanted my child. I just didn't want my daughter to suffer like I did. I wanted to make sure she would pick the right person to share the rest of her life.

The evening ended in a friendly manner, with Hector promising to stop by to say hello on his next break. I smiled politely and shook his hand rather than kiss him. He thanked me for a lovely meal and said goodbye to the rest of the family.

Everyone helped clear the table and I asked Baby to help me with the dishes. I wanted to talk to her in private. I waited until we were alone in the kitchen.

"He seems like a nice man," I finally said.

"He is, Mom. He really is a wonderful guy, unlike anyone I have met before," she replied.

"I'm glad you like him so much, but you don't need to rush. Besides, you need to get to know him better." I didn't want to make her feel I was against her.

"I know we have time. He doesn't want to do anything before he becomes a navy officer, and I want to finish school too."

"That sounds nice. It's important that you trust him before you make any decisions."

"I promise you I won't do anything stupid or disrespectful to you or Dad. But we are in love, and we want to be together," she said with determination.

"All I want is your happiness. I don't want him to hurt you. Please promise me you will be careful and you won't hide things from me anymore. You could have told me yourself. I'm your mother, not a monster. I want to know what is going on in your life. You and your sister are very important to me—both of you are my life. If anything happens to you, it would kill me."

"I'm so sorry. I was worried you would be upset and force me to end it. I know how hard it was for you growing up with your father, and I didn't know what to expect. Aunt Luisa told me all the horrible things he did to you and your sisters."

"He was a mean and sad man. But I would never be like him. I would never ruin your chance to be happy. I just want you to be with the right person. A bad husband is a death sentence that kills you a little each day." My own words resonated in my head.

"Mom, I know how much Dad hurt you in the past. But I see him trying now to make it up to you. Maybe he's not such a bad husband after all."

"You knew that? I thought you didn't notice his behavior," I replied, surprised at my daughter's awareness.

"Matilde and I are not little girls anymore. We see your sadness and we know how hard you try to hide it from us. You don't need to worry about me. I can take care of myself now."

"I know you can, but I still want you to respect the rules of the house. He's welcome to come to visit you when he's in town and you may go out with him, but no later than midnight. And Matilde has to go along. If you are okay with this, I won't stop you from seeing him," I said firmly.

"Of course. I don't have a problem with your rules if that's what makes you happy."

"You are a good daughter, Baby. You truly are." We finished doing the dishes in silence.

Luisa's departure was only a few days away. It suddenly hit me how much I would miss my older sister and the feeling of emptiness she would leave behind.

Both of us avoided talking about it and focused on our daily routines, but we knew every day we were closer to saying goodbye.

I helped her pack her two suitcases, and we sat on the sofa once we were done. Neither of us said a word. We simply started to cry in each other's arms. When we were done, we stood up and started making dinner. I refused to say goodbye. It was just too painful.

The next morning, Hans was supposed to come with us to help Luisa with her luggage. He had to run a quick errand in the morning, but before he left he promised me he would be back on time to go to the bus terminal.

We had breakfast and organized the house before we sat down to wait for Hans. Suddenly we heard someone honking loudly under our window. We ran to see who it was and saw Hans sitting inside a brand new car, a black Ford.

Between Luisa's departure and Baby's new boyfriend, I completely forgot about the money we put in our savings account after we returned from our vacation. After Hans deposited the money, we didn't talk about it again, and I simply forgot. There was too much going on at the same time.

Hans always wanted to buy a car and was waiting for the right time to do it. But I never expected him to surprise us like this.

We ran downstairs to see the new vehicle. We were absolutely speechless.

"What do you think?" he asked us. "Isn't she a beauty? I thought we should drive Luisa to the bus terminal like a queen."

"Oh, Hans, it's just great," I managed to say.

Before we could add anything, we were all admiring the interior and sitting inside the car. Everything looked shiny and new. It even smelled different. We were so excited we didn't notice how late it was.

"Hans, we need to get going. Luisa will miss her bus!" I exclaimed.

"Well, climb on board. I'll get the suitcases," he replied.

We did as he asked and were on the road in no time. The excitement about the new car made us forget about the sadness of her departure. We just made it on time and had to hurry up our goodbyes. I waited to be last.

Luisa hugged and kissed everyone. I held her in my arms and whispered in her ear, "I can't thank you enough, sister."

"I thank you. I will never forget our time together. Please come to visit soon."

"I will. I promise," I said and let her go to the bus.

"I love you," I managed to scream before she went inside and her figure got confused with the other passengers.

Matilde and Baby waited to see where she would sit and waved at her once they saw her face through the window. We tried to be brave and not cry, but I could feel the sadness building up and the tears sneaking up on us. The bus left right on time. We stood still on the platform, waiting for something to make us leave. We looked as the bus disappeared in the distance. One chapter closed and another one was opening up.

Chapter Fifteen

Empty. The house felt too empty. Baby started medical school in the fall, Matilde went back to high school, and Hans worked hard on his new business. I kept busy with my job and my responsibilities around the house, but it wasn't enough to make me feel better. Suddenly nobody needed me. Luisa had been a big part of my life the past two years and I had a hard time moving on. I remembered what she told me about giving Marta a chance, and I decided it was about time I had a friend. I was so used to putting everyone first that I forgot to have a life of my own. But it was up to me to change that. I could still remember the good times we had with Felipe and his wife back in Clorinda. There was no reason why we shouldn't have that again. And Marta and Julio seemed nice enough people. So I decided to make an effort and be more sociable the next time I saw them.

It took longer than I thought to overcome my shyness, but eventually we became friends. It wasn't like our friendship with Felipe. Marta and Julio were very different people, but nevertheless, we got along well and enjoyed each other's company.

Marta and I shared a common passion: movies. We loved catching a matinee before the rest of the family came home in time for dinner. We would exchange movie magazines and talk about the latest Hollywood affairs. We laughed a lot together, which was one of the things I loved the most about our friendship. But our lives couldn't have been more different. She didn't have any children. She had a career, and her husband had eyes only for her. What a lucky woman, I always thought. But she envied me my daughters. She mentioned once that she couldn't have children, and I didn't ask for details. She seemed healthy and strong to me and I thought maybe the reason was her husband. Maybe he wasn't able to get her pregnant. Be that as it may, she was okay with it. She put a lot of time and dedication into her job at the hospital and loved to have her own salary. She even mentioned that she made more money than her semi-retired husband, something very rare in those days.

She liked working with older people. She was very comfortable with death, she explained. She didn't mind watching her patients die in peace at the hospital. Life is difficult, she would say. Death is easy; you just stop trying so hard. I admired her vocation and selflessness.

It was the differences in our lives that made us friends. Hans didn't like Julio that much but didn't seem to care when we got together. Maybe he also missed having a friend like Felipe and just went along with it.

Most of the time, I would meet Marta alone, but when Hector came to visit Baby every four weeks, we would have everyone over for dinner.

It made it easier on me to have more people around as I was not comfortable with a boyfriend in the house. This way, I was distracted with other things, and the conversation was always light and friendly.

Baby and Hector took their relationship way too seriously for me. Both of them waited with excitement for the weekend when they were able to meet. It seemed that the long-distance romance had sparked an even stronger passion between them. I made Matilde sit in the room with them every time Hector was in the house, and they had to take her along if they wanted to go to the movies or out dancing. I knew they hated me for that, but I remembered those days vividly and what wild hormones can do to even the nicest girls.

Despite all my efforts to keep her close to me, I could feel Baby slowly separating from us; she was growing up. Her first year in medical school was going well, though I wasn't sure if she was happy with her choice. Some days she loved it, other days she wasn't so sure about it. I figured it was probably just a phase. It's hard to know exactly what you want when you are eighteen. But I had such high hopes for her. I wanted her to succeed in life and have every opportunity that I didn't have. Of course, those were my dreams, not hers.

For the moment, I was planning on staying firm and not letting her lose focus. I was her mother, after all, and I knew what was best.

Matilde, on the other hand, was still a free spirit. School wasn't her priority, and that frustrated me. But in my heart I knew what made her happy. She just needed to reach graduation, and after that, I would stop driving her crazy. She still had four more years to go and a lot of work to do. Music was the only thing that interested her. But I was willing to take it away from her if she didn't get good grades in school. That was the only incentive I had. As long as I had that weapon of persuasion, I knew she would stay on track.

Matilde liked to socialize with boys but wasn't interested in them yet. She had a few good friends, one of them a boy who lived on our same block. His name was Pablo. They walked to school and they did homework together, but it seemed to go no farther than that as far as I could tell. Pablo's father owned a small grocery store, and they went often for free ice cream and candy. Baby's hours at school or at the library were long, and Matilde was alone most of the time. I realized they were going through different stages in their lives and shared very little at the moment. That's why I encouraged Matilde to have other friends and spend more time with her peers. She enjoyed that as well and it made me happy to see her so independent. Baby was shy like me, but Matilde was comfortable with herself and was never afraid to speak her mind. Of course, sometimes it was too much, and she didn't know when to stop.

My daughters were growing up in a very different world than I did. I had a hard time understanding young people anymore—especially women. I didn't know what to think about all the changes taking place in our society. The music was getting louder, the skirts were getting shorter. Everyone talked about the women's revolution, but in my house everything was the same. Baby and Matilde loved the new fashion trends and started listening to English music. They were no longer interested in the traditional Spanish music I grew up with. Rock'n'Roll was taking over the radio, yet, I remained faithful to my tangos.

I liked some of the freedoms women talked about, but a lot of it really scared me. I was afraid things were going to go out of control soon. Keeping control of my home was a priority. Of course, that excluded Hans. I could never keep him under control. Maybe it was from him that Matilde got her free spirit.

He worked long days and always took care of our needs. But he liked his freedom. He had friends I didn't know anything about, and honestly, I didn't want to know. The '60s were very successful years for his business. He managed it well and was able to bring home new and modern things, such as a new refrigerator and a television set.

I missed having the ice man deliver a block of ice every few days, but my new refrigerator was amazing, especially on hot summer days.

The television also changed our lives. We still listened to our favorite radio shows, but to be able to watch them on the screen was surreal. The wildest thing Hans ever bought, though, was a racing horse.

His passion for gambling never went away, and on one of his trips to the casino, he met a man who needed money and offered to sell Hans his horse. He was desperate to pay off his gambling debts, and Hans had had a good night at the poker table.

The horse's name was "Milonga" (a popular dance style related to the tango). It was a beautiful animal, but it didn't win any races. It cost Hans more to feed it and rent the stable than what the animal was actually worth. But he kept telling me that the horse would make him a rich man. In the end, it never did, and Hans decided to sell him to a breeder. We saw the animal only a few times because Hans kept him at the race track stables. We certainly didn't miss him when he was gone.

The most significant addition to the family in those days was our dog, Lulu. She was a black Pomeranian, with a few white spots on her face and paws. Hans brought her home on a cold morning, wrapped up in blankets. We fell in love with her immediately. She became a member of our family and soon we couldn't imagine life without her. She loved to ride in Hans' car, but her claws always left marks on the seats. So I made her four little white gloves that she proudly wore every time she got in the car. It was truly a sight to see. I strongly believed that she saw herself as a human being, not a dog. She slept between Hans and me every night and sat for breakfast next to the girls every morning. For years to come, she brought so much joy into our lives.

Hans had a soft spot for her too, and she knew it. The minute he walked in the house, everyone else ceased to exist. She sat on his lap until it was time for dinner, and when he was done eating, she jumped right back on him. They both read the newspaper together or watched some TV. The only thing Lulu couldn't do was speak. But that didn't mean she didn't communicate with us. She made us understand her very clearly. It was like having a third child in the house.

For the first time in a very long time, life was good. We were all adapting slowly to our new routines and changes. And I went back to one of my old routines: my weekly calls to Asuncion.

Luisa had a hard time returning to her old life. Many things had changed in her absence. Elsa and Coco finally learned to live together, despite their differences and his bad habits. He started to teach Elsa about his business and let her help him with his clients.

Coco had made a place for himself in Asuncion's high society and was a regular at parties and social events. Elsa, on the other hand, had a difficult time adapting to her husband's circle of friends and clients. Nevertheless, she tried to please him and be the wife she knew Luisa wanted for her son.

It wasn't always easy. Coco took his work seriously and could spend hours locked up in his studio working on his paintings. He usually worked with one or two assistants, depending on the work load. He was very picky when it came to choosing an apprentice, and he always looked for a diamond in the rough, a young man to whom he could teach the secrets of his craft and not feel threatened. He spent a lot of time and dedication educating his assistants. Sometimes it took him years to trust them enough to let them work on a painting or project. He was so obsessed with perfection; no one could ever match his caliber of work. But he knew he needed the help and reluctantly agreed to have someone clean his brushes and prepare his paints. Since Luisa's departure, he was forced to hire someone on a more permanent basis. That way, he could spend more time with his clients and take care of other aspects of his business.

After trying out at least a dozen candidates, a young indigenous man with almost no education caught his eye. He was nineteen years old and had only finished elementary school. His name was Abel. He had no work experience besides a few odd jobs that didn't last long. But he was obviously gifted. He had a gift with colors and understood immediately the nature of the craft. He had come from the interior of the country looking for work so that he could send some money back to his mother and seven younger siblings. He lived in Asuncion with a very abusive uncle who forced him to hand him most of his pay. Coco and Elsa took pity on him and offered him a small room next to the studio. He got along with Antonia as well, and asked her to keep his money in a safe place, which she happily did.

Coco was very glad to have such a talented assistant, and Abel was delighted to have such a great teacher.

The only one not happy was Luisa. She didn't say much in our phone conversations, but I could sense her unhappiness. Antonia's health had deteriorated the two years she was gone. Her diabetes was getting worse, and she didn't take care of herself. Luisa realized for the first time how risky her situation was and couldn't do much about it. Antonia remained as stubborn as ever and wasn't willing to give up her food and wine for anything in the world, not even a premature death.

Luisa's relationship with Elsa hadn't improved much either. They remained cordial to each other, but they didn't like one another. They did try to get along on a daily basis just to keep the peace around the house, and for Coco's sake. He was the most important person to them and the only reason they avoided any kind of confrontation.

The atmosphere at the house was very tense, and Coco was aware of it. His mother's return was a reason for joy, but at the same time it brought back the tension that had finally gone during her absence. Coco didn't want to have to choose between his wife and his mother, so he did everything to keep both of them happy, but it was an impossible task.

Despite Luisa's complaints, Coco continued to share the same bedroom with Elsa. At least he didn't let her rule in that department. As long as Elsa felt she wasn't competing with Luisa for his affection, she would probably not get upset with Luisa's other requests and objections. But there was still no news about a pregnancy. Elsa wasn't getting any younger, and every year that went by reduced the possibilities of having a baby. I hoped that the minute she had a child, her relationship with Luisa would improve. Every week I said a prayer on my walk to the pharmacy and asked God to help her get pregnant. And every week I waited to hear the good news, but walked back home disappointed. I even got mad at God for not letting Coco have his own family. All my wishful thinking, all my prayers never materialized.

I asked Antonia to try any home remedies she knew to increase Coco's sperm count and improve Elsa's fertility. Antonia was the best at finding cures and preventing illnesses. She even had her own book of recipes, where she described in great detail the medicinal powers of plants, roots, and liquids. She gave Coco a daily mixture for breakfast to increase his sexual drive and prepared a special soup for Elsa to help boost her egg production. Nothing worked.

"It doesn't matter how many potions I give them. If they don't have any sex, there will never be a baby," she told me one day.

"But they are sleeping together, aren't they?" I asked, more puzzled than ever.

"They share the same bedroom, but that doesn't mean they are having sex. Besides, I can't see it in the cards. It's just not there, Chola."

"You and your cards! If they're both healthy, there shouldn't be a reason why Elsa is not getting pregnant. You just have to keep trying. Don't stop making them your remedies," I insisted.

"I won't stop, but don't get your hopes too high. It may never happen for them," she replied in a motherly voice.

Antonia was the oldest sister, and had a wisdom that we depended upon. She was never wrong, but I was going to stay hopeful for as long as possible.

On a rare occasion, Elsa picked up the phone and I tried to bring up the subject with her.

"How is Luisa behaving these days?" I asked, knowing what her answer would be. "Do you notice any changes since she retuned?"

"As long as we don't cross each other, we are fine. She's been trying hard to leave me alone, but I don't think we'll ever be on good terms," she explained coldly.

"It must be tough for you though. I tried my best to talk to her when she was here and make her come to her senses. I'm so sorry." I was not able to finish the sentence.

"It's not your fault. I'm very grateful to you for giving us two years of peace. Antonia has been very good to me and she tries to keep Luisa busy and under control. She's the only one Luisa will listen to," she continued.

"I heard Coco has a new assistant. How is that going?"

"Abel is wonderful. He even helps us around the house when Coco doesn't need him. He takes care of the garden and helps in the kitchen. He's just happy to be useful. We're very lucky to have him.

Of course, Luisa doesn't agree. She drives him crazy, asking him to do all kinds of things. She thinks he's up to no good, and we need to keep him as busy as possible," she added.

"Oh well, that sounds like her. She doesn't trust people outside the family that much, especially strangers."

"But Abel seems trustworthy and never minds working late hours until Coco is done with his work. Sometimes he'll be up all night helping Coco finish his paintings."

"It must get lonely for you when Coco works so much." I wanted to bring up the subject I was most interested about.

"I'm used to it by now. I don't wait up for him anymore. His work is his life and I've learned to accept it. I know I come in second, if not third," she said, with sadness in her voice.

"Don't say that, Elsa. I know how much Coco loves you. Maybe you two should take a vacation together, go somewhere nice. You should surprise him with a trip. It would probably be wonderful to take a break."

"That's a good idea, but he has deadlines with all his jobs. I would have to sit down and figure out a time when we could do it. But it would be so nice to escape, even for a weekend." She sounded a little more enthusiastic.

"Don't think so much about it and just do it. You won't regret it. All you need is a few days together to reconnect," I added, leaving the word "sexually" out of my sentence.

"Speaking to you is always so nice, Chola. I wish we could do it more often, but Luisa is like a watchdog over the phone, especially on the weekends when she knows you'll be calling her. She'll be disappointed today to hear you called earlier than usual. She just stepped out to get some groceries. She should be back any minute."

"Don't worry about it. I'm glad we had a chance to talk. Make sure you book that trip and tell me all about it next time we talk."

I looked at my watch and realized with panic how long I had been talking long distance.

"I have to go or this call will cost me a fortune," I added quickly.

"I'll tell Luisa you called. Stay well and thanks again for your kind words," she said before hanging up.

"You too. Hang in there and good luck!" I hung up the phone and ran home just in time to fix lunch.

Months went by quickly and soon we were approaching the first anniversary of Luisa's departure. I tried not to be preoccupied about the situation in Asuncion because there was little I could do about it.

The holiday season was around the corner, and there was a lot to be done. I invited Marta and Julio to have Christmas Eve dinner with us and told Baby she could invite Hector and his family as well. Suddenly we were no longer four for dinner, but nine. And of course, there was Lulu.

Our terrace was small, but I was sure I could fit nine people around the table. Luckily that December wasn't too hot. Every night we were able to open our windows to a refreshing breeze. The noise and smells of the city didn't bother us. It was a small price to pay for a little relief from the summer heat.

I was excited to finally meet Hector's family. Since Baby had introduced him to us, he came always by himself. I wondered if it was because of me that he tried to keep his distance or maybe he was just a reserved man. His mother became a widow relatively young, with two small children. I couldn't imagine how hard that must have been for her. To raise children on your own, without a husband, seemed unthinkable. But then again, I had done something like that myself. She worked full-time to provide for her children and always stressed the value of education. Hector's sister was seven years older and more capable of helping his mother growing up. But he too was a wonderful son, as well as an excellent student who took his career in the Navy seriously. I could see that Baby and Hector had that in common; both of them had strong wills and were dedicated to their passions.

Even when I didn't want to admit it, I started to like him, and I didn't mind their relationship so much anymore. They fit well together. The longer I thought about it, the more convinced I was that he was the right man for my daughter. But I was still determined to make them wait. Both of them were young and they needed a profession before they could start a family. I knew from my own experience how hard it was to support a family when you have no special skills or formal education. How strange to think about my child that way. Now it was her turn to create her own destiny. It just seemed impossible to me that she was old enough to do it. I was proud of her and thought she could do anything she wanted in life. The question was what she would do when the moment came.

It was still a few weeks until Christmas, and we were scheduled to visit Hans' mother to celebrate Hanukkah . I wasn't familiar with the Jewish traditions, but I always enjoyed spending the holidays with her. Most of the people living with her at the home for the elderly were European Jews. They loved celebrating every holiday because it meant they would have visitors come and go all day. The place would come alive with younger adults, children, and food—especially the food. I've never seen so much food in my life. I don't think I've ever met any other people that liked to eat as much.

The drive to the home was much more pleasant because we had our own car. It took us only about an hour to get there. The old Victorian home sat on a beautifully landscaped property that covered eleven acres of land. There was a pond at the entrance and a

wooded area in the back. The main building was a white histori-
cal house that had belonged to a wealthy family. After the patriarch died, his heirs fought over it, and they ended up selling the
property and dividing the money. It was a peaceful place. Hanna
lived in the main house where she could be close to her friends and
the common areas. They had tea every afternoon and played bingo
every night. It was a good place to spend the last years of her life.
I wondered where I would spend mine.

Everyone was treated with care and compassion. Most of them
were survivors of the war and spoke very little Spanish, but that
didn't matter much. They smiled and greeted us full of enthusiasm.
They loved every time the girls came to visit, and that made Hanna
proud.

Hanna's health had deteriorated in the last few years. She wasn't
as energetic as she used to be and couldn't take the long walks she
loved so much. But her mind was as sharp as ever. She would sit for
hours next to Hans to talk about every aspect of his life and ours.
She didn't want to miss a thing. She often asked for news about
Lotte, but we didn't know much about her either. We had recently
received a letter from her telling us that she was planning to marry
for the fifth time, and that she wanted to come to visit soon. Since
she went back to Germany, after the war was over, she returned
only once to attend her father's funeral. She wasn't the family type.
She was selfish and self-centered and was never affectionate to her
brother or nieces. I could forgive her for not liking me, but being
cold to the children was unforgivable.

After a feast of food and pastries, I sat with Hanna under the
shade of a sauce tree. Argentineans called this tree "the weeping
sauce" because its leaves grow downward from the branches, looking like a cascade of red little flowers. Its trunk is extremely wide
and its roots look like tentacles that break the surface of the ground

to show its power and might. Some of these trees can be hundreds of years old. They are a testament to time and endurance. Hanna picked her favorite spot, under the shade of one of her beloved trees. I sat on one side and Hans on the other. It was the end of a lovely and peaceful day. The sky was turning colors as the sun kissed the horizon for the last time: blue, white, orange, yellow. The colors of the Argentinean sky could be breathtaking. We sat silently admiring the beauty of the moment.

I was holding one of Hanna's hands when she looked at me and said, "*Gracias*, Chola, thank you very much."

"*Gracias de qué?* For what?" I asked, wondering why she was thanking me. If anything, I should be the one thanking her for such a lovely holiday together.

She turned to Hans, and I understood she needed him to translate. Her Spanish could go only so far.

"*Por todo*, for everything," she said and switched to German. "You are a gift from God, Chola. If it wasn't for you, we would never have survived the war. You opened the doors of your house and your heart to us when we needed it most. You supported us for years until we were able to get back on our feet," she told me, through Hans.

"I never forgot what you did for us, including Lotte. But most importantly, you gave me the most precious thing I could ever want: two beautiful granddaughters. I want to give them my few last possessions. I don't have much left, but I want you to give it to them when they get married. I don't think I will see that day, but I want to make sure they get a wedding gift from me."

She spoke slowly but firmly. This was her last living will. She let my hand go and opened my palm. She put on it her wedding band, her engagement ring, a pair of pearl earrings, and a pearl necklace. She closed my hand into a fist.

"These are for the girls. They can wear them or sell them. I won't be offended if they prefer the money. They are all I have left. I want them to know how much I love them," she added. She took a little break to catch her breath and continued.

"I also want to thank you for loving my son unconditionally, even with his many faults. You are the best thing that ever happened in his life. You deserve to be loved and respected by him," she said, and as Hans translated, I looked at him and saw his eyes tearing up.

I waited to make sure she was finished, unwilling to interrupt her. I had a strange feeling that she was saying goodbye. But she still looked strong.

"Thank you, Hanna, but you can give these to the girls yourself. You still have time." She interrupted me.

"Chola, I don't know how much time I have, but I'm not getting any younger. Please take these things with you. I prefer that you put them in a safe place rather than keeping them here. It's my wish." She looked right into my eyes and left me with no option but to accept them.

"Of course I will take them and keep them safe. You can give them to your granddaughters whenever you want," I added.

"I'm tired now. I think it's time to go back," she told Hans and stood up slowly, holding on to his arm.

We walked without hurry, enjoying the afternoon breeze and the perfume of the jasmines. I couldn't help but think about this wonderful woman walking beside me—her life, her struggles, her sorrows, her happiness. She had been through so much and here she was, walking tall and making sure we knew what she wanted.

It was getting late, and we needed to head back home. Hans went to get the car while we said goodbye to Hanna. The girls kissed her affectionately and she kissed them back. When I came closer, she held my hand and reminded me with just a look of our conversation. She kissed me and whispered in my ear, *"Gracias, Chola. Por todo."*

I couldn't respond. I simply stood there, looking at her, telling her without words that I loved her, that I would never forget her, that she would live in my memories forever. Hans honked the horn, and we left her waving goodbye from the porch.

We didn't speak much on our way home. We were tired after a long day and a lot of food. I couldn't stop thinking about Hanna's words. They lingered in my mind like little butterflies coming in and out of focus. She had told me similar things before. She thanked me many times for my help through the years. But this time it was different. She knew something we didn't.

We arrived home late and went to bed right away.

"You should check on your mom tomorrow," I told Hans before we turned the lights off.

First thing in the morning, I made Hans walk to the pharmacy and phone Hanna's home. He was back in less than half an hour. I forgot his legs were much longer than mine, and he could walk a few blocks twice as fast.

"How is she?" I asked, already knowing his answer.

"She died in her sleep last night."

I fell speechless on the sofa. I had my apron on and was holding an oven mitt.

"She was saying goodbye to us yesterday," I whispered.

"I thought she was just being an old person. I thought she was just ..." He didn't finish. He sat next to me and we both cried together.

"We need to tell Lotte," I finally said. "She needs to come for her funeral."

"I will send her a telegram later on today. But she may not make it in time." He stood up, wiped his tears with his handkerchief, and looked at me. "I have to go to work. We'll talk later." He rushed out the door.

I waited for the girls to wake up and told them the news about their grandmother. They started to cry, and we sat together on the sofa. We hugged each other for a long time, until all our tears were dry.

The sadness of Hanna's death was a constant presence in our lives that summer. After sending a telegram to Germany, we received a reply from Lotte letting us know that she was in the middle of her honeymoon and wasn't able to attend her mother's funeral. Of course, we were not surprised, simply disappointed. Hans made the necessary arrangements with a Jewish funeral home, and her body was laid to rest next to her husband's.

I wondered how she knew that her time had come. *Will I know when my turn comes?*

Chapter Sixteen

The week before Christmas I had no choice but to get ready. Hector's family was coming and so were Marta and her husband. Everyone was bringing a dish, but the majority of the cooking was left for me. I was never much of a dessert person, so I decided to ask Baby to take care of that part of the meal. Lately, I noticed she had been very excited and happy despite her grandmother's passing. I could only think of one thing: she was in love.

If there was one thing in life that could not be hidden, it was that volatile state of falling hopelessly in love. And Baby was without a doubt in love. I had to constantly remind her of obvious things, ask her everything twice, and call her name several times before I got her attention. It was funny but very irritating at the same time. I kept telling myself I had been there, I should be more patient, but sometimes I couldn't stand being in the same room with her.

Matilde had a good sense of humor about it and most of the time ignored her sister's absent state of mind. Hans was completely clueless about it. Or if he noticed, he chose to pretend nothing was happening.

On Christmas Eve, we followed our tradition and went to mass. I left the food ready to minimize the work on my return. Hector's family came to church with us, which made a good first impression. His mother wasn't a religious person, but when she found out that I was, she happily accepted our family tradition.

I liked Hector's mother instantly. She had a positive energy about her that I noticed almost immediately. She always smiled and never made a negative comment about anything or anybody. She seemed content and grateful for her life and her children. She looked older than her age, probably a result of having to raise her kids alone. Her face was sincere, and her expression seemed peaceful. Her daughter, on the other hand, was loud, vibrant, and alive. She overpowered everyone in her family. She compensated for Hector's quiet personality and her mother's tranquil manners. She liked to talk and discuss current affairs with great passion. She belonged to the new generation of women who didn't want to get married and have children. She wanted to rule the world.

It was a very interesting mixture of people that night. We ate, drank, and laughed. At midnight we made a toast and wished each other Merry Christmas, followed by a second toast in Hanna's memory. I had promised her that we would keep her memory alive, and I wasn't about to forget my promise. After I was done with my toast, Hector stood up with his glass raised.

"I would like to make an announcement," he said, and my heart stopped beating.

"Baby and I have decided to get married." I choked on my drink.

"I will be graduating from the Naval Academy next year, and we decided to get married right after that."

Hans stood up and gave Hector a hug that almost knocked him down.

"That's great news!" he shouted. "I can start calling you son-in-law!" he added, and my stomach fell to my feet.

Baby went to hug Hans and Hector, while the rest of the families clapped their hands and cheered for the couple. I was the only one paralyzed in my chair. My brain and my legs didn't want to coordinate. Somehow my brain waves were short-circuited. My daughter getting married? How can that be happening? She's not ready. I'm not ready. I wanted to shout STOP! This is crazy! But I had no voice. I didn't know how to react. Everything was overwhelming. I stayed silently in my chair and did not move until I was sure of what I was going to do. Baby made the first move. She came to me.

"Mamita, are you okay? Are you happy?" she asked me with such joy in her voice, I couldn't be upset about it.

"Of course, I am," I said automatically.

"I'm glad you are. I was afraid you would be disappointed."

"All I want is for you to be happy," I told her, knowing in my heart that it was true. "But what about school?"

"I don't know. I'm not sure about it. I will continue, but I'm not sure that's what I really want anymore", she answered.

"Don't rush. You have time to think and make a decision. We can talk about it tomorrow," I hoped that this night would end quickly and everything would go back to normal by morning.

"It will depend on where Hector gets based the first few years. He wants to be a pilot and there are only a couple of Navy bases with facilities for that type of training. I don't know where we will end up at the beginning."

I listened, and the more she told me, the worse I felt. She was going to get married and move away from me? What kind of crazy idea was that? I didn't want to hear any more. I stood up.

"I don't feel well. I think I need to go to bed." I left the party without saying goodbye to anyone.

As I walked away, I could hear Baby making an excuse for my inappropriate behavior, but I didn't care. I needed to escape and think. I wished for a fresh start in the morning.

Everyone slowly left after that, and the house became quite again.

Exhaustion took over and I finally fell asleep. I never remember my dreams, but that night was different.

Baby was dressed up in a beautiful bridal gown, and she was walking down the aisle. She looked amazing in her white dress and veil. I ran into the church, trying to stop her. I screamed and ran, but no one could hear me or see me. I tried to stop her, but I couldn't grab her. She kept walking until she reached the altar. Hector was standing there, waiting for his bride. He turned around, and I could see he was holding a long golden chain, but I was the only one aware of it. Everyone else saw just the wedding rings. I screamed even louder. I ran to the altar, but I couldn't reach Baby in time. She was standing next to him now, but I kept running. He kissed her and smiled. She smiled back. He took the golden chain and put it around her neck. He squeezed the chain gently. She didn't seem to notice. He kept squeezing. She smiled. He continued. She started asphyxiating. I kept running, but I wasn't moving forward. She was out of breath. She fell on the floor. Everyone clapped and cheered. The priest said, "I pronounce you husband and wife." I fell on my knees, exhausted, crying.

I woke up to the sound of my own scream.

"What's wrong?" Hans asked me, half asleep.

"It was just a nightmare, don't worry, go back to sleep," I replied, still shaken by it.

"Chola, you need to relax. I don't know what's going on with you, but it's got to stop."

"I don't want Baby to get married, that's what's going on. She's not ready. She's too young." I tried to keep my voice down.

"She's as old as you were when we got married. It's what she wants. She's happy, don't ruin it for her," he said, this time in a commanding voice. He turned over, grabbed his pillow, and inhaled loudly, putting an end to our midnight conversation.

The next few weeks I concentrated on other things. The January heat was so intense, I barely had any energy to finish my work around the house. I had taken a break from my job for the holidays but decided it was time to resume it, just to have something to occupy my mind.

That afternoon I went to see the tailor and his wife to wish them a happy New Year and to pick up some pieces to work on. I found his shop empty and the doors closed. I looked through the window to see if anyone was inside. The place looked like a bomb went off. It was heartbreaking. There was broken glass all over the floor. The counters were destroyed. It was a scary scene. I looked around trying to find a familiar face but didn't see anyone. I crossed the street and walked into a grocery store on the opposite side of the road. The place looked empty. I walked to the counter and asked to speak with the owner. An old lady came out from behind a door.

"Do you know what happened to the tailor and his wife?" I asked.

"They moved away," she replied coldly, avoiding eye contact.

"Where? When did they leave?" I needed to make sense of the situation.

"They left after Christmas. Luckily no one was there when they came," she replied.

"What do you mean? Who came?" I had so many questions I didn't know where to begin.

"The union people. I heard he refused to pay their new fees. He was a good man. I really liked his wife. They were good customers of my store. We will miss them. This country is a mess. No one can work like this anymore." "Do you know where they went? How can I contact them?"

"I'm so sorry, but we know nothing," she said and nervously walked away.

I understood immediately that she didn't want to talk any more. She was already risking too much by telling me what happened. The political situation was getting more volatile by the day. I feared for my family's safety. But there was nothing we could do. As long as Hans had his job, we would be fine. But I had to find a way to make some extra money, just in case.

I walked home preoccupied with the tailor's situation, hoping and praying that he and his family were in a safe place. Marta was at the front door when I arrived, and after listening to what had happened, she comforted me.

"Why don't you start your own tailoring business, Chola? You're very talented. I could be your first customer. I'm sure once we tell some people in the neighborhood what you can do, you'll have enough customers to keep busy and make some decent money," she suggested.

"Thank you, Marta, but I don't know that many people. I usually keep to myself. I wouldn't know where to start," I replied, toying with her idea in my mind.

"Don't worry about that. I will help you spread the word. I know a lot of people through the hospital and we can make a few flyers as well. You'll see. Everything will work out fine," she replied with confidence. "And don't worry about the tailor. He did the right thing by moving away from this place. Everything is so rotten. Julio and I are disgusted with it. Maybe we should all move away."

"Maybe we should. We came to this country looking for a better future and now everything seems to be falling apart," I replied.

"You're a good friend. *Gracias*, thank you for your help." I walked upstairs to start dinner.

The following weeks were quiet. Marta gave me a few dresses that she wanted shortened because the latest fashion trend was the mini skirt. I have to admit she was one of the few women I knew that could actually wear a short skirt with pride. She had long and attractive legs that truly deserved to be shown off. But not many women could do that. In fact, the majority of us Latin women have big hips and healthy-looking thighs. Generally speaking, we don't look good in a mini skirt. But when fashion dictates, you obey. Millions of women all over the world did. Even I had to give in eventually and move the length of my skirts above the knee. I was never brave enough to go higher than that, though.

Thanks to Marta's help, soon I had a nice group of loyal customers that kept me busy.

Since Christmas Eve, I hadn't spoken to Baby about her engagement. We both avoided the conversation and found every excuse possible to talk about other things. Sooner or later we would have to start planning a wedding. The first one to talk to me about it was Hector's mother. She stopped by one afternoon unannounced. It was hot and humid, and we were all sitting in the living room next to our only fan, trying not to pass out from heat exhaustion. She rang our bell and shook us out of our lethargy. We were happy to have a visitor but couldn't find the energy to express it.

She brought a tray of *facturas*—pastries—with her, but it was so hot we didn't want to eat anything.

"I thought I'd stop by and check on you," she said happily.

Baby hurried to welcome her and offer her a cold drink.

"Hector will be coming to visit next weekend, and he asked me to touch base with you to start talking about the wedding plans," she added, unaware of my resistance.

"That's very kind of you, but we still have a lot of time for that," I replied, hiding my annoyance.

"I was going to wait for him before I spoke to my parents about our plans," Baby interrupted, justifying her silence the past few weeks. I looked at her, obviously upset.

"Well, we need to get started if we want to find a good place for the reception. And of course, the most popular churches get booked months in advance. After he graduates, Hector will have only a few weeks before he gets stationed. That's why we have a small window to plan the event," she continued.

"I have a few tentative dates. I can start calling churches," Baby added, searching for a sign of approval in my eyes.

"I didn't know you were in such a hurry. I thought we had more time," I insisted, repeating myself.

"Time flies, Chola. Besides Hector wants to book the Naval Officers' Club for the reception and that can be pretty hard if we don't move fast," she added while she made herself comfortable on our sofa. "A lot of people getting married these days!" she exclaimed, giggling.

"That's right, Mom. The sooner we start, the better it will turn out," added Baby, trying to please her soon-to-be mother-in-law and annoying me in the process.

"Well, it looks like we are all on the same page. We will start right away. I will call the Club, Baby can contact the church, and Chola, you can work on the guest list," she said, ordering us around.

"We don't have a large family in Buenos Aires, so our side will be small. I'd rather focus on the dress, at least that I know how to do," I replied.

"Thank you, Mom, I'm so happy!" Baby looked very excited and relieved that this conversation was finally taking place.

Now everything was out in the open. There was no turning back. I had to come to terms with this new phase of my daughter's life.

I was very reluctant to do so, but I had no other choice. She had made up her mind and there was nothing I could do to stop her.

Hector's mother didn't stay long. She wanted to get home before dark. We had a year to plan and get organized. The next few months would be very busy.

I thought I might ask Coco for some advice on how to plan a wedding and what not to forget. Everyone in the family was excited, except me. I couldn't feel it. I was afraid. I didn't want her to repeat my mistakes.

The following Saturday, I went to the pharmacy to call Luisa and tell her the latest news, hoping she may have some good advice for me.

"Baby got engaged," I told her.

"That's great news! I always thought Hector was the right man for her," she replied happily.

"But she's so young," I repeated. "And they may move away to some Navy base who knows where."

"She will move out of your house no matter what. Maybe it's not such a bad idea to be away from your parents the first few years of your marriage, just to have a fresh start," she said.

"I hardly recognize you!" I exclaimed. "You can't have your son more than ten feet away, and you are telling me it's okay if Baby moves away from the city!"

"You are right. I can't live without my son. But that's my life, and it's too late to change it now. I should have known better, but I didn't and I regret not giving Coco more space. Now I have to live with the consequences of that mistake."

"Luisa, what happened? What aren't you telling me? Is Coco all right?" I rushed to ask, fearing her answer.

"Elsa left him. It happened a few weeks ago but I didn't have the courage to tell you."

"Why did she leave?" I managed to ask.

"She just left. She gave us no explanations, and Coco doesn't want to tell me what happened between them. I'm heartbroken. It's all my fault," she added.

"I don't understand. I thought they were doing well…"

"I never believed they were right for each other, but now that she's gone and Coco is devastated, I understand how much he needs her. I don't know what to do, Chola. It's killing me. She left him because of me, I drove her away!" She sounded weak, defeated. I had never heard her like this before.

"You did make her life very difficult," I said, pushing her to admit the truth.

"That's why I don't want you to make the same mistake. Let them live their lives. Let them go away if that's their choice. It's better that way. At least if it doesn't work out between them, they won't blame you, like Coco probably does me."

"Don't say that! He would never blame you. He adores you. Now you have to be strong for him and help him through this situation."

"I know. I just don't know how. He's like a lost soul since she left. He doesn't eat or sleep. He hardly speaks to me. He locks himself up in his studio and works nonstop. I'm afraid he'll get sick from it."

"He's a grown man. Let him mourn his loss. There is nothing you can do about it," I told her.

"And to make things worse, Antonia hasn't been feeling well lately. We will take her to the doctor this week. I'll let you know how it went when you call next Saturday."

"What's wrong with her?" I asked.

"She's in pain all the time. We are not sure if it's related to her diabetes. I will let you know. Now you should be going before this phone call becomes too expensive."

"Don't worry about the money. I've been keeping busy with my few clients. I'll call you next week."

"I'll be waiting for your call. Now remember not to make my mistakes. *Te quiero*," she said in a warm motherly way.

"I love you too," I replied and hung up the phone with a heavy heart.

I walked home, wondering why we keep making the same mistakes. What powerful force drives us to do the same thing over and over again? Why can't we break the pattern from one generation to the next? I couldn't think of an answer, but I knew I didn't want to be like Luisa or my father. Coco's failed marriage was a lesson for me. I couldn't ruin my daughter's happiness.

Chapter Seventeen

The last few years had been hard for Antonia. Since Coco's wedding, she had become the mediator between Luisa and Elsa, and that took a toll on her nerves. She became Elsa's ally in the house which, of course, caused a lot of tension with Luisa. But Antonia felt strongly about it. She recognized how hard the situation was for Elsa and felt sorry for her.

Antonia knew very well that Luisa was always going to take Coco's side, so she felt she needed to balance things by supporting Elsa.

When Luisa left for Buenos Aires, life became more pleasant in Asuncion. Antonia resumed her embroidery work, though on a much smaller scale. She started to spend more time with our other siblings and became closer with her nieces and nephews.

Because she never got married nor had her own children, she adopted her siblings' families as her own.

Antonia always had a gift for listening, which meant that everyone with a problem went to her. That was a good thing for everyone but her. She took their problems as her own and felt responsible for them like a mother would. In fact, she became the matriarch of the family. She was the first one to know if someone had marital or financial problems, if they lost their jobs, or had a mistress, if their children were doing well in school, or if they were up to no good. She kept reading the Tarot cards to anyone who was interested, but she tried to edit the parts that were not good.

She was tough as nails and as stubborn as always. If she made up her mind, nothing and nobody would be able to talk her out of it. She could be as strong as she was gentle. She was fair, decent, and honest. Even the neighbors called her to solve disputes amongst them. They trusted her like they would a judge. She was the only one with the courage to face Josefina's husband after he beat her up so badly that she ended up in the hospital. Antonia walked up to his face and with just a few words explained to him that if he ever touched Josefina again, he would be the one having to go to the emergency room. He never did it again.

Antonia was everybody's mother and friend. She made us all feel loved and protected. That's why when we found out that she was about to die, we were devastated.

A few months after Coco's separation, Antonia's health deteriorated rapidly. The first few visits to the doctor didn't help much. Nobody was sure what was causing her illness. Luisa kept telling us that they were running tests; that they thought it might be her diabetes; others thought it was her heart. But nothing they did helped Antonia.

Every week I would call and still no news of improvement. I was getting more worried every time and the feeling of impotence was killing me. Being so far away from my sisters was driving me crazy. I hated to be so helpless, so useless.

Luisa told me they couldn't get Antonia's high fever under control, and the doctors had decided to admit her to the hospital.

"They will keep her there as long as they need to, until they find out what's causing this," she explained.

"How can they not know? Are you sure you are going to the right doctors? Maybe we should consider bringing her to Buenos Aires," I wanted badly to be able to help somehow.

"She's too weak. She's been running a fever on and off for a few weeks. She wouldn't survive the trip. It'll be best if we treat her here," she added, and I could tell she was trying to be strong on the phone.

"Well, maybe I should come to you. I'm sure you could use my help right now," I offered.

"You are busy preparing for Baby's wedding. Let me see how things develop. I promise I will let you know if I need you."

"I will wait one more week. If her health doesn't improve, I'm coming to you," I said firmly.

"All right. We will speak next week again." We said goodbye.

The following days, I couldn't do anything but think about my oldest sister. I tried to remember my earliest memories of her, when we were all growing up under the same roof. I thought of the times when she helped me with my homework, taught me how to cook, and showed me how to embroider my initials on my underwear. She was the oldest; I was the youngest. There was an entire generation between us. We belonged in different worlds, and yet, we were deeply connected as sisters.

I used to feel sorry for her, for not having her own family. But I realized that she had so much love and affection from everyone around her, she didn't need it. I never knew if she ever fell in love, or if she regretted not having married when she had the chance. She valued her freedom and her independence more than anything, and she didn't care what price she had to pay to keep it that way. I admired her stoicism and her strength. She didn't feel sorry for herself so why should I feel that way for her?

Saturday came, and I ran to the pharmacy to make my weekly phone call to Luisa.

"She's not getting better," she said as soon as she heard my voice on the line. "But the good news is that they found the source of her illness."

"So what is it?" I asked impatiently.

"She has gangrene in one of her feet. It all started with an ingrown toenail that got infected. She tried to cut it herself and it got worse. It's the infection that's killing her." Her voice broke on the other end of the line.

"What do you mean?"

"She's dying. They will try to cut her foot off to see if that stops it, but there are no guarantees." She could no longer hide her sorrow from me.

"When will they operate?"

"As soon as they can. But they need to make sure her heart will survive the operation. Her diabetes makes everything more complicated. She put on a lot of weight the past few years, and her blood pressure is too high. If the infection doesn't kill her, maybe the anesthesia will," Luisa explained.

"I'm coming. I will take the first bus I can get. I can't be here while you deal with all of this," I said. "I need to talk to Hans but I don't think he'll have a problem with it. The girls are old enough to take care of themselves, and I will ask my neighbor Marta to help out. I will call you to let you know when I'm arriving."

"*Gracias*, Chola. I really need you now. I'm so grateful you can come." I knew she didn't want to take me away from my family, but at the same time she desperately needed my help in Asuncion.

"I will be there as soon as I can," I replied.

It had been more than four years since we moved away. I hadn't been to Asuncion in so long, I didn't know what to expect. Luisa was the only one of my siblings whom I had seen recently, and I was happy to be able to see the rest of the family. Of course, the reason for my trip wasn't a happy one, and the idea of losing Antonia was killing me inside. But I tried to stay positive. She was going to need our support and prayers.

I made sure I got everything organized at home before I left. Baby was going to be responsible for food, shopping, and preparing meals. Matilde was going to help out around the house, cleaning and doing laundry. Marta was kind enough to agree to lend a hand whenever the girls or Hans needed her. Hans promised me he would be back from work early to spend quality time with our daughters.

I had already started to make Baby's wedding dress but that would have to wait until my return. Nothing seemed more important to me now than my sister's health. She needed me, and I was willing to drop everything for her. I knew in my heart she would do the same for me.

A few days later, Hans drove me to the bus terminal. I was very tense and he noticed it.

"Don't worry about a thing. We will be fine. Say hello to everyone in Asuncion. And please take care of yourself." His voice was sincere.

"Thank you, I will. Make sure you call me every week to let me know how the kids are doing," I replied, feeling a knot building up inside my throat. "Hopefully, I'll be back in a few weeks." I kissed him softly.

I turned away to hide my tears and hurried inside the bus. He waited on the platform until the bus finally disappeared in the distance. I closed my eyes and took a deep breath.

It was the first time in my life that I was separated from my daughters. I knew it would be a test for all of us. It was very hard to let go of my protective ring around my family. That's the way it had been all our lives. I was their protector. I was responsible for them. Now that my daughters were almost grownups, I had to learn to let go. My job was already done. They were soon going to be on their own, making their own decisions, making their own mistakes.

The trip was long and tiring—at least that part hadn't changed much. I looked through the bus window, remembering our first few trips to Asuncion in Hans' trucks. I remembered the dirt roads and the children's faces as we drove by. Progress was finally finding its way up to Argentina's northeast. The roads had improved dramatically and were paved most of the way. We made several stops along the way for bathroom breaks and to stretch our legs. The landscape hadn't changed at all. The sky was the same. I inhaled slowly, taking it all in. I could see myself back in time, traveling these desolate roads, letting the views take me to another place and time, dreaming of a future that was still unknown.

Luisa and Coco were waiting for me at the bus terminal. We hugged, and they immediately took me down to the hospital where Antonia was admitted. The operation had been a success, and the doctors were very happy with the results. The fever was down, but she was still in critical condition. They explained to me that the infection was so severe they decided to cut her leg off above the knee. They didn't know how far up they had to cut to prevent the infection from spreading all over her body, if it hadn't already done so. The first signs after the operation were very hopeful. She would have to stay in the hospital for a few weeks, and after that, she would have to undergo a long rehabilitation.

Antonia was awake when I walked into her room.

"Chola, you came!" she exclaimed with joy in her eyes.

"Of course. How could I not be with you? You are my favorite sister!" I gave Luisa a quick wink and a smile.

"And you are mine." She laughed carefully, making sure she didn't move.

"I will stay here as long as you need me. You are an amazing woman, Antonia. We are so proud of you! Everyone can't wait to see you again. We all miss you so much, especially the girls. They wanted so badly to come with me," I told her.

"I miss them, too. I probably won't recognize them next time I see them." We noticed she was getting tired.

The nurse walked into the room and asked us to leave and let Antonia sleep and rest.

"Of course," I said. I turned to Antonia and asked, "Do you need anything before we go?"

"Yes, my foot is itchy. Could you scratch it?"

"Sure," I said, holding her remaining foot between my hands.

"No, not that foot, the other one. It's driving me crazy. It won't stop itching."

"Antonia, I'm already doing it," I said, unsure how to handle the situation.

"You have the wrong foot!" she yelled at me.

"I'm so sorry," I said, and I could feel my eyes tearing up.

The nurse noticed immediately and stepped in to help.

"It's time for your medication, Antonia. Your family needs to go home. They will be back soon. In the meantime you should rest," she said as we walked out of the room.

I stepped out of her room and broke down crying in the hallway. Luisa held me in her arms.

"Be grateful she's still alive. We thought we were going to lose her. Yesterday the doctors asked us to prepare for the worst.

She lost her leg, but she's still with us," she said, trying to calm me down.

"I don't know how to help her. I feel so powerless," I sobbed.

"You are here. That's the best you can do for her right now. The real work will start when she goes home. It will take a long time until she's used to her new life in a wheelchair."

"I just can't believe she will be condemned to a wheelchair. It's so terribly unfair," I managed to say.

"It's better than a coffin. She's alive. We need your help, Chola. Once you dry these tears, I don't want to see you break down again. You have to be strong. She will survive this—we all will," she said in her "older sister's" voice.

The following two weeks, we worked hard preparing the house for Antonia's arrival. Abel built ramps, Luisa cleared Antonia's bedroom to make it more accessible, and Coco ordered a new bed. I helped anywhere I could and visited Antonia at the hospital as often as possible.

Her doctors were pleased with the results of the operation. The fever was gone and her vital organs were stabilized. Her spirits were also improving. Once they reduced her dosage of morphine, she started to come to terms with her new reality. It was a terrible shock at first, but it got better every day. I was with her almost daily. When I wasn't allowed to visit her, I tried to spend time with my other siblings, Choli, and old friends like Ana Maria.

It had been many years since our last encounter. Ana Maria lived in a very different world. She belonged to Asuncion's high society and was married to a powerful and influential businessman. We shared very little. She invited me over for tea one afternoon at her mansion. Compared to my small apartment, every home in Asuncion seemed like a mansion to me. Her maid, wearing an impeccably white uniform, opened the door and showed me to the sun room. It was a beautiful day, and the sun was bright. Ana Maria seemed glad to see me after so many years.

"Chola, I can't believe you are here with me." She opened her arms to welcome me with a hug. It almost felt like old times.

"I know. I hardly believe it myself. It's been way too long, my friend. I missed you."

"I feel like it was yesterday when we both got married. So much has happened since. But how are the girls?" she asked, trying to lighten up the conversation.

"They are both well. Baby got engaged last Christmas. She will be married soon."

"That's great news," she replied. "Do you like him?"

"I do. Hector is a decent man. He is a Navy officer and wants to become a pilot," I added with a sense of pride I hadn't felt before while I watched the maid serve us some tea.

"I'm glad to hear that. Matilde probably looks very different as well. I'm sure she is a lovely young woman!"

"Yes, she is. I've been very blessed with my children. But how about yours?"

"Well, Isabel is at the Sorbonne in Paris. She loves it there. I don't think she would ever want to come back to this country, and Gonzalo will be graduating soon from Harvard. I hardly see my children these days. They are both grownups now," she said.

"It must be hard for you to be so far away. How do you manage?" I asked, feeling sorry for my friend.

"I'm fine. I'm very busy as president of a few charities, and I'm constantly entertaining for my husband's business. We also travel a lot, mostly to Europe—to visit Isabel."

"That sounds exciting." I had a hard time imagining my friend's life.

"I heard about Antonia. How is she doing?" she asked, once again changing the subject

"She's doing better now. It was very scary. We thought we would lose her. But the amputation went well, and hopefully, she will come home next week. It will take some time for her to get used to it, though."

"Send her my love and please let me know how I can help." She looked at her gold watch and seemed uncomfortable. "I'm so sorry, but I have to go. I'm in charge of organizing our next benefit ball, and I have so much to do. Maybe I could see you again before you return to Buenos Aires." She got up.

"Of course, I won't take any more of your time." I started to walk towards the front door.

"Can I ask you a question?" I said before I left.

"Sure," she replied.

"Are you happy?"

She thought for a minute and looked me in the eyes.

"I'm happy enough."

"One last thing," I said. "Do you still think of him?"

"Every day."

I walked away wondering if any of us was truly happy. I married for love; she married for social status. But neither of us had what we really wanted. We were not so different after all.

A few years later, I received a letter from Ana Maria telling me that her husband had died peacefully at home. After more than thirty years of marriage she was a free woman again. She told me she had finally reunited with her long-lost love: my brother Andres. I always wondered why she never wanted to tell me his name, why she insisted on keeping his identity secret. Andres waited patiently for her all those years and never married, dreaming of the day they would unite forever. They finally did.

The day before Antonia was supposed to come home, the house was busy with the preparations for her return. The ramps were finished, the bed had arrived, and we found ourselves ready sooner than we expected. Coco decided to work on a project he had neglected the past few weeks, and Luisa wanted to make one more trip to the grocery store, to make sure we had enough food in the house.

I found myself wondering if I should stay home and look for something to do or if I should visit Antonia one last time at the hospital. I had to admit I enjoyed our time alone, and once she came back, that privilege would be over.

I took the bus to the hospital, deep in my thoughts. I wondered about Hans and the girls, how they were doing without me. I knew it was going to take a lot more than the three weeks I had originally planned to help Antonia adapt to her new life. It killed me to be away from my family, but I was needed in Asuncion at the moment. My weekly conversations with Hans were brief and from what I could hear, everyone was doing well without me. Marta had been a great help, he told me, always checking on him and the girls, bringing them dinner and stopping by. I was so grateful to Luisa for having pushed me to make a new friend. I was glad to have her in my life, especially at this time.

When I arrived at the hospital, Antonia was sleeping so I decided to go to the cafeteria for a cup of coffee.

I walked in and suddenly I saw a familiar face. It was Elsa. I wasn't sure what to do or say. I sat down to wait for the waiter when she approached me.

"Chola, I'm so glad you are here!" she exclaimed and hugged me as if we were old friends.

"Elsa, this is a nice surprise," I replied timidly.

"I came to see Antonia. I owed her a visit. I knew she was admitted. I still keep in touch with my old colleagues," she said, reminding me about her past as a nurse.

"I'm so sorry about you and Coco. I should have contacted you before, but nobody could tell me how to reach you. You left so suddenly."

"I know. I'm sorry. I just couldn't talk to anyone. It was devastating, but I had no choice," she explained.

"I don't understand. I thought things we better between you and Coco. Last time we spoke—"

"After we spoke," she interrupted me, "I did what you suggested. I had it all planned. We were going to go away for a long weekend, just to be alone for a while. Coco seemed happy with the idea and I started to make plans," she stopped and looked away.

"What happened, Elsa?"

"You love him so much, I can't tell you," she replied as her eyes filled with tears.

"I need to know. I won't tell a soul, if that's what you want."

"I can't tell you what I saw. It will break your heart." The tears run down her face.

"Elsa, I respect you, and I won't push you, but you can trust me. I was always on your side—you know that."

"I know, Chola, and I appreciate it. It's just too painful to remember," she said.

"It's okay. You don't have to tell me. Don't cry." I opened my arms to hug her.

"I went to his studio one night," she said. "I wanted to tell him about our travel plans. I was so happy and excited I couldn't wait until morning to share it with him." She wiped her tears and took a deep breath. "I found them together," she continued.

"Who did you find?" I asked, knowing that Coco would never have another woman.

"Coco and Abel." Her voice went silent.

I was speechless. We both were. We sat next to each other. I held her hand for a long time. We didn't speak. We didn't have to.

After a few minutes she said, "I had to leave. I couldn't explain or tell anyone what happened. I don't want to ruin Coco's life. I still love him. But I couldn't stay either. Maybe one day I will have the courage to face him again. But I don't know when that will happen."

"I'm so sorry, Elsa. I don't know what to say. I can't even imagine the pain you must be feeling. Is there anything I can do for you?"

"Yes, there is something you can do. Please thank Antonia for me. She was the only one who supported me, besides you. She stood by my side and I will never forget that. I don't think I will ever return. I will file for divorce soon, and Coco will hear from me then."

"I understand. I hope you can find some peace one day," I told her and realized it was getting late. "I need to see Antonia before visiting hours are over. I'm so glad we met. Thank you for trusting me, Elsa." I could not believe what I just had heard.

"Thank you for listening, Chola. I will never forget you." She kissed me goodbye and walked away quickly, trying to avoid a long farewell. I didn't want one either.

Elsa left me alone with my thoughts. My mind was racing in all possible directions. I didn't know what to think or actually how to stop thinking. The waiter brought me back to reality by asking me for my order. I told him to bring me a strong black coffee to go. Maybe the caffeine would wake me up from this nightmare. I had so many questions, but in a strange way, my encounter with Elsa actually clarified a lot of my doubts. I had known Coco since the day he was born, and now he seemed like a stranger to me. Maybe we put so much pressure on him all these years to get married and start a family that we took away his chance to be happy in life. We all want to be loved, but we need to choose the right way. He married Elsa to make us happy. Or maybe he truly believed that she was the one woman who would change every-thing for him.

But the consequences were devastating for both parties. She would never be able to forget, and he would never be able to forgive himself.

My heart broke for him. I wished I would have seen him for who he really was, known his heart and desires better. But how could he trust any of us with such a secret? Homosexuality was a mortal sin. All I knew about it was what the priests told us. Homosexuals were an abomination, they would say. They don't belong in the Church or in our society. I always imagined these men to be disgusting creatures. But not Coco. He was the gentlest person I'd ever known. He was an artist—sensitive and tender, smart and creative. He was everything I would have loved in a man, and yet he searched for his happiness in a different way. I tried hard to understand, but I couldn't.

I decided the conversation with Elsa would die with me. No one would ever find out through my mouth what happened. Only if Coco decided to speak to me about it would I bring it up again. We were all accomplices in this terrible crime against love.

Love can come in different shapes and forms. Coco's and Elsa's lives would be forever ruined. And we were all, in part, responsible for it.

I finished my coffee and went to see Antonia. I told her about meeting Elsa and her message to her.

"Poor girl," said Antonia. "She must be suffering a lot right now. I wish things could have turned out differently, but maybe this happened for the best. I liked her a lot. I hope one day she can forgive us."

"Forgive us for what?" I asked.

"For not giving her a chance to be happy."

"What do you mean?" I insisted, not sure how much Antonia really knew.

"Coco and Elsa never had a real marriage. We were always in the middle. We were like a cancer in their married life. I will never forgive myself for not insisting that Luisa and I move out of the house."

"It's too late for that now. At least you tried to make things better for her and she's very grateful for that. But we need to focus on you and your health," I said firmly, trying to avoid any further conversation about Elsa and Coco.

"You're right, Chola. I'm ready to go home. I hate the food in this place and I can't wait to have a glass of wine!" she exclaimed, making me laugh. "Why don't you help me with my things? I don't want to forget anything at the hospital."

"I'll make sure we pack all of your belongings, don't worry. So when will they let you go?"

"Tomorrow, as long as my blood pressure is normal," she said. "I will miss the nurses and doctors. Everyone has been so nice to me. I even promised them I would read them the Tarot cards if they wanted."

"That could be fun," I replied, smiling at my oldest sister.

Antonia had aged so much these past few weeks. The operation took a toll on her health. She didn't look as strong and invincible anymore. It hit me suddenly that she was getting old, and it pained me to realize how fragile she was at that moment. Having her alive was such a gift, but nobody knew how long she would last in this condition. I never imagined that my oldest sister would one day celebrate her 100th birthday.

A day later, Antonia came home. And then the real work started. Luisa and I had to learn to help her take a bath, go to the bathroom, prepare her meals, and move her in and out of bed. It was important that she changed positions several times a day to avoid muscle soreness. A physical therapist came once a day to help with her rehabilitation. Most of the time, she was cooperative and tried hard to do her part. Luisa got her a little bell that she could use to call us when she needed anything. The doctors kept her on a few medications to ease the pain and anxiety and to keep her diabetes under control. The only reason for complaint she had was her doctor's orders against wine. She missed her daily glass of red wine, as if it was the air for her lungs. But as long as she was on pain killers, she would have to wait. It didn't last too long. A few weeks after arriving at the house, she decided she didn't need the drugs as much as she needed to taste the sweet flavor of the vines. We spoke with her doctors, and we all agreed that to make her happy was more important. So we celebrated by opening a bottle of her favorite cabernet.

Slowly life went back to normal, or at least to our new version of normal. Antonia became Luisa's new obsession, which gave Coco more room to breathe and work. Abel continued working as his assistant and helping around the house. I had a hard time looking him in the eyes, and I think he noticed because we hardly ever spoke, and when we did, it was only the necessary few words. I made a big effort to treat Coco as normally as possible, but it would take me years to come to terms with his choice.

I never heard from Elsa again. A few months later, their divorce was finalized, and Coco made sure she would never have any financial worries.

Soon, I started to feel it was time to go home. The three original weeks I had planned turned into four long months. I missed my daughters. I even missed Hans. Old habits die hard, I thought. I wasn't needed as much anymore, and I had to go back to help with Baby's wedding. It was going to be very hard to say good bye to my dear sisters. Our bond had grown stronger over the past few months, and I was going to miss them very much. But I had to take care of my own family. I spoke with Luisa, and she agreed it was time to go home. She came with me to buy the return bus ticket.

"You know, I would like you to stay forever, but the girls probably can't wait to have you back. You've been so wonderful, Chola, I don't know what I would have done without you."

"I'm glad I came. Now that I know you and Antonia are doing well, I can go home. Perhaps you could come for Baby's wedding," I suggested.

"I will surely try. I wouldn't miss it for the world!" she exclaimed, excited with the idea.

Saying goodbye to Antonia was going to be a lot harder. She was sitting in her wheelchair when I walked into her room.

"I heard you will be leaving us soon," she said, reading my mind as usual.

"Yes. I have to go home to my children." I sat next to her.

"They need you, I know. Thank you for being with me all this time, Chola. You bring so much joy to my life. I wish you and the girls would move back to Asuncion."

"That would be nice, but our life is now in Buenos Aires. I promise we will come back soon to visit you. You will always be in my thoughts and prayers."

"I never thought my baby sister would end up taking care of me. I still remember when you were a little girl. I'm blessed to have you in my life, Chola. *Te quiero mucho.*"

"I love you too, sister." We sat next to each other in silence for a long time.

Chapter Eighteen

The bus station was bustling when I arrived. My bus was a few minutes early, and I was afraid I would have to wait for a while until Hans picked me up.

I got off the bus, anxiously looking for my daughters' faces in the crowd. They were there, waiting for me, smiling, and waving. My heart started to race, and I ran to embrace them. I was so happy to be back, to have my girls finally in my arms, to be home. It felt like yesterday when my bus departed. Everything felt familiar and new at the same time. Hans waited patiently for his turn to welcome me. He did it warmly but I could tell he was anxious to leave the crowds of people behind.

I showed him where my suitcase was and started walking toward the exit, framed by my daughters on either side who bombarded me with questions. They wanted to know every detail of my time away. I gave them a brief version of the main events, thinking we would have a lot of time once we got home to talk about their aunts, uncles, and cousins.

My last days in Asuncion, I tried to see most of my siblings. I didn't know when I would return, and I didn't want any of them to think I forgot to say goodbye. The farewell process took days. It took me especially long to say goodbye to Choli. She was busy with her four children and we didn't have a chance to spend much time together during my stay. But we tried to make it up on the last day. She seemed happy and that brought me a lot of joy. Her husband was a good man and a great father. She remained the same—a gentle soul. Nothing seemed to affect her much, as if she was in her own happy universe. For a brief moment I envied her. Of course, she had been very concerned about Antonia's health but her children kept her away from the hospital. It didn't matter. We knew she had her hands full, and we never expected her to help much with Antonia.

I also managed to see a few of my other siblings briefly. Everyone made some time from their busy schedules to be with me before my departure. I was moved by their affection and love, especially because I had been gone for several years and didn't keep in touch regularly with many of them. Juan was still single and happy, chasing skirts all over Asuncion, while my brother Andres had gone into the circus business and was always on the road with his show of acrobats and clowns. There couldn't be a better place for him. When he and Ana Maria finally got together, years later, she embraced the circus life as if she had been in it all her life! Josefina remained with her abusive husband and kept to herself. She seldom visited with Antonia and Luisa. Maybe the shame was too much to bear. My sister Asuncion, the second youngest after me, was the last one I visited. She was living with her adoptive daughter, her husband, and their children. She had found peace in life and was very content being a grandmother.

It was interesting to see how all our lives had taken very different turns, some for the better, others for the worse. Some of them felt like strangers to me, as if we had never had a common denominator. With my sisters I had a strong bond, but with my brothers the relationship was more distant. I didn't fully understand what was so powerful between us women that united us and kept us going. We were all so different, and yet, we could relate so well to one another. I think in a way we were all the same. We were all survivors.

We arrived home, and I stopped at Marta's to thank her for her help during my absence. She wasn't there so I left her a little note telling her I was home. I unpacked my suitcase and gave the girls the few small presents I managed to buy before I left. Luisa also sent them a few typical Paraguayan-style blouses with intricate and colorful embroidery. Finally, after we ate, I started to feel the effects of more than twenty hours of travel and decided to take a short nap. I passed out almost immediately. Images of my time with Luisa and Antonia filled my memory, and I couldn't help but wonder how they were all doing right now. I was glad to be home, but felt sad to be so far away from them.

When I awakened, I noticed Baby had taken care of dinner, and Matilde was helping as well. Suddenly I realized that even though it felt the same, so much had changed when I was away. My daughters were no longer children. They were women now. I never noticed that change before. It took a long absence to discover that there were no more girls in the house. In front of me were two young women, independent and self-sufficient. I couldn't be more proud of the scene that was unfolding in front of my eyes. As I watched them, I asked myself, where did all the years go? Why did it happen so fast? It was only yesterday that they were babies in my arms. Now I could see only two beautiful women. What did I do to deserve them? I must have done something right after all.

Hans came early to have dinner with us and we all sat at the kitchen table like old times. We talked, laughed, and remembered when we used to live in Asuncion. Hans kept quiet, while the girls and I spoke about everything that had happened in my absence. Baby told me about her classes and wedding preparations. Matilde spoke about her music and her latest adventures in high school. Before we had finished dinner, Hans excused himself to read the newspaper. It didn't surprise me because I knew he didn't have much patience for small talk, especially when the conversation was between three women. We cleared the table and did the dishes.

The evening went by quickly and I began to feel tired again. I waited until Hans was finished reading and I asked him to join me in the bedroom.

"I noticed you were very quiet at dinner," I mentioned.

"Well, the girls monopolized your attention. There was nothing I could do," he said in his sardonic way.

"You're right. They wouldn't stop talking," I agreed. "They look so grownup to me. Maybe because I didn't see them for a few months, I'm beginning to notice some of the changes they're going through."

"They were amazing when you were away. I didn't have to do anything. They took care of me and the house, as good as you would have. They will be great women!"

"They already are," I added. "When did it happen, Hans? When did our daughters become women?" I asked as I undressed and put my nightgown on.

"I don't know, Chola. Soon Baby will leave the house and after that Matilde. Then, it's back to us," he said, with a hint of sadness in his voice.

"Maybe we will spend more time together." I wondered if we had anything in common anymore.

"We are both getting old, Chola. Look at us!"

"I know. But we still have time." I didn't understand what exactly he was saying to me.

"I don't feel my age, I still feel young. There is so much I want to do."

"I know what you mean. I feel young as well, though after twenty hours sitting inside a bus, all my bones hurt." I said, trying to lighten up the conversation but feeling the anxiety in his voice.

"I'm sure everybody feels this way at one point. I just never thought I would be admitting it."

"Hans, we are all afraid of getting old. I just spent four months with my older sisters. I saw how quickly it happens. Age can't be stopped. We just need to make the best of it."

"You are right," he said. "We missed you. I missed you." He kissed my forehead and turned over to his side of the bed, officially ending our brief conversation.

For the first time in a very long time, I wanted him to touch me, to want me. But he was snoring before I could even think about what to do. I was exhausted myself so I didn't do anything.

Maybe tomorrow, I thought, and closed my eyes.

The next few weeks were extremely busy. I contacted my old clients, hoping to restart my small business and have an income again while I worked hard on Baby's wedding dress. Things went back to normal, and before I knew it, it was as if I had never left. Hans' business was going well, and he was trying to build a client base in the interior of the country. He took a few short trips every month to cities such as Rosario, La Plata, or Santa Fe. It didn't bother me much because I was used to his trips when he had his trucking company. In fact, it represented a nice break.

Since my return from Paraguay he had been a little distant, absent minded, in his own world. I attributed it to his business and busy traveling schedule, but it worried me to see him so detached from us again. My mind was concentrated on finalizing the wedding preparations and meeting my clients' deadlines, so I didn't pay too much attention to Hans.

Hector's family had booked the Naval Club for the reception, and we reserved the church. We all met frequently to compare notes and make sure everything was running smoothly. Hector was away most of the time, and we had to make the best of every weekend he was around. Baby was also studying for her finals and had little time to waste. So I took charge of coordinating everyone's schedules. The closer we were to the date, the more nervous I got. Baby, on the other hand, seemed happy and relaxed. She seemed so sure of what she was doing. I wanted badly for her to have a better experience than mine, to shelter her from the heartache I had been through. But how could I ever do that? My job as a mother would finish the day she walked out my door; at that point she would take charge of her own life.

It was a hard thing to accept—my daughter as a married woman. I had no doubts she would be an amazing wife and mother herself; I just prayed she would have a good man by her side, and that Hector would be worthy of her.

Matilde, unlike her love-struck sister, had a strong mind of her own. She did well in school, but her passion was somewhere else. She played the piano regularly and went to her music classes religiously. For now, she didn't know what she wanted to do in the future, but a career as a music teacher didn't seem bad to me. I started to notice she was interested in boys. She was only sixteen years old but she handled herself in an exceptionally mature way. She liked going to the school dances and many times she would have friends over to listen to some music. I often wondered what kind of life was waiting for her.

Matilde and I worked together a few afternoons a week, and I taught her how to use my sewing machine. She was actually pretty good at it. She enjoyed copying the dresses we would see famous people wearing in magazines. Besides Baby's wedding dress, I had to take care of Matilde's and mine. I wasn't sure how I would be able to do it all in time. My routine fell back into place quickly. I resumed my weekly calls to Luisa who seemed to be dealing with Antonia pretty well. They were both determined not to let this disability rule their lives. We rarely spoke about Coco, just the necessary.

Everything went back to normal, except for one thing: my relationship with Marta.

Since my return we had seen each other only a handful of times, mostly on my way in or out of the house. She was cold and distant. I had a feeling she was avoiding me, and I didn't like it. I felt indebted to my friend for having taken care of my family during my trip to Asuncion. But I wasn't sure what was going, and I didn't know if I had offended her in any way. I decided to stop by one afternoon and confront her.

I bought some pastries at the local baker and headed to her place. I rang the bell several times. It took a while until I heard some footsteps and the door finally opened.

Marta was on the other side. She was wearing a pink robe and looked like she had just gotten out of bed—her hair messy and her makeup off. It was the first time I saw her looking like this.

"Chola, what a nice surprise!" She said nervously as she opened the door.

"I'm so sorry. It looks like this is a bad time," I admitted, looking puzzled.

"Not at all, I worked the late shift last night at the hospital and was trying to take a nap. My schedule has been crazy lately."

"I know I haven't had a chance to thank you properly for all you did during my absence. Hans told me how much you helped him."

"You don't need to thank me." She opened the door all the way, inviting me in. "It was a pleasure. You have a lovely family. It was no trouble at all."

"I brought some facturas for you and Julio. I won't stay—you look tired," I added, feeling like I was imposing on her.

"Thank you, it wasn't necessary. I know I haven't been much of a friend lately. I guess my late nights ruin my social life. I'm always sleepy and tired during the day."

"I understand. I was just worried that I might have offended you in some way," I admitted.

"How can that be possible? Don't be silly! It's me who's been too busy. But that's no excuse. I should have stopped by and had a cup of tea with you. Please forgive me for being such a bad friend."

"No problem at all. Whenever you want, just come upstairs, and we'll have a cup of tea."

"I sure will, Chola. Thanks for stopping by. I appreciate it, and Julio will love the pastries!"

"I'm glad you're well. I'll see you soon." I walked out of her house and went up the stairs.

I felt relieved after our brief conversation. A heavy weight had been lifted off my shoulders. Of course, she was a busy woman with a career. I should have known that I wasn't the reason for her behavior. But a lifetime of insecurities made me feel guilty about everything. I had to work on letting go of that bad habit.

Sometimes I felt sorry for my friend. She never had any children, and I had two beautiful daughters. I envied her freedom and independence, and she envied my family. Being away for so long from my children made me realize how much I loved them and how I could never live without them. I gladly traded my freedom for being their mother. There was no greater joy or pride in my life.

I knew I was far from perfect; in fact, I often felt insignificant, but being their mother gave my life a purpose, a reason. I was nothing until I had them. If being their mother was the only achievement of my existence, I would die a happy woman.

Until the very last days of my life, I knew I was loved by them. Even when I could no longer recognize their faces, I could tell in their voices that they loved me. Even in my old age and barely aware of the world around me, they never abandoned me. They became my constant pillars. Without their love I would never have been able to survive what was in store for me.

Chapter Nineteen

We were all excited, waiting at the bus terminal for Luisa's arrival. It didn't take much to convince her to come to Baby's wedding. She became so attached to the girls when she stayed with us and would have never missed such an important event. She agreed to have Coco hire a nurse who would move in and help with Antonia until her return. At first she didn't like the idea much, but it was the only way if she wanted to travel to Buenos Aires. Since Antonia's operation she hadn't had a break, and she was looking forward to spending some time with us.

Of course, we were overjoyed when we heard about her traveling plans, especially Baby. Luisa was more than an aunt; she was an extension of myself. But I have to admit she was a better listener than I was. She had an infinite source of patience for my children. And that made her their favorite aunt.

We picked her up in Hans' car and it felt immediately as if she had never left. She fit right in with all of us. We still had a few days before the wedding and a lot of details to finish up. Luisa and I went right to work touching up the dresses, ordering flowers, confirming the church and catering, checking the guest list. We felt like two young girls getting married ourselves—maybe for Luisa this felt like the wedding she never had.

Hector was scheduled to arrive a week before the religious ceremony. We couldn't book the church on the same day as the Justice of Peace. They would have the civil service a week before the religious ceremony. Hector would go back to the naval base and return for the church service.

Of course, I told them that until they were officially married in front of God, they would not be allowed to sleep together. The civil ceremony didn't count from my perspective. Baby would not be a married woman until she walked down the aisle.

When the day finally arrived, we all went downtown to the municipal building and waited patiently in a small room. The Justice of Peace sat behind an old-looking desk where a heavy book lay. Baby and Hector sat directly across from him and the rest of us sat behind them. The ceremony was brief and unemotional. After a few words of advice and a warm congratulation, the judge invited them to sign his big book. We all witnessed the moment when they wrote down their names and were pronounced husband and wife by the state.

Baby looked radiant in her ivory dress, with almost no makeup and her golden hair loose like she always wore it. She never needed makeup; her natural beauty was enough. She was holding a small bouquet of white calla lilies. Hector wore a dark suit that accentuated his happy face even more. They couldn't stop staring at each other and it reminded me of the first time I saw them together, and how Luisa felt they were meant for one another.

The circle was finally closing in front of my eyes, which were almost blinded by my tears.

Once the ceremony was over, Hans was the first one to hug the bride and groom. He couldn't hide the pride and joy in his smile. I hadn't seen him so happy in years.

"You have my daughter now. Love her and protect her all your life. I'll be watching you," he murmured in Hector's ear as he embraced him.

I was mesmerized by the whole scene until I heard Baby asking for me.

"Where is Mom? Where are you, Mom?" she kept asking for me as she tried to find my face in the crowd of people lining up to kiss her.

"I'm here, Baby, right here." I choked on my own words. "Are you happy?"

"Couldn't be happier, Mom." She wiped the tears from my face. "You will ruin your makeup if you keep crying!" she exclaimed.

"I don't care! I love you so much," I said between sobs.

"I love you too, Mom." We embraced each other.

We went back to the house and had a modest reception, just for our dear friends and family. Hector's best man was his closest friend from childhood. He was a year younger than he and went to the Naval Academy as well. He was tall, with dark hair and dark eyes. He had a presence about him that caught the attention of every woman in the room, especially Matilde. He and Hector were friends since elementary school and had always been as close as brothers. He was an only child himself. His name was Hugo.

I immediately liked him. He was funny and very friendly. He made everyone smile. It was hard not to fall under his spell. We heard from Hector that he had been engaged to a rich girl, but she called the wedding off only a few weeks before it was supposed to happen. A crazy thought went through my head: how ironic if the two sisters marry the two best friends. I shook my head and reminded myself that Matilde was turning seventeen in a few months, and she had all the time in the world to find a man.

Our home was small, but we all felt comfortable in it. Luisa was the only family member from our side; the rest were Hector's friends and family. The bride and groom held hands almost the entire evening, and I kept wondering how I was going to be able to separate them at the end of the night. Marta and Julio were there as well and I was glad to see my friend looking more rested and in a better mood. Hans was more social than usual, an obvious result of his happiness. I was glad to see my small family together.

Once everyone left, I reminded Baby of my expectations.

"I know, Mother. That will be my gift to you tonight. I will say goodbye to Hector and help you clean up," she said without letting go of his hand.

"Good night, Chola," Hector said. "Can I call you 'Mother' now?" he asked.

"Of course you can. Welcome to the family."

"Thank you for a lovely evening. Everyone had a great time. You are a wonderful hostess," he told me.

"It was my pleasure." I was a little uncomfortable with all the compliments. "Time to wrap things up. We'll see you in a week, Hector. Be well." I gave Baby a quick look, letting her know not to take too long.

"I'll be waiting at the altar," he replied with the biggest smile on his face.

The following week flew by quickly. I did the last few adjustments to the wedding dress and finished mine and Matilde's dresses as well. I was finally done. Now I could sleep at night. Baby had picked a dress she saw in a European magazine, and I had tried my best to copy it. The gown came out better than I had expected and most importantly, Baby was happy with it. Matilde's dress was simpler and inspired by Doris Day, her favorite actress. It was light blue and the skirt had several layers of tulle. Fun and fluffy, it was perfect for spinning around the dance floor. Mine was a little more conservative. It was black with a golden pattern on the skirt. Luisa decided to wear the same dress she had made for Coco's wedding, a dark blue satin dress that match her eyes perfectly.

Finally, we could relax a little. Baby completed her finals and was spending more time at home, which made me very happy.

We had never talked about the wedding night, and I didn't know where to start. I realized sadly that the subject was still taboo for me, and I was totally incapable of speaking with her about sex. I asked Luisa to do it for me because I was more nervous now than I was on my own wedding night.

I waited anxiously in the bedroom until they finished their conversation in the kitchen. Once they were done, Luisa came in the room.

"You have a very smart daughter. She knows everything she needs to know," she said and left me without saying another word.

I exhaled.

On the morning of the wedding, I woke up early to make breakfast and have some time for myself before everyone else got up. I needed a few minutes to absorb the magnitude of the moment and what lay ahead.

The house was silent and peaceful. It was a sunny spring morning, and I could feel the warmth of the sun's rays coming through the windows. I sat at the kitchen table, trying to imagine life without one of my daughters. She will do just fine, I kept repeating to myself. She will be happy. It was like a little prayer in my head

I kept repeating, as if this small action would guarantee a good ending.

I had always been a woman of faith, and that would never change. Even though there were times in my life when I felt abandoned by God, today I felt his strong presence in our lives. Luisa interrupted my peaceful moment when she walked into the kitchen looking for me.

"Are the girls up yet?" I asked.

"No, still sleeping," she replied. "But maybe we should get them up."

"I'll do it. Will you go ahead and get the coffee ready?"

I walked into their room and stopped for a moment to watch them sleep. They looked so grownup and yet so small. Through my eyes, they were still little girls clinging to my skirt. I opened the curtain to let the light in and waited until they opened their eyes. I sat on the side of the bed and watched them. Matilde woke up first and jumped into my arms like a toddler. Baby woke up with the commotion and hugged me as well. The three of us sat on the edge of the bed locked in a long embrace.

Luisa called us from the kitchen, and we all sat down for our last breakfast together. Hans drank his coffee too fast, burning his tongue and cursing in two languages. We all laughed at the scene, all too familiar for us.

Baby and Hector were planning to go to Uruguay for their honeymoon, and after that, they would return to Buenos Aires for a few weeks until Hector found out where his next post would be. I was hoping for a post close by, but there were only a handful of places where he could train to be a pilot and none were close to the city. The nearest naval base was more than 400 miles away. I cringed at the idea and tried not to think about it, at least for the moment.

Another thing that worried me was how Baby would be able to continue her studies. Maybe she could transfer to another university. I brought up the subject during breakfast—something I later regretted.

"I don't know yet what I'm going to do," she replied casually, as if the subject didn't matter at all.

"If you are getting a transfer, you should start researching your options," I suggested, trying not to be imposing or patronizing.

"Mom, there is a chance I may not go back at all next semester. We don't know which naval base Hector will be stationed at. It's hard for me to make plans right now." She focused on the cup of coffee sitting in front of her.

"But you can't quit!" I regretted that the words came out of my mouth so abruptly.

"I already told you I don't know what I'll do. I didn't say I would quit." I could tell the conversation was escalating into a full discussion.

"But you are thinking about it. I thought medical school was your life." I tried hard not to raise my voice.

"Hector is my life now, Mom. His career is important to him, and I will go wherever I need to go to support him."

"All I know is you can't quit! Your life and your future are important too," I exclaimed, feeling the anger coming up my throat.

"That will be a decision that Hector and I will make together. This matter doesn't include you, Mother." She looked into my eyes with defiance, something I had never seen her do before.

"You are right," I replied. "What I say doesn't matter anymore. I raised you well and you are an intelligent woman. You will know what to do." I left the kitchen to avoid a confrontation on her wedding day.

I was angry with myself for having brought up the subject, but I was even more frustrated with Baby for not valuing her life and career more. Here she was with all these amazing opportunities in front of her and still reluctant to take them. She belonged to the generation of women destined to change the world, with all the possibilities I didn't have. It was too late for me, but not for her. Was she going to give it all up for a husband? Maybe I did something wrong after all. I should have pushed her harder to achieve her goals. Now it was out of my hands. She was in charge of her own destiny, and I had to watch from the sidelines. This wasn't what I wanted for her. But we live the life we choose, and we choose the life we live. And I knew that better than anyone. Baby would have to choose.

The day went by among hair appointments and last-minute preparations. Hans was supposed to drive Baby to the church, and because we couldn't all fit in the car, he would have to make two trips.

I helped Baby get dressed. She looked like an angel more than a bride. Her blonde hair was pinned up, with a few small daisies peeking out. Her dress was simple yet elegant. She didn't want any tulle nor a veil, so I made it out of a soft pearl-colored organza that dropped to the floor like a water cascade. The different shades of ivory accentuated her deep blue eyes even more. I stared at her, wondering how someone so perfect and beautiful could be related to me. I checked one last time that her hair was pinned correctly, her dress wasn't wrinkled, and her makeup wasn't overdone. Radiant—she looked simply radiant. Hans walked in the room with his mother's pearl necklace in his hand. He put it on Baby and took a long look at her.

"This is a wedding gift from your grandmother. She wore it on her wedding day. She wanted you to have it today." He was obviously touched by the intimacy of the moment. He stroked her face gently and said, "Now you look perfect."

I gave Baby one last careful hug. "*Te quiero,*" I murmured in her ear.

"I love you too, Mom," she replied, and we both apologized with our eyes knowing that our conversation this morning had put a bitter note on this special day.

Hans dropped off Luisa, Matilde, and me first. The church looked festive with fresh white flowers on the altar and on the aisle side of the benches. Hector was waiting proudly, wearing his formal uniform and saber, flanked by his best man, also in Navy uniform. His mother was standing by his side. He couldn't hide his joy. He always seemed reserved, but this evening he was all smiles.

We found our seats at the front of the church. Hans and I would stand next to Baby during the ceremony, but I had to wait for him to walk her down the aisle. Suddenly we heard the nuptial march and stood up to watch Baby make her entrance. She walked slowly, holding on to Hans' arm. He was walking tall, wearing a black tuxedo. He looked as handsome as when we first met more than twenty-five years ago. When they finally arrived to the altar, he kissed Baby on both cheeks and gave her hand to Hector. I joined them and the ceremony began.

As the priest spoke the all-too familiar words, reality sunk in. This is it, I thought. I wondered what Baby was thinking or feeling at this moment and wished I could peek into her head and her heart. All my fears disappeared momentarily, and I let myself enjoy this special occasion.

Three years later, I would be standing at this same place to witness Matilde's wedding. Life passed me by all too fast. But I was satisfied. I had done my job the best I could, the best I knew how. My family was changing and I had to change with it. But the biggest challenge of my life was yet to come.

The wedding reception at the Naval Club was a complete success. It was everything I dreamed of and more. The room was majestic.

Big mirrors lined up elegantly on each side, making the already tall ceilings look even taller. The tables were masterfully decorated with white and pink roses and distributed in a big circle around the dance floor. I was amazed at the results of so many months of preparation. I had to admit Hector and his family had done an unbelievable job organizing the reception. We enjoyed every minute of it. Baby danced with her brand new husband and tears of joy came down my face as they moved around the dance floor. Theirs were the pure faces of love.

Hans had his turn but kept it short and sweet. He kissed Baby and passed her on to the best man, who was eagerly waiting for his turn. He turned to me and extended his hand.

"Dance with me," he asked.

I walked toward him without taking my eyes from his. I took his hand and let him pull me gently closer. His strong grip surprised me for a second and we started moving like we were one. No words could describe the moment. I just felt the music and didn't speak at all. Hans was the one who broke the silence.

"You are quiet tonight. Are you all right?" he asked me.

"I'm full of contradictory emotions. I'm happy and sad at the same time. It's just harder than I thought it would be," I replied close to his ear so he could hear me above the music.

"She will be fine, you'll see." He tried to lighten up the moment.

"I'm not worried about her—she's a woman now. I'm more worried about our family. How will life be without one of us?"

"She is not disappearing from our lives. Nothing will change. You will move on, just as we all will." I could hear in his voice that he didn't want to talk about it much. He was probably full of emotions himself; seeing his little girl leave wasn't easy for him either.

"You're right. It's just a matter of time, and I will be fine." I decided to keep the rest of my thoughts to myself.

Throughout the evening, I tried to move beyond my shyness and be a gracious hostess. Hector's family was eager to meet our side of the family. Luisa and I made an effort to introduce ourselves and speak a few words to everyone.

At five o'clock in the morning, while the younger crowd was still dancing and singing to Beatles songs, I sat down exhausted and decided it was time to take my shoes off. Forget the formalities! I was in so much pain. I regretted picking new shoes for the occasion.

Hans offered to drive Luisa and me home and I took his offer without blinking. Most of the adults had already left, so I didn't feel bad for leaving the party early—I knew some of their friends would stay until it was time for breakfast.

Baby's hair was a reflection of how much fun she had. There were still a few daises attached to it that had survived the dancing, but most of her hair was down now, floating on her shoulders. I had removed in a very discreet way some of the pins through the night, but a few still remained tangled up in her hair. By now it didn't matter any more.

I walked barefoot to Baby to let her know I was ready to leave. Earlier during the day we had brought her suitcase to her hotel room where she and Hector would spend their first night together. Later in the afternoon, they would be taking a ferry boat to Uruguay where they would spend a week on their honeymoon. I reminded her briefly of the plans and told her I was leaving.

"Mother," she said, stopping me from walking away too fast. "*Gracias.* Thank you for everything. For my whole life," she said.

I nodded and kissed her. And all the emotions I was trying to hide the entire night came down my throat and overwhelmed every part of my body.

Chapter Twenty

The morning after the wedding was peaceful. Months of prep- arations and stress were finally over. There were no more dresses to finish, calls to make, flowers to pick up. Life was normal again. Luisa was sleeping on Baby's old bed and I decided not to walk into the bedroom to avoid seeing her absence. Because I was the first one up on Sunday morning, I decided to go by myself to an early mass and stop at the bakery on my way back home to pick up some fresh croissants for breakfast.

That morning was fresh and cool, anticipating the beginning of fall, my favorite season of the year. I felt good. I inhaled deeply with every other step I took and savored my solitude. I walked slowly to make the moment last a little longer, trying to absorb this new phase of my life. In my heart I always knew this day would come, and I embraced it for the first time, without the urge to fight back.

There was so much for be grateful for. All the sacrifices, all the heartache, everything had been worth it. Today was a good day, I told myself. And I repeated it a few times until I reached the steps of the church. I sat through mass and thanked God for giving me the strength to go through life with grace and dignity. I remained concentrated in my thoughts, thinking about my daughters, my family, my own mother, and her struggles. The hour-long mass seemed to last only a few minutes. I stood up to receive the last blessing before heading back outside.

The sky was darker when I walked out of the church, and it smelled like rain. The weather had changed dramatically in only one hour. I walked faster to beat the rain, but it caught up with me anyway. I took refuge in the bakery and decided to wait until the downpour slowed down.

The smell of fresh bread overwhelmed me. It was one of my favorites since I was a small child. It brought back so many wonderful memories of my siblings waiting impatiently at the kitchen for my mother to pull the bread out of the oven, of my aunt Nira baking her raisin bread for Christmas, of Antonia's old habit of dipping the bread in her wine before she ate it. I smiled at my memories and wished I could go back in time and relive some of those moments.

The rain stopped, and I hurried to buy the croissants and be on my way. By now, everyone would be awake and hungry. A light drizzle kept coming down, but it didn't bother me. It was actually refreshing because the temperature hadn't gone down. It was humid but not unpleasant. I walked quickly the few blocks in front of me. By the time I reached the house, I could feel my wet clothes sticking to my skin and my nice salon hairdo losing its puffiness. This new style of beehive hairdos was driving me crazy!

I opened the door and walked in slowly just in case they were still sleeping. Matilde had come back from the party at seven o'clock in the morning. I knew she would probably sleep until noon. I heard some noise in the kitchen and assumed it was Luisa and

Hans making coffee. I went straight to our bedroom to change out of my wet clothes and try to rescue what was left of my hair style. I undressed and put a robe on before I headed back to the kitchen.

But something stopped me on my way. Luisa and Hans were not talking—they were murmuring. The sound of their voices worried me. I didn't want to interrupt their conversation, wondering if they were trying to hide bad news from me. Maybe something happened to Antonia, maybe Coco got hurt. My head was spinning with infinite possibilities. I stood behind the door and listened.

"Hans, think about it before you do anything you will regret for the rest of your life," I heard Luisa say.

"I've been thinking about it for too long. I have to do it—I have to go," Hans replied.

"You are making a huge mistake. You have no idea of the consequences this decision will bring," she added.

I could hardly make out their words, but I didn't like what I heard. I kept silent while I listened.

"For years I've been trying hard to make it better, but it hasn't worked out. This is my chance to have a life, a different life," he said.

"How can you be so selfish? Is that all you care about? You will hurt everyone around you and once the damage is done, there will be no way to take it all back," Luisa implored him.

"I gave them all I had. Now it's my turn. I love her, and I will be with her no matter how high the cost."

My legs started to shake and weaken. They finally gave out on me and my whole body slid down until I was on my knees. I was petrified. I couldn't think, I couldn't move, I couldn't react. My heart started racing furiously, while my hands started shaking uncontrollably.

"She's waiting for me. We will go in an hour to the train station. I can't face Chola—you have to do it for me."

"You are out of your mind if you think I will help you," Luisa said firmly.

"It doesn't matter anymore. I'm leaving, and that's that. You can do whatever you want," he replied, sure of himself.

"But Chola loves you," Luisa murmured with pain in her voice.

"I don't love her anymore. She left me a long time ago. Now it's my turn to go."

"She stuck with you for more than twenty years. She took you in time after time despite all the pain you caused her. She gave you two beautiful daughters, she raised them, and this is how you repay her, by stabbing her in the back? You are a miserable man, Hans. You don't deserve her, you never did," she replied.

"I know that. I never deserved her. I thought I could change for her—maybe I could be somebody else. But it only made me angrier. I can't change who I am. But I can be myself with Marta."

When I heard her name, overwhelming fury took over me. My hands turned into fists, and anger built up inside me. All the months I was gone, thinking she was looking after my family, she was in fact seducing my husband, stealing him from us, destroying the only happiness we knew. My best friend—my only friend—who was dancing last night at my daughter's wedding, knowing she would run away with my husband the very next day, was now killing me. I couldn't hear any more. I ran to the bedroom and tried to calm myself enough so I could get dressed. My hands were shaking, my pulse was racing, my head was spinning. I couldn't get his words out of my head, "I don't love her anymore." All the years I had suffered his perversions, his addictions, his infidelities. He was walking away from our life as if it never had any meaning at all.

The signs had been there all along, and I didn't see them—I chose not to. I was as much a coward as he was. But what was I supposed to do now? I sat on the floor to try to figure out my next move.

My instinct was to run, to scream, to yell in his face all the profanities I could think of. But I had to think. Think, Chola, think!

After a few minutes I walked out of the bedroom and into the kitchen. I was surprised to find Luisa alone.

"Did he leave?" I asked and Luisa didn't have to wonder if I knew exactly what was happening right now.

"He just left," she replied. "I'm so sorry, Chola. I tried to stop him."

"I know," I sat down as if in a trance. "I want to know where he is going," I added in an artificially calm voice.

"Don't do it, Chola. Don't follow him. It will kill you," she pleaded with me.

"I'll do what I have to do. He will have to tell me to my face that he's running away with the whore downstairs."

"You are wasting your time! Don't do it, please," she begged.

"Tell me now, Luisa, and stay out of it." My voice put fear in my older sister.

"They are taking the train to Rosario. They are going to the train station," she murmured.

I stood up without looking back at her, grabbed my umbrella, my purse, and walked out of the house.

The streets were still wet from the rain. The sky shared the same color as my soul. The deep gray seemed to sink into my chest and push me down with it. It kept getting darker and darker inside of me. Fury, pain, anger, everything mixed and turned into the most disgusting flavor in my mouth. He wasn't going to get away so easily. He would have to face me one last time, even if it was just to tell me to go to hell. He owed me at least that much.

As I walked out of the house, I saw Hans and Marta getting into a taxi cab right in front of me. I ran, but they sped away. I couldn't remember if I had enough money for the taxi fare but that seemed irrelevant at the moment. I stopped the first taxi that drove by and ordered the driver to follow the other car. This crazy person inside my body wasn't me. As if in a trance I kept yelling at the driver to go faster, not to lose them! Everything was coming to an end and I could feel it. Every bone in my body could feel it. I wasn't sure what I was going to do when we reached them. I was blinded with fury and couldn't think clearly.

I ordered the driver again to go faster. He probably thought that I was a madwoman, that I had completely lost my marbles, that I couldn't think straight, that I was a danger to everyone around me. And he was absolutely right.

The traffic on *Avenida 9 de Julio* slowed us down and I panicked. What if I missed him? What if he left before I could confront him?

"Find a way around it," I yelled at the poor driver who was losing his patience.

"Lady, this is a cab, not a plane. I'm doing my best," he replied and started pushing the horn in the hopes that the traffic would open up for us.

My stomach was knotted up and I thought I would throw up. When we reached the train station, I gave the driver a handful of bills without counting them, and I jumped out of the car. It was a busy Sunday, and the place was crowded with weekend travelers, pedestrians, and sidewalk stands that sold food and trinkets. I walked as fast as my legs could carry me and tried to avoid the people that crossed my path.

I finally reached the majestic entrance of the building, which, despite the dirt and years of neglect, still showed signs of its original beauty. I ran into a man with an expensive suit and briefcase. I asked him for directions to the ticket office. Maybe I would find them there; maybe Hans was buying their tickets. The attendant told me the train to Rosario was sold out and a gentleman had bought the last two tickets a few minutes ago. I turned around as if in a trance and looked frantically for the train to Rosario. Platform 5. Platform 5, I kept repeating in my head. The train was leaving in nine minutes. I ran like a madwoman until a man in a uniform stopped me and asked me for my ticket.

"Lady, you need to show me your ticket to continue to the platform," he said.

"My husband..." I said and didn't finish my sentence—the gun shots interrupted me. Once, twice, three times. Three bullets.

Somehow I knew. He's dead. Hans is dead.

I froze on the spot, and the chaos in the station took me with it. Everyone around me was screaming and running in panic to safety. I didn't move. I couldn't. I fell on my knees. I'm not sure what happened next. I didn't hear the sound of sirens and the screams of policemen and paramedics asking for people to stay out of the way. I didn't speak when one of the station guards took me by the arm and walked me to the waiting room. It was over.

The fury I had felt just minutes ago turned into paralysis. I sat silently on a wooden bench, incapable of moving, until the sound of peoples' voices next to me brought me back to reality. I heard them say it. Two people dead, one badly wounded. That was the aftermath of this crime of passion. I lifted my head up to listen carefully to what they were saying.

A man and a woman were standing on platform 5, waiting for the train to open its doors, when a crippled man with a gun approached them. He shot the woman first, right in the heart. Immediately after that, he shot the man who was standing next to her. The shooter then turned around and put the gun to his head, taking his own life.

At that moment it hit me: Hans may still be alive. Instinctively, I stood up and walked to the first policeman I found.

"My husband was shot. I'm his wife! I need to see him," I exclaimed.

"Follow me. I'll take you to the paramedics. They just left with the only survivor. We can ask where they took him." He held me tightly by the arm, making sure I didn't fall on him.

We walked together to the main exit, asking the crowd of morbidly curious bystanders to move aside and let us through. It took a few minutes until we finally reached the road where three ambulances were parked and paramedics were running around. Chaos was all I could see. The policeman still holding me by the arm asked one of them about the man who survived. "He was taken to the nearest hospital," he was told. An ambulance was about to depart. "We will take his wife," I heard them say.

I sat inside the empty vehicle and wished for a second that the bullet had reached me instead. Dying would be so easy. Living, surviving, was hard. Both paramedics were sitting in the front, and I was grateful I was alone. The traffic wasn't a problem at all for the ambulance, and we reached the hospital in just a few minutes. They opened the back to let me out, and one of the paramedics extended his hand to help me. I appreciated the gesture—my body was still in shock. He was a tall, dark young man. He took pity on me and didn't leave me until he made sure I was in the right hands. The doctor who came out to speak to me was wearing his green operating clothes. He explained to me quickly that Hans was still alive but in critical condition. He was going to operate on him to extract the bullet from his chest. He didn't know how severe the damage was and suggested I prepare myself for the worst.

His words didn't register completely in my brain. I could hear him but I wasn't listening. All I could think of were my daughters and the pain they would feel if their father died today. Not once did I think of myself. I had removed myself completely from the picture.

I went to the waiting room and sat patiently in a corner. I didn't have the courage to call Luisa and explain what had just happened.

I decided to endure it all alone. Matilde and Baby shouldn't find out until I knew better what his condition was. I prayed to God to spare his life not for my sake, but for his children's.

The hours went slowly by. I sat and waited.

The doctor finally came out to tell me his condition was stable, but he would remain in the ICU until he was out of danger. "Go home and come back tomorrow. You will be able to see him then," he said kindly. I couldn't leave. I insisted I needed to see him. The doctor reluctantly agreed but just for a few minutes.

Hans lay still on a hospital bed, his body covered with tubes and wires. He looked helpless, vulnerable, insignificant. His fragile humanity was all he had left. He didn't seem like a man to me anymore. He looked more like a child who had just lost his innocence.

I came closer to him and noticed he was trying to open his eyes.

I touched his hand gently and told him it was me.

"You came," he said softly.

"Of course I came. You were not going to leave me without an explanation."

"I was stupid and selfish," he murmured with much difficulty.

"Don't talk anymore."

"Chola..."

"What, Hans?"

"Don't let me die alone."

"I won't," I replied.

As I walked out of the hospital, I realized how empty I was. I didn't feel anything anymore. Something inside of me had disappeared. I was crazy to think that I could ever change him. It took a bullet to see that. It took a bullet to realize how wrong I had been all my life. In my heart, Hans was already dead.

I walked away from the hospital, from Hans, and never looked back.

Epilogue – Matilde

Baby and I visit my mother every day. We make sure she's never alone. She's 95 years old, and at this pace, she will reach 100 like both of her oldest sisters. Longevity runs in her side of the family.

I don't know how she made it this far. I would have died long ago if I had suffered only half of what she had.

I stopped trying to understand why she took my father back. She stood by his side until the day he died, at age 84.

Now that I'm a mother of three girls and a grandmother of four, I feel closer to her.

I understand her dreams better and I'm willing to forgive her mistakes. Maybe her mistakes don't matter so much anymore. Why is it that we pass on some of the best aspects of ourselves to our children but also some of the worst?

I see her in everything I do. I see my father in me as well. I inherited his wanderlust and his stubbornness. My children adored him until the day he died. He made them laugh with his thick German accent—which he maintained even after spending a lifetime in a Spanish-speaking world.

For a long time my mother suffered in silence. Their last few years together were peaceful and friendly, as if they were lifelong friends and roommates. We buried the shame of his actions in the deepest corner of our closet, locked the door, and threw away the key.

I sit next to her at the home where she lives and wonder if she still knows who I am.

Sometimes she recognizes me; other times she just stares. Maybe her dementia isn't such a bad thing after all. Her brain decides what memories to keep and which ones to forget. She speaks to me clearly and lets me know her thoughts in the random order that they appear in her brain.

I can't make much sense of it all, though I never tell her that. I just keep up with the conversation. Sometimes I feel as if we traded places, and now I'm taking care of her just as she once took care of me.

Every week that goes by she gets smaller and smaller. She's slowly disintegrating in front of my eyes. But there is a luminosity about her that strikes me every time I arrive. She shines beautifully, and her light always stays with me after I leave.

I will never know how much she sacrificed for us or how hard it was to pick up the pieces of her broken life. She spent her best years with a man who didn't deserve her, and yet she found the strength to persevere. She loved a man who disappointed her again and again. And despite it all, she lived her life with grace and dignity.

Hans never measured up to her. He was a bad husband and a mediocre father. But his redemption finally arrived when he became a grandfather. He loved his grandchildren more than anything in the world.

I guess there is redemption for everyone after all.

The End

Acknowledgments

I grew up in a predominantly female household, surrounded by strong, independent, smart and loving women. To them, specially my mother, I owe who I am today. They paved the way for me and all the women of my generation to be able to succeed in life and reach for the stars.

To them, I will be forever grateful.

I'd like to thank my grandmother; without her there would be no book. She is the real flower. Thanks for inspiring me to write this story – your story. Your grace, dignity and perseverance have been a major influence in my life. Gracias, Cholita!

Thank you, mom, for always pushing me to get out of my comfort zone and follow my dreams. You made me believe in myself and showed me that life can be an extraordinary journey, with ups and downs, but mostly ups. And to you, dad, for your wisdom and your unconditional love.

To all my wonderful friends, who helped me and encouraged me to keep writing, especially Melissa, Ingrid, Eugenia and Sheila.

Finally, to the three men in my life: Dave, thank you for 19 years of friendship, love and support. Nick and Seb, I am so proud to be your mother. I love you!

Book Club Guide

Thank you for choosing my book to read and discuss. Here are some questions that may guide you through your discussion. Please feel free to check out my website at www.myriamalvarez.com for more interesting facts about the book and to give me your feedback. I would love to hear from you!

Guide

Why is Hans attracted to Chola?

What effect does Chola's upbringing have in her decisions?

Despite the language, what other cultural differences do Chola and Hans have?

Why can't Hans give up his addictions?

What impact does Hans' family have in their marriage?

Why does Hans have survivor's guilt?

How does motherhood change the way Chola feels about herself?

Why can't Chola leave her husband?

Who is the weaker character of the two? Why?

What's at the root of Luisa's obsessions?

What role does religion play in Chola's society?